A PLUME BOOK

TALES FROM THE YOGA STUDIO

RAIN MITCHELL began practicing yoga as a teenager and is currently at work on the second novel in the series. Rain's favorite pose is corpse.

TALES FROM THE YOGA STUDIO

A Novel

Rain Mitchell

A PLUME BOOK

PLUME
Published by Penguin Group

Penguin Group (USA) Inc., 375 Hudson Street, New York, New York 10014, U.S.A. •
Penguin Group (Canada), 90 Eglinton Avenue East, Suite 700, Toronto, Ontario, Canada
M4P 2Y3 (a division of Pearson Penguin Canada Inc.) • Penguin Books Ltd., 80 Strand,
London WC2R 0RL, England • Penguin Ireland, 25 St. Stephen's Green, Dublin 2,
Ireland (a division of Penguin Books Ltd.) • Penguin Group (Australia), 250 Cam-
berwell Road, Camberwell, Victoria 3124, Australia (a division of Pearson Australia
Group Pty. Ltd.) • Penguin Books India Pvt. Ltd., 11 Community Centre, Panchsheel
Park, New Delhi – 110 017, India • Penguin Books (NZ), 67 Apollo Drive, Rosedale,
North Shore 0632, New Zealand (a division of Pearson New Zealand Ltd.) • Penguin
Books (South Africa) (Pty.) Ltd., 24 Sturdee Avenue, Rosebank, Johannesburg 2196,
South Africa

Penguin Books Ltd., Registered Offices: 80 Strand, London WC2R 0RL, England

First published by Plume, a member of Penguin Group (USA) Inc.

First Printing, January 2011
10   9   8   7   6   5   4   3   2   1

Ⓟ REGISTERED TRADEMARK—MARCA REGISTRADA

LIBRARY OF CONGRESS CATALOGING-IN-PUBLICATION DATA

Mitchell, Rain.
  Tales from the yoga studio / Rain Mitchell.
    p.   cm.
  ISBN 978-0-452-29691-6
  1. Women personal trainers—Fiction.   2. Yoga—Fiction.   3. Female friendship—
Fiction.   I. Title.
  PS3613.I8628T36 2011
  813'.6—dc22

                                                                    2010030045

Printed in the United States of America
Set in Horley Old Style

To Denise Roy—extraordinary editor and inspiration—I hereby dedicate all of my gratitude poses to you

PART ONE

It's at moments like this—when she's put the class through their paces and has them settled back onto their mats in a state of collective peace, contentment, and deep relaxation, when their bodies are glistening with a light sheen of sweat, when the afternoon sun is glinting off the end of the Silver Lake Reservoir, which she can see through the wall of windows she and Alan had installed on the southern side of the studio, when all seems temporarily right with the world—that Lee starts craving a cigarette.

"Inhale through your nose into whatever traces of tension you're still holding on to, and sigh it all out through your mouth," she says. "Let it go."

The craving is just a ghost from the past that visits her from time to time, drops in from the years of misguided study and too much stress at Columbia University Medical Center, when, like a quarter of the students, she would rush out to 165th Street from a lecture on emphysema, abnormal cell growth, or heart disease, light up, and huddle against the buildings in the gray dampness of those New York afternoons.

"One more long, luxurious inhalation, one more compete exhalation."

And that wasn't even the worst of her behavior. Thankfully, those days of rote memorization, trying to prove something to her impossible mother, always feeling as if she'd stepped onto the wrong flight and was hurtling toward an unknown destination, are long past and gone for good. No regrets, no second-guessing.

The fact that on the night Alan moved his stuff into a friend's spare room, unannounced, explaining only that he needed some space to get his "head together," she stopped at the convenience store on her way home from the studio and bought a pack of Marlboro Lights was a blip on the radar screen. She'd rather give herself some slack and say she wasn't in her right mind that night. "*Om shanti*, Yoga Lady," the Indian store clerk had said ironically, rubbing in the contradiction.

"They're for a friend," she'd lied, which made it even worse somehow.

She smoked only two and was about to throw the pack out before she considered how expensive cigarettes have become in the past ten years (who knew?) and told herself it was a horrible waste of money to dump them. She locked them in the glove compartment. Maybe she'd pass them out to a few homeless people. Except wasn't that like handing out lung disease? Talk about bad karma. So now she didn't know what to do with them except leave them safely out of reach until she figured out the best course of action.

How long has she had the class in savasana?

She watches fifteen rib cages rise and fall in unison in the beautiful golden afternoon light, ignores one awkwardly timed erection courtesy of Brian—"Boner," as Katherine and a few students refer to him, he of the white spandex yoga pants—and closes her own eyes. If she thinks herself into it, she can get a contact high from the class. A deep breath in, a long breath out, a reminder that even if life has suddenly gotten way more complicated in the past few weeks, even if for the moment— might as well face it—it kind of sucks, it's still better than it was back in those dark New York, failing-med-student days in her twenties—before Alan, before the twins, before Los Angeles. Before yoga.

She opens her eyes and sees that she's run seven minutes over. Fourth time this week. Or is it the fifth?

She brings the class back, has them sit up cross-legged, and then, with the sudden feeling of warmth and tenderness for all of them that inevitably comes over her at this point in class, she says, "Take this feeling with you, wherever you're headed. This calm is there for you when you need it. If something totally unexpected comes up, don't let it knock the wind out of you. You can't control the other people in your life. But you can control your reactions to them. You can't predict what the hell they're going to do all of a sudden, out of nowhere, with no advance warning, just when you think everything is running so smoothly and perfectly, and then . . ." *Uh-oh.* "Have a really great afternoon, folks. Don't get bent out of shape. *Namaste.*"

D idn't I tell you she was the best yoga teacher in L.A.?"
    This is Stephanie, crowing in her loud and endearingly hyperbolic style to the friend she brought with her to the studio this afternoon. Stephanie can't help it; brash hyperbole is what has made her successful in film development. Or so she's told

Lee. When it comes to the movie business, Lee has learned to filter out the superlatives, lop eighty-five percent off most claims, divide by two, and then believe any of it only when she's seen the film on Netflix.

Stephanie's friend, still on her back on the floor, stretching out her spine like a cat, is a young, dark-haired beauty with the long legs, perfect muscle tone, and unmistakable signs of injuries past and present that Lee knows all too well from observing students. A dancer, there's no question about it.

"You're embarrassing me, Stephanie," Lee says.

"Give me a break," Stephanie says. "You love it."

"You're right, I do. But for my sake, try to be a little more subtle about it?"

"Subtlety is so overrated. You're fantastic."

Lee stacks the purple Styrofoam blocks neatly on the shelves. Alan has held a couple of kirtan workshops at the studio, and in addition to the inexplicable injury of moving out two weeks ago, he's added the insult of complaining to her about petty house-keeping chores. The mats aren't neatly stacked; the blankets haven't been properly folded; the straps are tangled. "I'm trying to create a sacred space with the music," he said the other day, "and it doesn't help to have everything look so disorganized."

"Are you *kidding* me?" she felt like screaming. "You think I'm worried about messy *blankets* right now? How about telling me what's going on? How about talking about the mess you're making of our marriage?"

Instead, she's been breathing, tidying, and trying to give him some sacred space so he can get his fucking head together.

"I mean, Chloe and Gianpaolo are great teachers, too," Stephanie says. "But you've got the magic, Lee. If I could convince Matthew to come out here one of these days, he'd get hooked, I guarantee it."

Last week it was "Zac" and the week before it was "Jen" or some other single name that's supposed to convey the impression that Stephanie is on a first-name basis—and carries clout—with the Hollywood A-list. Maybe she does.

Lee has no idea if Stephanie or any of the other regulars have heard whispers of what's going on in her life. Alan practices at the studio, and he does a lot of fix-it projects around the place—he's a good carpenter when he puts his mind to it, and pretty skilled at dealing with small plumbing problems—so with all that and his music workshops, everyone knows him. Lee's asked Alan to keep their personal life between them (and anyway, the relocation is just temporary!) but ever since he read *Eat, Pray, Love,* he's had this annoying new need to "process" and "discuss" his feelings, which might mean complaining about her to total strangers. She shouldn't have suggested he read the book. It was like giving a loaded gun to a kid. She wanted him to understand *her* a little better, not to use it as an excuse to dodge the responsibilities of the studio and the twins and revisit the same old regrets about his songwriting and performing disappointments.

Stephanie, like a lot of the women who come to the studio, has idealized Lee's marriage. Lee and Alan, perfect couple, perfectly coordinated schedules, perfect bodies, perfect kids. This was somewhat less embarrassing to Lee back when Alan and the marriage seemed more ideal. She's pretty sure Stephanie comes to Edendale Yoga partly to soak up the aura of happiness and stability (in short supply in Stephanie's own life, Lee would guess) that hovered over the studio until recently. Lee is doing her best to maintain some of that uplifting aura while making sure the classes don't suffer at all. No more subtle references to her marriage in class! How did *that* happen?

Lee watches Stephanie walk out to the reception area. Before the door has closed behind her, she's checking her BlackBerry.

Lee worries about Stephanie. She gives off the air of someone who is working twenty-four/seven, making calls, arranging meetings, trying to set up something on a film project she
frequently refers to, dropping way too many names. She often
comes to class looking as if she needs a good night's sleep, and
it wouldn't shock Lee if it turned out Stephanie does more than
yoga to help her relax at the end of the workday, and maybe in the
middle of it, too. She claims twenty-eight, but Lee has a feeling
it's more like thirty-three, that tricky in-between age. At least she
hasn't gone "freeze-frame," Lee's expression for the faces in class
that remain surprisingly immobile when Lee has them do lion
pose and asks them to stick out their tongues and scrunch their
eyes. Or try to, anyway.

It's L.A. She's not judging. The last time she went to a yoga
conference, half the teachers over thirty were complaining
that their gyms and studios were encouraging them to keep up
appearances "at any cost," since students like to think yoga is
going to keep them looking young from the outside in—and if
it's just the outside, that's okay, too, at least for some.

In class, Stephanie pushes too hard. She's fit but not naturally
flexible, and one of these days, she's going to hurt herself. She's
short, with a cropped haircut that seems to be more about getting
out of the house quickly in the morning than flattering her face.
When Lee looks at Stephanie struggling through class, she sees
a body that would look more natural and comfortable draped in
another five or ten pounds. She's been coming for six months or
so, and Lee has formulated a plan—not that she'd tell Stephanie.
Her goal is to slow her down, calm the inner voices telling her she
needs to push harder, talk louder, all in an effort to outrun age
and whatever demons are hunting her down.

Lee has a plan for a lot of her students. Occupational hazard.
Way easier than trying to formulate one for yourself.

When the dancer friend is up and rolling her mat, Lee introduces herself. The dark-haired girl is even more striking close up—emerald green eyes, a (naturally) lush mouth, silky brown skin, and an effortless grace in her every movement. Except when she winces.

"When did you injure your Achilles tendon?" Lee asks her.

The girl—Graciela—does a surprised double take. It always amazes Lee what people think they can get away with.

"How did you know?"

"I got suspicious during your first down dog. The right and left sides of your body are in two different universes. You're not big on backing off from pain, are you?" Lee says it with a smile. She's learned how to make comments like this without having them sound like judgment or criticism.

"Not my forte. I'm sure you know how it is; Stephanie told me you have a lot of dancers practicing here. We don't exactly get points for backing off."

"Modern?" Lee asks.

Graciela tips her hand side to side. "Contemporary. Hip-hop, mostly." This is what Lee suspected—the muscular arms, the strong shoulders—but because Graciela is obviously a Latina, she didn't want to seem as if she was making assumptions. "I've got an audition for an important video shoot in three weeks. A Very Big Deal. I'm not even allowed to mention whose video."

She pauses, a wicked grin on her face, obviously waiting for Lee to venture a guess.

"Beyoncé?" Lee asks.

Graciela squeals. "Oh, my God. Can you believe it? Do you know what a break this is for me?" She does a little leap and winces again. "I have to either heal or . . . well, there is no 'or.'"

Graciela's trying for a light touch, but the false optimism in her voice is something Lee knows well and is yet another thing she's happy to have left back at Columbia med school, along with the snow, the self-starvation, and the antidepressants.

"Promise me you're not doing anything crazy to 'heal'?" Lee says.

"Yeah, well, I think you're going to have to define 'crazy.' I go to a psychic in Venice Beach who told me I'm going to be fine, so I'm running with that. My doctor's an alarmist, anyway. I was doing some yoga at the gym, and I was about to try one of those superheated classes. That's when Stephanie insisted I come up here. I sometimes work shifts at a coffee shop she goes to."

"Welcome aboard," Lee says.

Graciela slings her bag over her shoulder. She has truly gorgeous dark hair, all ringlets, bounce, and shine. As she's gathering it back behind her head, she looks up at Lee and says, "Do you really think I'll be ready for the audition? I'm not kidding myself, am I?" The sparkle is gone from her voice, the cheery bravado. It's been replaced by that dancer despair Lee knows so well from listening to some of her students.

She studies Graciela for a minute. Part of the hell of being a dancer is that all that strength and beauty Graciela has, all the hours of training and practice, can be rendered insignificant by a little tendon problem or something else equally small, painful, and vital.

"Go out and make an appointment with Katherine," she says. "She's our masseuse, and she's got a million little tricks. And then I want to see you here at least four times a week. We'll start you out in restorative poses. But I warn you, I'm going to keep my eye on you. I'm going to rein you in, and if I catch you pushing too hard, I'm calling you *out*."

Lee gives Graciela a hug and holds it for longer than she meant to. When she pulls away, she sees a look of such intense anxiety and sadness on Graciela's face, she wonders what else is going on that she's not saying. There's so much she never learns about her students' lives outside the studio. "Oh, honey," Lee says. "I know. But trust me, you just have to slow down and stay focused and have a little faith. We'll do our best, okay?"

"My budget's tight right now," Graciela says. "I'll try to come as often as I can."

Lee thinks about Alan, about his lectures on Lee's soft spot, how the studio is not a nonprofit organization. But what's one more person in class? And if Graciela can't afford it, she just won't come, and then, somehow or other, Lee loses out, too. She likes this girl. To hell with Alan. She founded the studio; she's the owner.

"Pay me what you can. And if that means nothing, that's fine, too." Lee walks out to the reception area, then, having second thoughts, sticks her head back into the yoga room. "Just don't tell anyone. Especially a handsome guy with long hair you'll see around sometimes carrying either a tool chest or a harmonium. My husband."

Among the improvements Alan has made at the studio is creating a lounge area, complete with room for retail, out of what had been a storage closet back when the studio was the showroom of a rug dealer. There are a couple of comfortable sofas and chairs where students hang out between classes and shelves that Tina keeps stocked with a growing collection of yoga-related products. The lounge is one of the best improvements they've ever made, as far as Lee is concerned. A little funky, admittedly (where would she be without the Furniture for Sale page on Craigslist?), but it's gone a long way toward helping build the community feeling Lee always dreamed about creating at the studio. In addition to the friendships, people have used the space and spirit of the practice to organize fund-raisers for a handful of local causes and a couple of international disaster relief efforts.

The retail area is another matter. Lee hadn't wanted to take on the responsibility of ordering and keeping track of the finances of what has become a small (very!) store, but Tina talked her into going ahead with it, claiming students need a convenient place to buy mats and headbands and a few other practical items. She would handle everything for Lee, split the profits with the studio, and get a free monthly pass for classes. The problem is that every product, no matter how mundane and seemingly straightforward, creates a controversy.

Tina is standing behind the counter when Lee walks into the lounge area, and she beckons Lee over.

"I need to talk with you about something," Tina says.

"I'm a little pressed for time. . . ."

"It will only take a minute."

Here we go, Lee thinks. Tina is one of those young, superfit yoginis with too much nervous energy and a tendency to get anxious if Lee asks the class to go into child's pose or to modify a handstand or back off on one of the more extreme twists. She's definitely competitive—mostly with herself. She was a platform diver in high school, and Lee is always reminding her that she's not going to have her poses scored. "I'm not a judge," she keeps telling her. "I want you to work on enjoying it." So far, she's seen lots of work and not much joy.

"It's about the tea," Tina says and maneuvers her body so that no one in the lounge can hear. "I ordered this new organic brand that everyone is raving about, and without thinking, I ordered five boxes of *this* along with the herbal."

She holds up a package of Earl Grey.

"Okay," Lee says, waiting to hear what kind of debate was inspired by a box of tea. Tina recently graduated from UCLA and is back living with her parents, so Lee suspects it's a matter of too much time on her hands.

"It's caffeinated," she says. "Which I didn't really think about at the time, but Isabella Carolina Paterlini—she was at Chloe's seven a.m. class today—said she's trying to get off coffee and that seeing a caffeinated tea on the shelf was a trigger for her. I wasn't sure what to say, so I told her I'd ask you."

"Good thing you didn't decide to go with Red Bull," Lee says.

Tina has a nervous, pinched face and, as far as Lee can tell, not much of a sense of humor. Although admittedly it wasn't much of a joke. A lot of people seem to get self-righteous about things like diet and drinking when they get into a yoga studio, and Lee can't tell if it's coming from some genuine feeling or because they think it's how they ought to behave. In the grand scheme of things, Lee is pretty abstemious, but she's not above the occasional turkey burger and fries (and the *very* infrequent cigarette) and she thinks most people would be a whole lot happier and healthier if they relaxed around these issues instead of trying to adhere to a strict policy. What is "perfection" anyway?

"Have you tried it?" Lee asks.

"No. But all their teas are amazing."

"I'll tell you what," Lee says. "I'll buy the five boxes. I love Earl Grey, and I can always send my mother a box or two for her birthday."

"Oh, Lee. That's so great. I'll put them in the office. Have you got time to talk about something else?"

"I have to get to school to pick up the twins," she says. "What is it?"

"Someone asked if we'd stock Kegel exercisers. I didn't even know what they were, and then I looked it up online. I was wondering . . ."

"Let's put that one off until tomorrow." If a box of tea is inspiring this much conversation, she can only guess what would come of this item. There are moments when she'd like to close down the retail section—too much trouble—but some of the students have expressed a real appreciation for it. Lee starts to walk to the office and then turns back. "You're doing a great job, Tina," she says.

In most ways, she is, and it's amazing to Lee how well people respond to a little much-needed praise. Positive reinforcement. Why, she wonders, hasn't Alan figured that out yet?

It takes Lee twenty minutes to walk from Edendale Yoga to the school to pick up the twins. Alan dropped them there this morning and went downtown to work with his writing partner on a song they're hoping to sell to another reality show about addiction on VH1. He was supposed to leave the car for her and walk back to his new digs. She'd bet anything it's not in the lot. Fortunately, she's not a gambler, so she'll just stay focused on what's right with the day.

Growing up in suburban Connecticut, Lee never imagined she'd live in a place as urban as Silver Lake. California had never been on her radar screen, period. She always dreamed she'd end up in Vermont, some pretty, small town where she could have a private practice as a GP, raise a family, and go pond skating a few months a year. Basically, the full Currier and Ives fantasy. The last time she was in Vermont, she got stuck in a traffic jam outside a strip mall of outlet shops. Oh, well. Now she can't imagine leaving Silver Lake. It's just the right mixture of fun and funky, boho and beautiful. And yes, people do walk in this neighborhood and ride bikes to work and sit around drinking coffee (caffeinated!) at sidewalk cafés. It's probably in the low seventies today, and as she strolls down the street from the studio, she can see the reservoir spread out before her like a shimmering mirror framed by the green of palm trees and the stucco houses with their red tile rooftops.

She breathes it all in, trying to store up some of this calm (*this feeling is there for you when you need it*) before the twins storm back into her life and make every moment an exercise in accepting the unacceptable. Systems? Plans? No point with two eight-year-old boys steering the ship. Still, she couldn't have picked a better place to raise kids, even if Silver Lake is a little scruffy around the edges once you take a good look, even if the air can be a little thicker up here. Her own path would have been a lot clearer a lot sooner if she'd grown up in someplace as diverse and fun as this instead of Darien.

As she steps onto the sidewalk around the reservoir, the breeze picks up, freshening the air and making her think, for one moment, that everything really is going to work out all right. Alan is just being moody and childish in the way he can be sometimes. It's his most unappealing quality, but she's dealing with it. At least he started working on some new songs. That will make him feel good about himself until there's one of those rejections that always send him into a spiral of self-doubt expressed as anger at someone else. It was her idea for him to pick up the harmonium and start playing live music at a few of the classes in the studio. He has a surprising flair for it, and students love it. True, it's not what he imagined doing with music, but it gives him an audience, and Lee has gotten him a couple of gigs at other small studios around town. If he needs a little time to look at what he's doing and reevaluate, she can deal with it. He told her it's not about her and it's *definitely* not about an affair. For the moment, it's easiest to believe he's being honest. *It's all going to work out. It's all going to be fine.*

She rounds the corner and the school comes into view. The entire student body is lined up on the sidewalk, and there's a fleet of police cruisers at the door, blue lights flashing, and the sound of fire trucks in the distance.

That's when she starts to run.

The fast was incredible," the woman says as Katherine kneads her calves. "After the third day, I had absolutely no hunger whatsoever. I mean, what is *that* about? And for the ten days, ten whole days without a bite of food, I was still . . . you know . . . a few times a day. Amazing amounts. I'm so happy to have *that* out of my body."

"Who wouldn't be?" Katherine says.

Cindy's monologue, which began even before she lay down on Katherine's table, has officially crossed into TMI territory. No surprise there. Katherine guessed what was coming as soon as Cindy told her when booking the appointment that she couldn't wait to describe an "amazing experience" she had during a ten-day cleanse. This is Cindy's fifth massage with Katherine, and each time she comes, she has a new amazing experience to recount in detail; most of them involve getting something out of or off of her body. A new diet, sinus rinsing, high colonics, a sweat lodge.

What is *always* a surprise to Katherine is finding out yet again how boring it is to listen to someone's dietary and digestive adventures. Katherine is no stranger to all this (flirting with "healthy" fads helped her kick her more dangerous addictions), and she has to admit that Cindy looks good, her skin taut and glowing. But sometimes Katherine thinks she ought to post a sign reminding clients that she doesn't need to know about their bathroom experiences in quite so much detail. She reaches over and turns up the music a few notches, hoping to send a subtle message.

"You're probably wondering what I ate to break the fast, right?"

Not really.

"It's usually the first thing everyone asks."

Assuming they're able to get in a word.

"I was supposed to start off with a day of this green juice. I'm not sure what was in it, but it tasted like I was drinking hay and it made me so nauseated, I reached for the first thing I could get my hands on to try and get rid of the taste, and that happened to be a chocolate chip bagel that Henry had left on the counter in my kitchen."

Here comes the requisite attack on Henry.

"Thanks a lot, right? I mean, he knew I was going to break my fast that day. He's into sabotage. But, hey, I love him anyway. Omigod, his ass is so beautiful, like a marble statue. I'm not thrilled about his wife, but at least he was kind enough not to tell her that there's another woman in his life, which I think is kind of sweet of him. So the bagel wasn't what was on my plan, but

I figured since I'd already eaten it, I might as well enjoy it, and then—have you been to that new bakery on Hyperion? . . ."

There's a weird disconnect Katherine has noticed among some of the people she works on. They talk about their bodies as if they're temples of purity they want to honor by getting massage, doing yoga, eating only organic foods. But at the same time, they spend half their waking lives trying to empty out their systems and purge them of normal bodily fluids and effluvia, as if they're at war with their most basic and healthy functions.

The good thing about the talkers is that you can tune them out and focus on your own obsessions, like, oh, let's say figuring out a way to make a connection with the redheaded fireman who just started working at the station up the street. Big Red. Now *there's* someone worth obsessing about.

When she's finished with Cynthia, Katherine puts a scented eye pillow over her eyelids, tells her to take her time, and goes out to the reception area. She strolls behind the desk and nearly bumps into Alan. He's kneeling behind the counter, going through the class sign-in sheets from last week. Lately, he's gotten more and more insistent about checking the sign-in sheets against the receipts, trying to prove that Lee isn't collecting from everyone or is offering a sliding scale to some students. Katherine is keeping her mouth shut on that.

"Hey, babe," he says.

There are so many reasons that being referred to as "babe" by Alan makes her slightly ill, Katherine wouldn't know where to start complaining. Instead she says, "Heeeey," with exaggerated flirtiness she hopes he finds insulting.

She's never entirely trusted Alan—the amazing body, the long hair, the too-handsome, chiseled face, the way he preens in front of classes when he's playing live music—as if it's all about *him*. Since Lee confided that he moved out on her and the boys, she trusts him even less. Lee is better off without Alan, but he hasn't earned the right to walk out on her. As for the reasons behind that move, Katherine has a few suspicions of her own, but she's keeping her mouth shut about that, too.

"Do you know how many people are signed up for my kirtan workshop next week?" he asks.

"Three," Katherine says.

If Alan had his eye on his own business instead of counting up Lee's receipts, he'd know this. Katherine rents her massage space at Edendale Yoga, and she ends up spending more time at the studio than anyone else, including Lee, waiting for clients and killing time between appointments. Out of fondness for Lee, she tries to keep her eyes on as many things as she can, but in a low-key way—she's committed to not getting overly involved in anyone else's life. Still, too many people have their unskilled hands on things around here—mostly studio assistants who trade front desk duty for free classes. In addition to having minimal knowledge of how to work the computer programs, they're always in such a rush to get into class, they leave money on the counter, credit card receipts scattered around, and the computer screen littered with Post-it Notes with questions, requests, and assorted details about unfinished business. Last week, Katherine saw one that said: "I cldn't figger how 2 print rcpts, so let evry1 in free. Hope OK. ☺ Tara."

"Three," Alan says. "Perfect. I was hoping it would be a small group. That makes it so much easier to work with them."

Katherine says nothing, the best way to let him know she isn't buying that comment. He's a good musician and has a nice voice, but after the last workshop he gave, she heard a lot of complaints from students that he mostly performed and didn't let them sing much.

Katherine also knows that Alan was supposed to leave the car at the school for Lee today, but she can see it outside the studio.

Classic passive-aggression and an issue she is not going to get in the middle of.

He walks into the studio, and through the glass doors Katherine can see him "stretching," a routine that involves a lot of preening and prancing, a few push-ups to get his biceps pumped, and a handstand that he holds for almost a minute. Supposedly he was a runner or something in college, and he *does* have a great practice, one that would be a lot more impressive if it wasn't so obviously intended to impress.

Alan's music career is the reason he and Lee moved out here. The fact that it didn't work out as he planned doesn't say anything about his talent; show business didn't work out as planned for most residents of this city—herself included. Katherine has sat through enough of his coffeehouse and private performances to know that he's a skilled musician and a capable songwriter. But sadly, he tends to oversell himself in front of an audience or let out a trace of bitterness about the disappointing size of the crowd, so you end up feeling like a jerk for having shown up. "I had confirmation from forty people that they were coming tonight," he once said from the stage to an audience of ten. "I guess they had something better to do."

As far as Katherine's concerned, Alan's behavior toward Lee is just a lot of unattractive acting out. The spoiled boy who's used to being the center of attention needs some space to lick his wounded ego. As for what she saw him doing in the office two weeks ago . . . more acting out.

She gathers up the sign-in sheets and goes back into Lee's office, turns on the computer, and pulls up the receipts for the past week. Because she's a body worker and a former junkie, everyone assumes her computer skills are basic. Sometimes it helps to keep expectations low.

The last thing Lee needs right now is to have Alan breathing down her neck about all the free passes she hands out and the bartering she does with some of the regulars and the sloppiness of the studio assistants. She tries, whenever she can, to get rid of the Post-it Notes and bring a little sanity to the accounting side of things. Alan would probably be upset if he knew, but it's not like he's going to handle the job himself.

Katherine is so absorbed in what she's doing, she barely notices the sound of sirens. When they register, she heads out to the sidewalk and sees the fire trucks headed down the hill. Another brush fire somewhere, no doubt. And no sign of Big Red on the truck.

L orraine Bentley intercepts Lee as she's dashing across the street to the school.

"Don't freak," she says. "It's just another false alarm."

Lee isn't having any of it. "Where are the twins? Have you seen them? What's going on, Lorraine?"

The two of them jog down the line of kids, most of them in giddy recess mode. A little voice in Lee's head is telling her everything's fine and she's overreacting, but a louder voice is shouting, *Where are they?* All the pent-up tension of the past couple of weeks is beginning to squeeze her in the chest.

Then she spots four boys off by themselves in the playground, clearly not where they're supposed to be. She sees Michael push a boy off the jungle gym. Marcus dashes over and helps the boy get up.

Lorraine grabs her arm and says, "Don't let them see fear on your face, Lee. Don't get them worried."

As she steps onto the playground, the boys rush over to her and grab her legs. Even Michael. "Someone tried to blow up the school," he says, proud rather than worried, but the fact that he's clinging to her like this means he smelled trouble.

Miss Marquez appears from around the corner, looking even more harried and exhausted than she usually does. "I'm sorry, Lee," she says, trying to catch her breath. "They were all supposed to be on the sidewalk. I don't know how the boys got over here. Didn't you boys hear the announcement? Didn't you hear me calling for you?"

They're still clinging to Lee, not even bothering to respond. Miss Marquez has lost what little influence and control she had. "What happened?" Lee asks her.

Miss Marquez can't be more than twenty-five. Teachers use the school system here as a résumé builder. Two or three years and they're out with a badge of honor, moving on to greener pastures. There's sweat beading up on her forehead, like little blisters. She speaks quietly, so only Lee can hear. "A call about someone with a gun. This was just a precaution. They were pretty sure it was a prank right from the start."

It's the third unnerving "prank" since January. And it's only March. There was a bomb scare, rumors of a new superflu that caused a two-day closure, and now this. It's just what happens these days, but what worries Lee most is that the overstressed faculty and administration don't seem to be able to control the situation. For the past year, she's been telling the principal that she'd love to come and give yoga classes for the staff, to help them deal with the stress, but there were objections from a couple of teachers that the practice conflicts with their "religious beliefs." *Breathing*, she asked, *conflicts with their religion?* This just renews her conviction that she's got to keep pressing the issue. Maybe she could offer one week of free classes at the studio for teachers. Alan would love that.

Back on the sidewalk, Lorraine has Birdy's hand. Birdy is a sweet little girl who seems to be living up to Lorraine's odd choice of name. Pale, thin, and decidedly sparrowlike. Predictably, the twins call her "Turdy." Lee's had no success getting them to stop, but at least they no longer do it to her face. And let's face it, the kid is . . . unusual?

"Garth and I are calling in all our chits," Lorraine tells Lee. She's the only real California blonde Lee is friends with, and, with her Joni Mitchell coloring and cheekbones, Lorraine makes Lee hear strains of "Ladies of the Canyon" every time they meet. "His parents, mine, every relative we can think of. I can't do this anymore. I don't care how expensive it is or how I'm supposed to support public education. One of these times it's not going to be a false alarm."

Birdy is staring at Lee with her preternatural gaze, her watery blue eyes too limpid and ethereal for an eight-year-old. She really doesn't belong at this school. At least Michael is a tough kid. And even if Marcus isn't, he has his twin around to (hopefully) help him out.

"You look sad," Birdy says.

"No, no, honey," Lee says. "I'm happy that everything's okay here, that's all."

Birdy gives Lee one of her eerie silent stares, and Lee knows she understands that she's being lied to.

Garth and Lorraine are both artists with a big studio behind their modern house by Shakespeare's Bridge. They play an active role in the local gallery scene, and Lee's lost count of the number of openings she's gone to for them. They're one of those couples who seem to spend all of their time together and to be constantly holding each other's hands. She once heard Garth refer to Lorraine as "Mommy" in a way that made Lee a little uneasy.

She finds Lorraine's big, muddy canvases incomprehensible

and unattractive, which makes them a lot more appealing than Garth's embarrassingly homoerotic nude self-portraits. They claim to be struggling artists living hand-to-mouth, but it's hand-to-mouth at a pretty high level. Lee guesses they call in their chits a few times a year.

"Do you have another school in mind?" Lee asks.

"We've got applications in at three," Lorraine says. "They're all interested, but we're waiting to hear."

In other words, they've been planning this for months, long before any of the recent incidents at the school. This makes Lee resent Lorraine in some inexplicable way and, at the same time, feel like a bad mother for not having investigated the same options herself. But she's always been one to try to fix a situation instead of running from it.

She heads to the lot with the boys and searches for the car. As suspected, it isn't there. She's tempted to call Alan and start ranting, but it's always best to just deal on your own, she's found. Especially now. She's afraid that showing Alan she needs him will only drive him farther away.

Michael is poking his brother, and as she walks back to Lorraine, she separates them a few times before they settle down. Lorraine has on a casual, slightly shredded, gauzy skirt and a crisp blue shirt. Lorraine has a look. Maybe Lee needs to acquire one, too.

"I forgot that Alan has the car today," she says. "It's been so busy at the studio, I'm more scattered than usual, which is saying something."

"Do you need a ride?"

"If it's not too inconvenient."

Lorraine looks at the boys. "We'll put Birdy up front," she says. "If you don't mind riding in back."

"I insist."

They get the kids arranged and strapped in, and Lee sits between the boys to keep them apart. Michael immediately starts swatting at Marcus and she gives him a look.

"So I've been meaning to invite you to an opening Garth's having in a couple of weeks." Lorraine names a date as she pulls out of the lot. Lorraine is one of the overly cautious drivers whose hesitation at every turn is meant to be safe but is actually a hazard. "He's just finished some new work and the gallery is so excited about it, they shifted their schedule around to give him a show. We'd love it if you and Alan could come, if that's possible?"

"I'm pretty sure that week is open." Something about the way she asked the question makes Lee a little paranoid that she's heard rumors about Alan's move. They've told the kids he's just staying with Benjamin so they can get some work done and they don't need to talk with anyone about it, but you never know what's going through their heads. As for the opening, the idea of standing around Garth's paintings with a group of people talking about his technique while pretending not to see the garish depictions of his dick that are always front and center on his canvases is pretty excruciating. But there are a lot of things Lee likes and admires about the couple, and it might do her and Alan good to appear together in public.

"I'll send you an e-mail," Lorraine says. "It'll have to wait until Thursday. Garth and I have Wednesdays as a techno-free day. No cell phones, no computers, no TV. You guys should really try it. It always ends up being our most romantic day of the week, if you see what I mean."

"Sounds good," Lee says. She starts playing with her hair nervously, thinking about Alan and the fire drill and the last time she and her husband had a romantic day of the week. (And "most" implies there's more than one day a week that's passionate!) She's always telling her students not to compete and to let go of ego, but sometimes Lorraine makes her feel as if her own life is going off the rails.

"Are you okay, Mom?" Marcus asks. He's her worrier.

"Oh, sweetie," she says. "Of course I am. I just got a little nervous when I didn't see you on the sidewalk."

Michael starts kicking the back of Birdy's seat and chanting, "Ice cream, ice cream, ice cream, ice cream."

She reaches over and puts a hand on his thigh. Does Alan take them out for ice cream when he picks them up? She thought they had an agreement about the kids' diet, but she thought a lot of things that aren't turning out to be what she imagined.

"We've got some tofu pops in the freezer at home," she says.

Even Marcus screams in protest at that suggestion and joins in with his brother's chanting.

To hell with it, she thinks. She could use a little indulgence herself. "What do you think, Lorraine? My treat?"

"Let's go to the new gelato place," she says. "Birdy's lactose intolerant and they have sorbet."

Michael makes farting noises on the back of his hand, but hopefully not loudly enough for Lorraine to hear.

The thing that Katherine likes best about the new Dutch bike she bought online is that it's pink. It's true, she paid too much for it—and extra for the designer color—but her massage practice at the studio has really caught on in the past few months, and she figures she owes herself a little pampering, a treat. She ordered it on the second-year anniversary of her sobriety. Why not?

It's sturdy, it's solid, and she feels cool riding it around Silver Lake. Complete strangers sometimes wave at her. It has a great classic design, and she gets off on dressing to match the bike's style, if not its color—a little more girly and retro-chic, a little Zooey Deschanel. She's been getting back into sewing and has taken apart and restitched a couple of vintage dresses she had stored away in a closet. It's true the bike is a target for thieves, but in her mind, that only confirms its value. She's got a very good lock.

What she likes least about the bike is that it really doesn't show off her ass.

Under most circumstances, she'd consider this a plus. She's had way more than her fair share of wanted and unwanted attention all her life, and there's no use pretending that thirty percent of her massage clients at Edendale Yoga aren't guys (and one or two girls) who think she's hot. Almost a year ago, after she put an end to her relationship (to be generous about what was in fact more like an exercise in low self-esteem) with Phil the Impossible, she decided to take a break from men and dating and sex altogether. It's been among the most relaxing stretches of time she's had in years and the most centering, but lately, as she's biked down Hillhurst Avenue to the studio and past the station house and spotted the redhead—two days ago she chatted up one of the other firemen, who told her his name is Conor—she's had a sudden desire to be leaning over the handlebars, flaunting the results of all those utkatasanas she's been doing over the past couple of years.

The way she sees it, there's a big fat connection between sex and yoga (well, sex and *everything*, but who's counting?) that a lot of people don't like to own up to. A lot of people she knows come for the body sculpting (sex appeal), combined with the flexibility (sexual enhancement), and the muscle control (duh!). The boyfriend before Phil also turned out to be a total shit (actor!), but after one month of Lee's classes, his staying power increased dramatically.

And if people aren't using yoga classes to enhance their sex lives, they're using them as an alternative to sex after a divorce or a bad breakup (Stephanie, she's guessing) or a long dry spell. How else do you explain the popularity of Gianpaolo's classes at the studio? His Italian accent is so thick, it's hard to understand a lot of what he says. But *man*, does he give amazing adjustments, especially in paschimottanasana, when he more or less drapes himself over you backward so you can get your forehead closer to your knees.

There are a few tragic types, like Brian/Boner, who come to class to show off their wares, but they usually end up the resident joke at Lee's studio. The white stretch pants that scream *I'm serious about yoga, ladies—and circumcised.* She's guessing he'll either finally hook up and (mission accomplished) stop coming or realize no one's buying and head off to a big commercial studio with a singles bar atmosphere. There is no shortage of those in this town.

It's another perfect morning, and since she's got a few extra minutes before Lee's 9:30 Intermediate Vinyasa class, she circles the block twice, hoping to spot or be spotted by Conor. Nothing. It's a shame. She has on a yellow cotton dress and it looks great with her pale skin, and she's finally learned how to ride while wearing a skirt. (Carefully, but not *too*.) She's tempted to stop and adjust the basket she has on the front to see if Conor ventures outside, but that's too obvious. She let one of the guys know she wouldn't be disappointed if Conor contacted her, so maybe she'll just leave it at that. And there's always lunch break.

As she's locking the bike up behind the studio, she sees Lee through the window of her office, talking on the phone with her head down. Katherine always suspected that something was up in that marriage, never bought into the conventional wisdom that it was a perfect match. Like those exist? She's been around the block a few too many times, had her heart broken too often, and seen the darker side of the way men really act to buy into fairy tales.

The truth is, Lee's marriage is none of Katherine's business. She knows that. But if it wasn't for Lee, Katherine would probably still be using. She'd still be working for the escort service. Assuming, that is, she was still around. For a while there, that wasn't certain. How much Lee knows about the specifics of *that* tawdry chapter is not clear. Not that it's such a shocker. Just another L.A. story: tough, clueless girl from Detroit heads west with totally half-baked ideas about acting, ends up "dancing," leading to escorting, leading to self-loathing, leading to self-medicating, and culminating in one long slide into self-destruction. Where would she be if she hadn't met Lee? Hadn't been welcomed into the studio free of charge? If Lee hadn't lent her the money for the massage school? More to the point, where would she be if Lee hadn't shown her unconditional belief in Katherine's talent as a healer and her ability to keep herself clean?

In the reception area, she can see from the number of shoes in the cubbies that it's going to be a packed house. This is Lee's most popular class, but it's a crowd, even for her. Katherine goes into her massage room and peels off her dress, hangs it in the closet, and gets into her old tank top and the cotton drawstring pants she bought at a street fair at Venice Beach. She absolutely refuses to go the trendy-yoga-outfits route. Even if she secretly craves some of the practicality of those pricey outfits.

At the reception desk, she bumps into Lee.

"It looks like a big crowd in there, Miss Lee. You up for it?"

"I can't wait."

Katherine slips on a headband, not that she really needs one with her current hairdo. Six months ago, a client of hers gave her a gift certificate for an obscenely expensive haircut in Hollywood that came out looking as if she'd hacked her hair off herself. So now that's what she does. Scissors, mirror, and voilà. Maybe a little punky, but it suits her, and it is kind of surprising with the retro clothes and the twirly skirts. Lee has dark circles, not the way she usually looks. Exhausted? Or has she been crying? As causally as she can, Katherine asks, "Everything okay?"

Lee smiles. "A little distracted. Something at the kids' school last week. The Alan stuff catching up with me." She looks away from Katherine and says with enough sincerity to break Katherine's heart, "You think I'm a good mother, don't you, Kat?"

"What's this about? Why would you even ask me that? As for Alan, he's going through some early-onset midlife thing that will pass."

"I'm just trying to keep my options open, that's all."

This seems to refer to something specific, but Katherine has no idea what. She'd like to ask, but it's 9:30, and Lee never starts class late.

If Katherine were a painter, she'd do a series of portraits of people on their mats before class begins. It's incredible how much you can tell about someone's personality just from those first couple of minutes. If Bosch were around, she's pretty certain this is what he'd be painting—a little microcosm of the world, with so many types crowded into one little space.

There are five people lying flat on their backs, two of them using blocks as a pillow, and one with her hands folded on her stomach, actually (though lightly) snoring. Tina of the endless retail drama is sitting up in a tense lotus, twisting her head from side to side to see who else is in class and how much space she's going to have to do her splits. There's a couple she sees every once in a while, their mats close together, lying on their sides, heads propped up in hands, very quietly talking. They met here, he's married, and if they're not having an affair they will be long before they can do headstands. It's easy to see from the way they're looking at each other that if Lee started the class half an hour late or just scrapped it altogether, they'd barely notice.

Boner is at the front of the room, *facing the class*, loosening up his lower back by thrusting his hips (etc.) forward. A woman in a purple leotard who comes at least five times a week is "politely" asking someone if he'd mind moving his mat over "just a hair," all with a smile that's so hard and tense it could cut glass. And two guys Katherine has never seen before are executing a series of warm-up sun salutations in a "watch us, aren't we amazing" fashion. One short and muscular, the other lean, so they look like a Mutt and Jeff team. Where'd they come from?

Lee gets things going by asking, as she always does, if anyone has any injuries she should know about. Purple Leotard's hand goes up, and before Lee can even acknowledge her, she's off and running.

"I'm not sure if you'd call it an injury, but I've been noticing this little crick in my neck when I wake up? It's kind of annoying? I'm not sure if it's related, but my boyfriend just moved in and we're still using my double bed. His furniture is in storage back in New York? We'd been planning for him to move out here for years, and then finally, last month, he did it! Yay! It's been so great having him here. At first I didn't think I'd like sharing my place. . . ."

"Congratulations," Lee says, interrupting, but sweetly. "Go easy on the twists, and look down at your mat when I'm telling everyone else to look up. We'll start there. Anything else?"

"I went to Chloe's class last Monday," someone says—nasal voice, but Katherine can't see the speaker. "And someone I've never seen before was teaching."

Katherine thinks of this portion of the class as optical-asana since she spends so much time rolling her eyes.

"That was Melissa," Lee says. "She stepped in at the last minute when Chloe had an emergency root canal. Did you like her class?"

"She only did three sun A's at the start of class, and Chloe always does five, so I was kind of disoriented. I mean, not just in class, but all day. It really freaked me out."

"I noticed that," Tina says. "It was weird."

"Whatever," the nasal voice says. "I think the studio should have a policy of more uniform classes so we know *exactly* what we're getting."

Katherine wonders why Lee bothers to start the class this way. Half the time, people just want to discuss their private lives or make irrelevant observations or veiled complaints. Most people with real injuries talk to her privately before the class begins. It's probably part of Lee's desire to create a community, and it's true, it does tend to make people feel they have input into what goes on in class, makes them feel as if they're part of the process, even if, cases in point, it's an annoying part.

"Melissa is a wonderful teacher," Lee says. "I prefer to let her, and all the teachers here, decide how they want to teach their classes. I think it's best to forget expectations and try to get as much as you can from what's being offered. Otherwise, you risk ending up missing out on something potentially great. Are we ready to begin?"

Fifteen minutes into class, Katherine has one of those experiences she thinks of as her Katherine-has-left-the-building moments. Although really, it's much more than a feeling of escape. She's floating somewhere above the hardwood floor, feeling a curious combination of physical challenge and complete release. It's Lee's magic. She started off the class with an intense series of sun salutations. You never know how long Lee is going to have the class hold a posture, so you just have to let go of expectations and past classes and give yourself over to her expertise. Katherine didn't count the sequences, but by the second one, she felt as if she was dancing and her breath was the music. Not *her* breath, but the collective breath of the class. Lee can have thirty people breathing in unison within minutes. It's a strangely powerful, sensual experience. She has a way of making you concentrate on the smallest movements and adjustments of your own body, while still feeling connected to the whole group.

The sun salutations slid into a series of balancing-stick warrior postures that made Katherine feel strong and perfectly grounded, and a few minutes later, they were doing half moons. It was during these, when Lee's deep, musical voice and clear metaphors had everyone curving deeper and deeper, that Katherine noticed the woman practicing next to her and was shocked she hadn't noticed earlier. There was no mistaking the fact that it was Imani Lang, *the* Imani Lang. There couldn't possibly be two women in the world that looked that uniquely gorgeous.

But even standing next to a bona fide TV star (unless, given recent events in Imani's life, she's been demoted to "former TV star") doesn't keep Katherine from going to that strange, beautiful place where she can think of nothing but what she is doing right now, stepping out of time and leaving all of her usual concerns outside. It's this moment and Lee's ability to bring her back to it again and again that helped her stay off drugs back when it

was an uphill battle to do so. Now it's what keeps her on the right
path. She feels an intense combination of happiness, gratitude,
respect, and a few other less defined emotions that add up to the
feeling that there's just nowhere else she'd rather be at this very
moment. Unless maybe . . . except, no, she doesn't even know the
big redhead. Here is perfect.

Imani's underpants started creeping up her butt ten minutes
into class, and by the time the teacher has them on their stom-
achs doing back bends, she can't help reaching down and adjust-
ing them. Not a pretty move, but necessary. Next time—if there
is one—she'll remember to wear a thong. Although God knows
what problems that might present. There are two women in the
front of the class who could join Cirque du Soleil tomorrow if
they wanted to. What are they wearing, she wonders. *Very spiritual inner monologue*, she thinks, and then decides to drop the
self-criticism. Half the people in the room are probably obsessing about their underwear. The other half are probably focused
on the guy in front who's clearly not wearing any.

"Don't worry about lifting up your chest," the teacher says.
"Focus on pushing your feet back and feeling how you rise, softly,
as if your heart is starting to swell with love and compassion."

She comes over to Imani and, while still talking, gently moves
her arms in a way that makes Imani feel as if her upper body
floated off the floor.

"You're doing great," she says quietly. Imani takes this to mean that she's doing so badly and making so many clumsy moves, it's obvious that she and this rubber mat are new acquaintances.

At the end, as everyone is lying on the floor in "corpse" pose—cheerful image—Imani decides that if she had to rate the experience, she'd give it a C minus. Or maybe a big fat D for "disappointing." Like she needs one more disappointment.

The problem is, the class was better than she was expecting and she's actually feeling pretty calm and loose and relaxed, which means that she's going to have to tell all the people who've been advising her to try a yoga class—Cameron, Drew, Becky Antrim—that they were *right*. That's disappointing.

When everyone starts filing out, she stays on her back and starts doing some sit-ups. There's probably something anti-yoga about doing a sit-up, but too bad. Plus, it lets her stay a little low-profile. She hates it when she gets recognized and someone starts making a fuss over her and hates it even more when no one does. Lose-lose.

Ever since she lost the baby eight months ago and went into a very well-deserved depression, everybody's been saying: Try yoga, try yoga, try yoga. Like what? That's going to make her un-miscarry? It reminds her of the kinds of moronic things people said when her mother was diagnosed with breast cancer. Her mother should be drinking green tea. She should stop eating sugar. Has she tried aromatherapy? *It's not a headache*, she always felt like screaming. *It's cancer!*

Good old L.A. Everyone's got the answer to everything, and she wishes that just once it didn't come down to the same hocus-pocus New Age holistic bullshit. There's nothing she loves more than hearing advice about an herbal cure for cancer and the horrors of the *legitimate* medical profession (*Western medicine is inhumane!*) from someone whose face, body, and teeth indicate she's spent more time in hospitals than Dr. Kildare.

She's up to one hundred sit-ups and she's not stopping until she does another one hundred.

Another thing is Silver Lake. She'd never been up here before, even though she lives nearby in Los Feliz, but two weeks ago, when she was driving around in the aimless way she's taken to doing in the past month or so—afternoons can be surprisingly long when you're not working and your husband is a doctor— she headed up this way. She was shocked by the laid-back atmosphere, a crazy mix of new hippie, old-style rock-and-roll, and California cool, all blended in with sidewalk cafés and vintage clothes shops, loopy murals, and a surprising lack of chain stores. Everybody seemed to be hanging out. Like her, but less guilty about it. She made a mental note when she passed the yoga studio. Maybe this was what she needed. An out-of-the-way place where everyone was low-key and artsy-fartsy enough to guarantee a small class of eccentrics who never watch TV and wouldn't recognize her from her *X.C.I.A.* glory days. Wrong again. The classroom was jammed, half the students looked as if they stepped off the cover of *Yoga Journal* or *Vogue*, and a few of them did a double take and whispered when they saw her walk in. And okay, she still gets a charge from that, but not when she's about to make an ass of herself trying to stand on her head. (Who knew she'd find it so easy?)

Out in the reception, the crowd has thinned, but the beauty with the black hacked-off hairdo and tribal tattoos on her biceps who was practicing next to her is still there, chatting with a little group, including the teacher. Who, Imani must admit, is also a beauty. She has dirty-blond hair and well-bred bone structure, intelligence and kindness that radiate off her in waves.

The tattoo girl introduces herself—Katherine—and is so friendly, Imani doesn't mind when she says, "I recognized you right away. And awesome padangustasana, by the way."

Imani can't help but laugh at that. "Pada*what?*" she says. Half the poses were referred to with animal names and the rest with this pretentious language that was obviously Sanskrit. Or meant to sound like it.

"Wait. You don't mean that was your first class, do you?" Katherine asks.

The incredulity in her voice is maybe the most flattering thing Imani's heard since the *L.A. Times* TV critic referred to her as "Halle Berry—if Halle Berry could act."

"Guilty."

"Oh, my God! You were amazing!" This is from the short, brown-haired woman giving off heavy "wannabe" vibes. D-girl, obviously. "You are a total natural. And can I just say, Thursday nights have *sucked* since you left *X.C.I.A.* I'm Stephanie. And this is Graciela, an amazing, amazing dancer."

"When I'm not laid up," the dancer says.

"We're working on her," Stephanie says. "And tomorrow, Katherine is going to be literally working on her."

Katherine makes some exaggerated gestures like a mad scientist kneading bread. Masseuse, no doubt. With those looks, she definitely gets great tips.

Stephanie says, "It's funny seeing you here. I was talking with David Caruso a couple of days ago. He was so great when he did those episodes of your show. He's dying to work on a project I'm setting up."

"Uh-huh." Typical development girl. This translates into: *I've been begging Caruso's agent to read a crappy script that's been shopped around for the past five years.* Still, there's something appealing about the woman, unless it's maybe a feeling of connection carried over from having been through the rigors of the class together.

Imani's a little disappointed the teacher hasn't said anything to her. She was always a bit of a teacher's pet, a feeling that's carried over into a desire to please directors, earn for her manager, and be her doctor's best patient. Two out of three isn't bad. The yoga teacher has moved behind the reception desk and seems preoccupied. When Imani catches her eye, she smiles and says, "You did a great job. And I hate to tell you, but I think there's a guy lurking outside with a camera. I'm assuming that's about you?"

"Oh, shit. I didn't think it would be an issue up here."

She's always had a love-hate thing with the paparazzi. During the height of her *X.C.I.A.* days, when it was all relatively new, she actually loved the attention. The noise and flashbulbs were like exciting background music for the most mundane chores, and suddenly, life was like an exciting movie. And she was the star. She'd really made it, and who ever thought *that* would happen?

But when she lost the baby and they kept coming after her—at the hospital, weeping as she left her therapist's office—she began to think of them as vultures. *Please,* she'd beg, *leave me alone!* But of course that only made it worse. Something else for them to photograph. The dark side of the Hollywood dream, another cliché she'd stumbled into. It was one of the reasons she went back to Texas to be around her family for a month, leaving Glenn alone in L.A. When she came back, she vowed she'd never let them get to her again. Her manager hinted that a little attention from the tabloids might actually be useful at this moment, get people talking about her, if nothing else. But the last thing she wants is to be photographed minutes after she's been sweating her ass off. And isn't wearing makeup.

"Where's your car?" Katherine asks.

"Up the street. There's no way I can get past him."

"We have our secrets," she says, taking Imani's hand. "Follow me!"

She leads Imani out through the back and starts unlocking a big pink bicycle from a post. "You go straight up this alley, up around the block, and left at the Midnight Café. Give me your pack and the keys to your car and I'll meet you in front of the art gallery next door to the florist."

"On the plus side," Imani says, "I'm better at biking than I am at yoga."

"Which you were great at."

It's not until Imani is cycling down the alley that she realizes she's just given her backpack—with her wallet in it—and the keys to her *car* to a complete and total stranger. She starts laughing. Crazy, crazy. For some reason, she trusts Katherine more than she's trusted anyone in a long time. She looks like one of those reformed bad girls that are usually the most honest people you can run into. The bike is amazing, a combination of an old clunker from childhood and deluxe modern efficiency. Maybe Katherine made the real leap of faith by giving her the key to her lock. There's just no way you can feel depressed pedaling along on a pink bike. She might not come back to yoga class, but she probably should rethink that D rating. The day is rapidly turning into a B plus.

Katherine has to admit she got a special kick out of plotting with *Imani Lang* and then driving *Imani Lang's* car up the block. She hasn't been on TV in close to a year (Perez Hilton was full of items about the miscarriage) but she's still gorgeous and it isn't like they get a whole lot of celebrities at the studio. Does it make Katherine shallow to be a little starstruck? Well, that and everything else about her, probably. The tabloids always portrayed Lang as a megadiva with an iron will. Not so. She was like a kid when Katherine complimented her poses. An exaggeration, for sure, but everyone has to start someplace.

Katherine has a noon client coming in for a hot rock massage, a policeman who's constantly making get-your-rocks-off jokes. She has a strong feeling it's all protesting too much and that he's a closet case, but at least he never makes a move. She heads back to the studio instead of circling the block again and checking for Conor. *He moved out here a month ago,* one of the other firemen told her, smirking, yesterday. *And no, he hasn't got a girlfriend.* "I didn't ask," Katherine said. *Believe me,* he said. *You did.*

Down the street from the studio, she notices the Mutt and Jeff guys who were showing off with their routine before class this morning getting into a car. When they close the door, she sees the logo for YogaHappens stenciled onto the side. (Prius, it figures.) She knew there was something about the two of them. The smug way they folded deeply into their paschimottanasanas, their showy ujjai breathing.

YogaHappens is the Starbucks of yoga studios, a corporate concern that's rapidly gobbling up small studios or opening a superstudio next door and forcing them out of business.

Katherine knocks on Lee's office door and rushes in, too steamed to bother with formalities.

"You know those two guys showing off on the right side of the studio today? Tall and short, perfect everything? I *thought* they were a little Stepford Yogi. Guess where they're from? YogaHappens! Can you believe it? Probably scouts, looking to see whose business they can destroy next. Why don't they just change their name to Walmart and get it over with? Jesus."

Lee bursts out laughing, not what Katherine was expecting.

"I feel as if I'm watching ninety minutes of deep breathing go right down the drain."

"Overreacting? You know how I get. But I hate how all these big chains come along and turn everything into a *business*. And what's with that logo of theirs? It looks like a big boob, which is probably a subliminal message they're trying to send. Do you have to let them in if they come back?"

Suddenly Lee isn't laughing anymore. She looks stricken, in fact.

"I'm sorry, Lee. Just ignore me."

"It isn't that, Kat." She runs her hands through her hair. "I invited them to class."

"You *what*?"

"Close the door, will you?"

Katherine closes it and sits down in front of Lee's desk with a bad feeling. It's never a good idea to assume you're on the same wavelength as someone else. It's never a good idea to assume *anything*, a lesson she ought to have learned by now.

"They originally got in touch a couple of months ago. They heard about me and wanted me to 'audition' or something crazy. I didn't pay a whole lot of attention."

Get to the point, Katherine wants to say. She's always hated backstory, no matter how necessary for the plot.

"Please don't give me that face, Kat. I'm just trying to keep my options open, okay? I've got two kids, and the school they're going to is one mishap away from disaster."

Katherine has always hated the way kids trump everything. What's she supposed to say to that? *Forget about them? They'll live? I went to public school—in Detroit, for God's sake—and I turned out all right—once I got off the heroin?* Katherine feels like reminding Lee that her plan was to work *with* the school, not abandon it, but sitting across the desk from her like this,

Katherine suddenly realizes it's probably as much about Alan and whatever is going on with him as it is the kids. And Lee's posted a big Danger: Stay Away sign in front of that part of her life.

"It's still yoga," Lee says. "They're not bad people; they just have a different idea of how to run a business."

"Yeah, marketing research, cookie-cutter classes, and buy, buy, buy. Don't you know how special you are, Lee? You saved my life. About half the people who come here feel the same way, even if the reasons aren't as dramatic. I know that means something to you."

"I'd still be teaching. That's the deal."

Deal? Things have gone that far? "They'll have you doing their spiels in six months, I guarantee. They have forty-five studios between here and San Francisco, they're planning to go national, and they have enough lawyers on staff to roll over you at every turn." Okay, so she's riffing, but the essence of what she's saying is true.

"I've got to think about Alan," Lee says. Katherine knew this was coming. Kids and husbands. What an unbeatable combination. "He's been interested in this for a long time. There might be something in it for him, too. I'm just exploring the options. All right?"

Katherine stands up and opens the door. "It's your studio, Lee. It's your decision. I've just gotten a little hooked on feeling like family."

"I'm exploring, Kat. They're exploring. They want to look over our books, see how much we're actually bringing in."

"I'm sure they'll have fun with your bookkeeping system," she says. "I've got a client in a few minutes."

As she's closing the door, Lee says, "I almost forgot . . ."

Katherine leans back into the office. "Shoot."

"You got a call while you were out."

"Appointment?"

"No. A message from somebody named Conor. He said to tell you he likes your bike."

The demographics on this project are through the roof," Stephanie says. "The novel got the most amazing reviews of the year, everyone is comparing the writer to a young Bret Easton Ellis, and the author *himself* is working on the screenplay. It's got love, Las Vegas, and poker. What more can you ask?"

The producer, Lon Borders, is a handsome young guy with fine, light hair and the kind of freckled skin that is probably going to put him at high risk for something malignant once he hits forty. Stephanie has always had a thing for guys who look like this—swimmer's body and sun-damaged skin, not that she's been anywhere near a beach for twelve months now, not since she and Preston broke up. (*Cheeseburger, cheeseburger,* she silently chants, as she always does when Preston pops into her head.)

Lon produced a couple of so-so horror movies that made money, but *Hello, Pretty!*, an indie hit two years ago, is what got him this office on the Paramount lot. American girl goes to Tokyo and gets involved in Japanese beauty pageants. It did *not* deserve the two nominations it got, but it was cute and a lot smarter than most movies of its sort. He would be perfect for this project. He thinks outside the box and he needs to do something a little more hard-hitting. Another reason he's perfect? He's the last top-tier producer in Stephanie's list of possibilities. If she can't snag him, she's going to have to shift into desperation mode and start working on private investors and grants from Canada and every unlikely place she can think of. Not the way she planned to spend her spring—not to mention the next year and a half. She's running out of steam at exactly the moment she's going to need the most.

Stephanie optioned the book, *Above the Las Vegas Sands*, right around the time she and Preston broke up. She paid more than she should have, but there was a lot of interest, and it was a matter of pride. Preston told her she'd never be able to get the rights. He'd just sold a script and she'd just gotten downsized out of Christine Vachon's development stable.

"Our careers are going in different directions," he'd said. "Let's not get in each other's way." Total creep.

But she showed him (*cheeseburger*), even if she broke rule number one to do so and paid out of pocket. Almost all of the $150K she'd inherited from her mother. Talk about pinning all your hopes on one thing. She was depressed at the time. And even though she's pretty sure she didn't make the offer while she was drinking, she can't quite remember the whole process that led up to the final, way-too-high figure.

Lon's assistant is a little brunette who looks like she graduated high school last year. She's supposedly taking notes on her laptop, nodding at everything Stephanie says, wide-eyed and eager. It wouldn't surprise Stephanie to learn she's really answering e-mail.

The only person who seems engaged is Brady, a spindly guy in skinny jeans sporting a shaved head. He's made a few comments that indicate he actually read the novel before the meeting. Imagine that. He clearly gets the book and appreciates how it could be made into an amazing movie. Too bad he obviously has no power whatsoever.

Lon, the swimmer type, taps his fingers together and glances down at his watch. A small gesture that says way too much. "Tough working with novelists adapting their own books," he says. "In my experience."

No kidding. The way she got the option was by outbidding Christine Vachon, promising the writer he could do the screenplay himself, and then paying him Let's-not-get-into-it up front. Only to have him prove to be a spoiled diva, a type she knows well from her days studying creative writing at Iowa. He cranked out fifty pages that were basically the opening chapters of the novel with different punctuation.

"I think this material would really appeal to Diablo Cody," bald Brady says, God bless him.

"I've already sent her the book," Stephanie says. "She promised she'd read it this weekend."

Stephanie talked to Cody's agent two months ago and was told Cody is booked with writing projects for the next two years and can't even look at anything else. An Oscar can do that. Lying like this is pointless, but it's pride rearing its dangerous head again. She gets the feeling Lon is wasting her time, teasing her along because it gives him a kick to make her perform for him and see her sweat, let her believe he *might* be interested if she jumps through enough hoops. She's seen this dynamic too many times already. Since the contraction in Hollywood, there are about forty-three thousand, two hundred and seven freelancers like Stephanie bopping around town trying to get some traction, and most of them are spinning their wheels. She knows it, Lon knows it, but they still have to do this dance.

Then again, he *might* be interested. You can't burn any bridges.

"Not only that," she says, improvising, "but I was talking to Imani Lang the other day—we go to the same yoga studio—and she's a huge fan of the book and is dying to play the singer."

"I thought she quit the business," Lon says dryly, opening a desk drawer in a random way.

Gossip wakes up the young assistant, who rattles off a monologue about Imani littered with facts (you can put quotes around that), some of which Stephanie didn't know. She's married to a pediatric surgeon and quit *X.C.I.A.* at his suggestion when she got pregnant. Then came the very public miscarriage and the very publicized depression. Come to think of it, Imani *would* be perfect for the singer, a character with so many ups and downs they could name a ride at Disneyland after her.

"Interesting," Lon says. "But Imani can't open a movie."

"She has an amazing voice," Stephanie says. Who's to say she doesn't? "She originally wanted to get into music. She would be a natural for the soundtrack and tie-in video. Anyway, *Vegas Sands* is an ensemble piece."

She decides to stand up before Lon makes his move. The more she thinks of it, the more excited she gets. Even if the author is a pain in the ass, the novel is brilliant, and it *is* going to make an incredible movie. If Lon isn't interested, she's not spending another minute here. You can't burn bridges, but you can cut your losses.

As bald Brady is ushering her down the hall, he says, "This has fabulous potential. I'm going to talk to Lon about it some more."

"Thanks," Stephanie says. "I appreciate that. It has the kind of characters that would attract a really great cast. And believe me, we could do it cheap."

"You don't have to talk me into it. I loved *Silver Linings*, by the way. It's a big favorite with me and my friends. I've watched it four times."

She can't help but wonder if this is true, but why not take the easy way out and believe that it is? *Stop judging and start feeling,*

Lee said in class last week. *What would it feel like if we just accept things as they are instead of judging them?*

She's not going to let it show on her face, but listening to Brady crow about the movie, she could easily tear up. *Silver Linings* came out five years ago, a small, intelligent movie about a troubled family. She got the project to the producer, and even though she didn't make anything, she got a producing credit. The movie was a big hit at Sundance, and if you believe the reviews, a lot of that was thanks to the uncredited work she did on the screenplay. The scenes she rewrote from top to bottom are the ones they always praise.

Unfortunately, all the excitement, prestige, and promise was followed by a lot of heartbreak with distributors, deals that didn't materialize, and a commercial run that never got off the ground. It was through the movie she met Mr. Cheeseburger. Still, the film continues to open doors for her, just not as widely as it once did.

Outside, the sun is too bright and there's something dry and suffocating about the air. She woke up with a headache this morning and psyched herself into believing this meeting with Lon was going to change her losing streak, even though she knew the chances were slim. She loves being on the Paramount lot and always has. It's a kick. Unless, that is, you've just been kicked in the pants. Then all the classic Hollywood fixings—the stucco buildings, the cute little golf carts—start to grate on your nerves.

Her car is roasting hot, and when she turns on the AC, she hears that funny ticking noise the engine's been making for the past few weeks. Like she needs another expense. According to careful calculations, she can live off her savings for another two months. If she's careful. After that . . .

But she's not sure what happens after, and she's not going to drive herself crazy thinking about it. She'll *get* the money. She will make this movie. She'll show . . . *Cheeseburger, goddamn it!*

Stephanie is supposed to meet Graciela this afternoon, but if she hits any traffic at all, she'll probably be late anyway. She's not entirely sure if she's eaten yet today. She was nervous about the meeting and rushing around. Oddly enough, she's not hungry. What she really wants is a drink. There's a restaurant not far from here that serves great salads and the kind of fun, frothy cocktails you can pretend are smoothies.

But as she's heading down Melrose, all that sunlight and sparkle start to get to her, and she can feel the headache creeping up on her again. She decides to head up to Santa Monica Boulevard and go straight back to West Hollywood. She's got a list of a dozen names of people with no credentials but a few extra dollars they want to use to buy their way into the movie business. She never thought she'd have to sink this low, but it is what it is. Might as well plunge in. She'll pick up a bottle of wine, head home, pull the shades, and start making calls.

Lee takes it as a positive sign that Alan has agreed to go to the gallery for the opening of Garth's show. She couldn't get out of attending since she sees Lorraine at school almost every day, and to have gone solo would have been humiliating and the start of rumors and gossip. At least this way, they'll present a picture of domestic stability. She's surprised that this matters to her—the picture—but right now, it seems important. There's no need to make this temporary move of Alan's look more significant to friends than it is.

The night of the opening is so cool and beautiful, that when

Alan shows up at the house, they decide to walk. Another positive sign. It should only take them about thirty minutes. Barrett, one of the interns at the studio, has agreed to babysit for the twins. Barrett's a senior in college studying early childhood education. She was a gymnast up until a few years ago when she aged out of the sport and made a canny decision to transition to yoga. She's studying with another gymnast-turned-yogini at school and she has an impressive (if maybe *too* athletic) practice. Someday she could be a great teacher. The twins like her. Lee does, too, even though she doesn't always trust her. Sometimes Barrett gives indications of being envious of other people's lives—Katherine's massage practice, Chloe's teaching skill—in ways that make Lee uncomfortable.

"Katherine spotted the YogaHappens people at the studio the other day," she says to Alan as they stroll along.

"It'll be all over the studio in a week," Alan says.

"She's the most discreet person I know," Lee says. "I didn't even ask her to keep it quiet. It's understood."

"It's understood until she decides to blab," he says. "People like her get better, Lee, but they don't change."

Lee decides to keep her mouth shut. Alan is thirty-four, two years younger than Lee. He's been on the fringes of the music business since he was twenty. Although squeaky clean himself, there's no question that he's hung out with his fair share of drinkers and druggies, but the fact that they're *musicians* somehow excuses the substance abuse in his mind, even when it's ongoing. The fact that they're men helps, too. At Alan's level, there's a lot of sexism in music—it's a bit of a boys' club—and he, like a few of the guys he plays with, has a very thinly veiled resentment of women who get the attention he thinks he deserves. The same old arguments about women not being *real* guitar players—as if—what?—you play guitar with your penis? (Grudgingly, they admit that women can sometimes be real pianists and, of course, violinists.) If Katherine were a man, he'd be more understanding about her past and her transformation.

"There are a lot of bad feelings about that YogaHappens," she says. "Too corporate, too aggressive."

"It's about us, Lee. It's not about Katherine. It's good for both of us."

She's grateful that he's talking about them as a couple. "Let's have a nice time tonight," she says. "And speaking of discretion, I'd really appreciate it if you don't say anything about your current housing situation."

"Give me a little more credit than that," he says.

"How's the work going on the songs?" she asks.

"Jesus, Lee. You sound so suspicious when you ask that. Like you assume things aren't going well."

"I'm not assuming anything. I just asked how your work is coming along."

"It's in the tone. It's all about the tone." He moves away from her slightly. "And it's coming great. We've finished three songs. One of them is definitely right for a new reality show that has a soundtrack. Ben's agent is going to be sending it off soon."

"I can't wait to hear."

He shakes his head slowly, another indication that he's taken offense at her tone again. Maybe she did reveal something. When she hears Alan's songs or sees him performing, she can see and hear the talent, no question of that, but also has a strong sense that there's some small but crucial missing piece. Maybe he knows it, too, and that's why he's so defensive. It's probably best to keep quiet.

The gallery is on the fringes of downtown Silver Lake, a former curtain shop that's been painted white from top to bottom and is, if you can believe Lorraine and Garth, becoming one of the more important galleries in a neighborhood known for its artists. There's a crowd of thirty or more people inside, most holding wineglasses, dressed primarily in jeans and stylish little print dresses, listening.

The gallery owner is in the middle of introducing Garth when they walk in. He's a rotund man with huge black eyeglasses that cover half his face.

"... And so we're caught in this miasma of tertiary malignancy. The question isn't *whether* the artist responds, but *how*. And Garth's way is to contextualize the incumbent ... voluptuary ... *solemnity* of the current ardency. That's why this series of paintings is so important, not only to his body of work, but also to our very existence. The malevolent *betrothal* we all feel when we look at this work makes it possible to say: *Yes*."

There's a smattering of polite applause, and then Garth is introduced. He and Lorraine are wearing identical outfits—untucked navy blue shirts over white jeans. And Birdy, standing beside them, is color coordinated. Garth holds up his hands and lets his head drop. He's a handsome man, probably in his late forties, with graying hair he keeps plastered to his scalp.

"I am truly humbled by Tony's words," he says. "They're obviously unearned, but if"—he throws up his hands"—this work keeps the planet spinning on its orbit for even ten seconds longer, I will be happy. I'm grateful to all of you for coming and giving me the opportunity to move you in some small, small way with this work. Now for Christ's sake, let's enjoy!"

Lee sometimes wonders if her own inability to appreciate art is the problem. In style, Garth's painting are somewhere between David Hockney and gay porn. Cool California blues and greens, lots of water, and lots of male flesh. This series of twenty or so paintings depicts Garth sprawled nude (of course) in a variety of positions—faceup, facedown—on a reclining webbed lawn chair. She's not sure what "malevolent betrothal" means, but she's pretty sure it doesn't mean the combination of embarrassment and faint revulsion she feels when she looks at the paintings. What does Lorraine make of all the lurid images of his ass that seem to be invitations? And what about Birdy? She's dressed in a lacy white dress and navy blue Chinese slippers, and is looking at a painting while her father kneels beside her, pointing to something or other on the canvas. Hopefully a palm tree.

When she whispers some of this to Alan, he says, "Don't be such a prude, Lee. You're around bodies all day. You wanted to be a doctor."

"It's not the nudity," she says quietly. "It's that you're supposed to pretend you don't see it and comment instead on the malignancy or whatever it is."

"A minute ago, you were asking me to pretend I hadn't moved out."

Lorraine comes over and gives them big hugs. She smells lemony and sweet, not as if she's wearing perfume, but as if her golden hair and skin are emitting this lovely fragrance.

"We are *so* delighted you could come," she says. Again, there's the emphasis she gives to her words that makes Lee think she knows or suspects something. "Isn't the work amazing? The show is causing a sensation. You're looking as devastating as always, Alan. Don't let him out of your sight, Lee."

Although Alan is (deservedly) vain about his looks, he has begun to express regret that he never gets complimented for anything other than his appearance. People don't even ask him anymore what he's doing musically. Lee wouldn't say so, but she sometimes wonders if this is a matter of friends politely not wanting to rub salt into wounds, since he often reacts in the hostile way he did to her questions.

"There are a couple of people who are dying to meet you, Lee. They all want to start doing yoga."

Lee grabs a glass of wine, takes Alan's hand, and follows Lorraine. There's a group of three women, probably in their forties, standing near the back of the gallery, laughing uproariously about something, maybe a little sloshed. Lorraine introduces Lee, and the first thing one of them says is: "You *drink?*"

"In moderation," Lee says.

"That's so funny. I thought you yoga teachers were all so *pure.*"

Uh-oh. Lee can hear the drip of condescension in her voice, as if Lee has been berating her with a lecture on temperance for hours.

"I guess it depends how you define purity," Lee says. She'd love to tell them she has a pack of cigarettes stashed in her glove compartment, but she'd rather Alan didn't find out about that. "This is my husband, Alan."

"Now *he* doesn't look so pure."

"Alan's a musician," Lee says. "And a songwriter."

"How interesting. Anything we've heard?"

This question is always a slap in the face to Alan. People assume that you're legitimate only if they've heard something you've written on the sound system at Trader Joe's. Lee rattles off the name of a song that was used over the end credits of a movie five years ago.

"Don't know it," one of the women says.

It was a hit with young *people*, Lee longs to say, but that's so catty and also, sadly, untrue.

"Do you ever worry," a woman with bracelets says, "that the yoga 'thing' is like the aerobics fad, and it's going to die out in a year or two?"

This again.

"The practice has been around for thousands of years," Lee says, "so it's already outlived Jane Fonda."

"Really? I heard the Indians cobbled it all together from watching the British soldiers do calisthenics. I'd happily stand on my head if it made me look as good as you two. You're so *fit*."

Somehow or other, this woman makes the word sound obscene. Lee is all too familiar with this kind of thing, being treated with envy and, at the same time, as if she were a freak. It's easy enough to ignore, and at least the condescension toward her balances out a little of the sting Alan probably feels right now.

"I'll bet it's good for your *marriage*," one of the others leers.

"You're welcome to come by the studio anytime you like," Lee says. "Try it out. Bring your husbands."

"There's a laugh," one says. "I'd have as much luck trying to get him to wear a tutu!"

Lee smiles and takes Alan's hand. They go over to Birdy and Garth and congratulate him on the show. He puts his arms around Lee's waist in a way that makes everyone uncomfortable.

"Do you like the incumbent ardency?" he asks.

Lee doesn't say anything and Garth winks. "It's all showbiz, folks. You gotta pay the bills somehow. Nothing sells like selling out!"

Lee is relieved. This is the first time he's given any indication that he knows how all the pretentious talk about his work sounds. It's really the first time he's ever been ironic about himself. "How do you like your daddy's paintings?" she asks Birdy.

Birdy stares at her with her limpid, ethereal gaze. "Mommy said you were getting divorced. How come you're here together?"

Lee tries to smile and looks at Alan. It's definitely time to make a move. If talking with YogaHappens brings Alan home sooner, she's all for it. She'll make an appointment with them tomorrow.

～✤～

Imani is driving through Beverly Hills when she decides to check out a cupcake bakery that opened last month and maybe get a couple of treats. The whole cupcake craze is annoying—and brilliant. She would never allow herself to stop at a bakery and buy a slab of chocolate cake, but a nice little bite-size treat seems way less decadent. She's telling herself the second one she intends to buy is for Glenn, but she knows for certain she'll have it finished before she's anywhere near Los Feliz and home.

The bakery (Cookie's Cakes) is owned by Cookie, a super-skinny white girl who probably wears a surgical mask when she's baking, just in case it turns out smells have calories. Everything in the place is white, and Cookie's dressed in a white lab coat. It feels more like a weight-loss clinic than a place to indulge. Cookie (as likely to be her real name as Imani is hers!) has her head practically shaved, with the remaining stubble dyed platinum blond. This makes her look even skinnier but strangely feminine and girly, too.

Imani forces herself to smile at her and orders a Banana Daiquiri and a Dulce de Leche and then, because the name sounds kind of light and semi-low-cal and the swirl of frosting on top is an appealing pale purple, something called a Lavender Breeze.

"Oh, that's my favorite," Cookie says.

"Really? You eat a lot of these?"

"I taste tiny slivers." She holds up thumb and index finger to the thickness of a credit card. "I'm totally neurotic about my weight, and basically, I started baking because I like being around the temptation, and proving to myself I can resist it. I know, total eating-disorder kind of thing, but not dangerous or life-threatening."

This is such a brutally honest, full-disclosure mouthful, Imani immediately shifts from finding Cookie irritating to being touched by her and admiring of the way she's efficiently packing the cupcakes into a little white box. "At a certain point," she says, "you gotta figure a few pounds don't matter one way or the other."

"Not there yet. But working on it." She hands Imani the box, tied up with a silver ribbon.

"It's brilliant the way you have the place decorated," Imani says. "So clinical, it feels like it's good for you to eat this stuff."

"I know. Smart, right? And feel how chilly it is in here? Same thing. Like someplace you'd do surgery. And I hope you don't mind me saying, but *X.C.I.A.* went way downhill after you left."

"Mind? I'm surprised she didn't *pay* you to say it!"

Imani spins around, and Becky Antrim is standing there, beaming. Imani gives her a big hug, and they walk out to the sidewalk, arm in arm. "Damn, you look good," Imani says. "What's your secret?"

"I don't buy cupcakes," Becky says and flips her world-famous hair off her shoulder. "Which doesn't mean I don't eat them. I just walk back and forth in front of this place until I spot someone I know buying them. Give me one of those little fuckers."

Becky has been holding the title of America's Sweetheart for longer than Imani can remember. She skyrocketed to fame on *Roommates*, one of those iconic TV hits that actually deserved its reputation. Imani met her when Becky was dating one of the guys on *X.C.I.A.* and used to come by the set. Two things surprised Imani: Becky's way more gorgeous in person than she is on screen and, despite being trashed by the tabloids for fifteen years now, despite having more money than God *and* Oprah, despite having had her heart broken in the most public way possible by the most handsome (white) man on the planet, she's still one of the sweetest people Imani's ever met.

They go to a Starbucks around the corner and sit at a sidewalk table, open up the box, look at each other, and start laughing.

"Straight to hell," Becky says. "Let's go, *mon amie!*"

By the time they've polished off the third cupcake, Becky has brought her up to date on the latest love disaster in her life, not in a self-pitying way, but with the ironic, "what else is new" stoicism she uses to deal with everything. No interest in another TV series, she explains, but lots of interest in continuing to do quirky little indie films. "They keep me relevant," she says. "Whatever that means. And they're fun and I've learned more about acting from doing them than I learned all those years on *Roommates*."

"But don't they hurt your career?"

"There are two ways for someone like me to get respect in this town," Becky says. "One is to get paid a fortune for a blockbuster and the other is to get paid nothing for a smart little indie that hits big at Sundance. I alternate between the two."

She licks off the last of the frosting from her fingertips and rests her cheek against her fist. "What about you, sweetie? Are you doing okay?"

Becky's tone, soft and gentle, leaves no doubt that she's asking about the miscarriage and subsequent meltdown. What else would she be asking about?

"I'm doing a lot better," Imani says. She's not sure the "lot" is accurate, but it might help to say so. And eight months after *all that*, she's started to realize that people expect her to be better, so she's doing her best to fake it until she makes it.

"You know what?" Imani says. "I finally started doing yoga."

Becky pops up out of her chair and gives a little cheer. Becky is a famous yoga fanatic. Someone on the street snaps a picture with a cell phone, and Becky turns and gives them a goofy grin and then the finger. She's definitely made peace with the gawkers, something Imani needs a little help with.

"Are you loving it? Where are you practicing? Do you have any idea how long I've been waiting for you to start practicing?"

In truth, Imani only went the one time. And even though she liked it, the idea of getting it all together to go again has kept her from a return visit. Figuring out when to eat and shower and which level class to take and then loading the mat and towels and all that into the car makes her feel exhausted. She got such a warm welcome, she was afraid she was going to get sucked into a social scene she's not sure she's ready for or interested in. It just seemed simpler *not* to go.

"I'm not exactly a fanatic yet," she says.

"Doesn't matter. You will be. What style?"

Shit. How's she supposed to know? "Masala?" she says, snatching the only Hindi-sounding word that comes into her mind.

From the look on Becky's face, she's trying to decide if Imani is joking or not. There have been rumors for a while now that Becky is a big pothead, but Imani's never paid attention to them. If she's stoned right now, there's at least a chance she'll forget the comment. Or maybe she just saw through Imani's exaggeration.

"Well . . ." She waves it off. "The style doesn't matter. It's all good. I have no plans for this afternoon. Let's make a day of it. I have got tons to show you. It's really a good thing we had that high-protein snack!"

Becky takes her to a store in Beverly Hills where she says she does all her shopping these days. It's packed with customers, and not only women, and has a staff of the most fit and beautiful clerks she's seen in a while. The really crazy thing is, they're actually nice. Imani feels like asking if she could have a serving of *that* Kool-Aid, for sure, and maybe they could distribute it around town?

"What do you wear to classes?" Becky asks.

Imani isn't about to tell her that the one time she took class, she wore a tank top and a pair of silk boxers that she bought for Glenn but that he refused to wear. She'd heard you were supposed to wear something loose and they were that!

"Oh, the usual," she says.

Becky purses her lips. "I can tell we're going to need everything," she says. "Let's start off with pants."

She holds up a pair of what look to Imani like pedal pushers. "These are amazing, They hug your legs, but don't bind or anything. They're great when you're doing, I don't know, let's say ardha chandrasana," Becky says.

"Let's you say," Imani tells her, "because I have no idea what you just said."

"And look." She holds out the tag. "Not that you need them, but 'anti–muffin top.' Is that awesome or what?"

What Imani notices mostly is that the customers, all these women of assorted ages and shapes, seem so completely confident about themselves when they're trying on the clothes, even the tight pants and the tank tops. It's the exact opposite of the way she usually sees women acting in sportswear stores. Almost as if they like their bodies . . .

The other thing she notices is that while there's the usual flurry of giggles and double takes upon spotting Becky—and, to a lesser extent, her—there's a palpable camaraderie in the air. People just talk to them. "Did I see you at that Rodney Yee workshop last month?" "Have you tried the new ashtanga studio that opened in Brentwood?" "You have got to check out this teacher at the Sports Club. He's amazing!"

One hour and more money than she wants to think about later, they leave the store loaded down with enough equipment to nearly fill the backseat of Imani's car. Pants, tops, underwear guaranteed not to give her a wedgie. Maybe she went overboard, but she figures if it inspires her to actually get to classes (to show off all the damned stuff) it will be money well spent.

Becky tells her to follow her, and so they wend their way down Santa Monica Boulevard in tandem. Becky, who never uses her directionals, makes a sharp right that Imani nearly misses, and they end up on a quiet side street. Imani's been expecting her to take her to some yoga palace out here for an extravagant class, but Becky turns into the parking lot of a little stucco church.

"I know," she says as she gets out of her Prius. "I know it's not exactly glamorous, but don't say anything until afterwards. I'm on a list, and they e-mail notices of new classes. This one's supposed to be incredible. The teacher is descended from Swami Somebody or Other. At least, that's the buzz."

They go in a side entrance to a little assembly hall that looks and smells like the kind of place Imani's mother used to take her for rummage sales when she was a kid back in Texas. There are about twenty people sprawled around the room, mostly ultra-skinny women that look vaguely familiar. Fashion models, is what she'd guess. There are a few aging trophy wives thrown in, too. Same shape and basic package as the models, but a little more worn and weary looking. A few people smile at them, but it's all in an "I'm not impressed" kind of way.

Becky helps her set up her mat along one wall and goes to sit cross-legged in the middle of her own mat, with her eyes closed. For some reason, Imani starts to get nervous. There's an unspoken intensity wafting off these women that is palpable and a little threatening. She slipped into one of the funky little bathrooms and put on one of her new outfits, but she looks down and realizes she didn't take off the tags. *Look at me! I've never done this before!* Why has she been pretending with Becky all day? What's the point? She feels as if she's about to be thrown into the middle of a very wide lake and told to swim to shore.

She leans over and whispers, "I was exaggerating about the yoga thing. I've only taken one class. And I wasn't very good. I think I should leave."

Becky touches her hand. "You're not going anywhere. Just start breathing and everything else will be fine."

When Lee walks into the lounge at the studio, Tina is loading a carton with tank tops and yoga shorts. They're from a small local company that makes simple, nicely designed workout clothes in cotton. They've been after Lee for months to sell their line and, given the quality of the clothes, she's disappointed to see they're going back.

"No interest?" she asks Tina.

"Not in these."

Lee takes a tank top out of the carton. It's a beautiful shade of light blue, and the body is long so it goes past the hips and doesn't expose your stomach when you're doing inversions. "It's too bad," Lee says. "They're nice."

"It's the company's own fault," Tina says. "I told them they wouldn't sell, and they sent them anyway, and now I'm the one who has to ship them back."

"And it's their own fault because?"

"Because they sent a bunch of mediums. Do you think anyone in here is going to buy medium? They really need to size them right."

Lee thinks it over. She's proud of the fact that her classes attract both men and women, and people of all sizes and shapes. "I'm sure a lot of people would fit into these."

"No kidding. But I told them that women who do yoga aren't going to buy something labeled 'medium.' It's like a slap in the face. Even 'small' is beginning to get iffy. They have to start at XXXS. Some companies have what they call 4XS."

There was a time, Lee thinks, *when this kind of thing made sense to me.* But fortunately, that time is over.

She goes into her office and tries to focus. It's shaping up to be a full day. She has a class in twenty minutes and after that, she has to head up to the house to meet with Alan and the businesspeople from YogaHappens for a preliminary discussion.

She used to prepare for class by making notes on index cards with poses she wanted to cover, metaphors she wanted to use, and, sometimes, a quote or part of a poem she wanted to read during savasana. She trained with a yogi in New York, has all that med school anatomy background, and studied dance semiseriously when she was in college. But she's convinced that what makes her a good teacher is a strange ability she has to look at someone's body and be able to tell where they're holding tension, where they're being fearful, and how they could let go of both. She doesn't make as many notes anymore, preferring instead to have a rough outline of what she wants to cover in her head then simply going with what feels right during class.

There are only eight people in the room today, Graciela included. Lee knew she had potential, but she truly didn't expect her to be as diligent and restrained as she's being. Lee sits on the floor at the front of the room, rests her hands on her knees, and says, "Does anyone have any issues or injuries I should know about?"

In the silence that follows, Lee hears a voice from somewhere inside her own head saying: *Me! I have injuries. You should know about them. I want to be taken care of! Give me a modification and an adjustment. Me, me, me!* But she does her best to ignore the voice and says, "Remember, this is your practice. I'm just here to guide you and take care of you when you need assistance. Let's begin."

Under Lee's guidance, Graciela has been sticking to restorative poses. What this translates to is settling into a pose—one that wasn't that hard to begin with—for a *very long time*. While the rest of the class is doing something else (like moving!) Lee keeps checking on Graciela to make sure she's . . . restoring. The weirdest part of the whole experience is that it's physically some of the easiest stuff Graciela has done in years, and, at the same time, relaxing and remaining quiet and patient feels almost impossibly difficult.

She's lying on her mat now, propped up with a bolster under her hips and a block under her forehead, both of which Lee put into place. Basically, she's not doing *anything*. She didn't even have to do much to get into this position since Lee manipulated her arms and legs. And yet, she's having such a hard time remaining still, she's afraid she's going to burst into tears.

"Whatever comes up for you in these poses," Lee says, "try to let it go. Maybe anxiety? Maybe sadness? Anger? They're just thoughts. Let them go. They only control you and have power if you let them. They're parasites—they can't live on their own."

In the time she's been coming to the studio, Graciela has started to wonder if Lee is a mind reader. In many ways, she's better at judging Graciela's moods and feelings than the tarot card reader she goes to.

"Remember *The Wizard of Oz*? 'Your magic has no power here. Be off with you!' Negative thoughts? Fear? Self-loathing? They have no power here. Be off with you!"

What's coming up for Graciela is Daryl, and more specifically, what really happened when she screwed up her Achilles tendon. The way he pushed her, the way she's pretty sure it wasn't really an accident, the weird way his face got contorted right before it happened and she found herself on the floor. Or is she just imagining the whole thing? Did she just trip? Was he just trying to help her, like he claimed? She felt that pop in her ankle and the combination of pain and awareness of what it meant for her whole career just took over and everything went a little fuzzy.

Lee comes over and lays her hands on the small of Graciela's back. Just her touch—warm and reassuring—is enough to make Graciela let go of the tension she's been holding in her shoulders. Her weight drops down onto the bolster. Okay, she thinks, she's going to let the floor do its work and her body melt. It's so bizarre to be in a room with people doing physical activity (the rest of the class, anyway) and not have any competition or showing off, not even having the *option* of showing off or strutting your stuff that it's almost confusing. *Yoga's about union,* Lee once said. *Union of mind and body. But not your mind and someone else's body.* That was a revelation. And now, really, this is *all* that's expected of her? Sink? Drop? Let go?

But thinking about that, feeling a kind of crazy gratitude, all while Lee is pressing into her back, tears start to come. And before she knows it, she's all-out weeping. Actual sobs. There's no way Lee can miss this, but somehow, Graciela has enough trust in her to just let it go.

"Were you in pain?" Lee asks after the class.

"No," Graciela says. "I mean, I haven't been in pain—much pain—for the past week almost. I got a little emotional."

Lee is looking at her with a smile, her head tilted, almost as if she's asking her for more information. Unless maybe she really *can* read Graciela's mind and is sympathizing with her. Lee has some crazy combination of wholesome beauty—the clear skin, the bright eyes, the fine bone structure—and an undercurrent of quiet fire that makes it hard to take your eyes off her. She *looks* like she came from Connecticut, as Stephanie told her she did. Not that Graciela knows anything about Connecticut. She's spent her entire life here in L.A.

"That happens," Lee says. "It's not a bad thing. Just let it all out." She touches Graciela's hair and winks. "It'll help heal your ankle."

Graciela is tempted to say something about Daryl, but she feels funny already about accepting Lee's generosity. She isn't going to exploit her kindness any more by laying that on her.

Lee looks at her watch and does a little double take. "Shit," she says. "I have to run. I'm due at the kids' school in half an hour and I don't want to be late."

"Let me give you a lift," Graciela says. "Please."

"Are you going in that direction?"

"Whether I am or not," Graciela says, "I wish you'd let me."

Before coming to yoga, Graciela hadn't spent any time in Silver Lake, quite possibly hadn't even been to this neighborhood. She and Daryl share a loft downtown, in a great old building that gives them more space than most of her friends. She's been there for five years and let Daryl move in when one of his roommates got married. It was supposed to be for a couple of months, but it has pretty much worked out. As much as she likes the grit and old-L.A. glamour of downtown, she has to admit it's nowhere near as relaxed and welcoming as this neighborhood.

Graciela's still driving the beat-up VW Golf one of her girlfriends sold her for two hundred dollars right before she moved back east. Graciela doesn't even know what year it is. She looks inside as she's unlocking the door.

"Sorry about the mess," she says to Lee. "My boyfriend's a deejay, and he tends to leave a lot of stuff in here between gigs." She tosses a box of CDs into the backseat. Maybe she shouldn't have been so quick to offer Lee a ride.

"I have twins," Lee says. "You call this a mess?"

"Yeah, but kids are supposed to be messy. It smells like he was eating popcorn in here, too. Sorry."

"You are *so* hard on yourself, honey. Will you stop?"

Graciela wants to apologize for that, too, but manages to keep it in check.

"How long have you two been together?" Lee asks.

Graciela fills her in on the details as they drive down around the reservoir, the sun glinting off the silvery surface of the water, the air hazy and warm. As she's talking about Daryl—mother with drug problems; made a career for himself with raw talent, charm, and drive—she feels a swell of pride and love for him and, at the same time, has the uneasy sense that she's leaving out the most important details.

When they get to the school, Lee asks her if she'd like to meet her kids.

"I'd love to," Graciela says, "but I'm supposed to go visit my mother. Since I was forbidden to rehearse for a while, I've been trying to help her out. She's going through a rough period. My stepfather died last year, and she's still trying to make sense of things."

"I'm sorry to hear it," Lee says. "And Graciela, honestly, I'm proud of what you're doing. This is going to work out fine. Believe me. And I love your car! Popcorn and all."

As Graciela is driving off, she calls Stephanie, but once again, her phone is shut off. She's been trying to get in touch with her for two days. Usually she's the type who's glued to her phone. It's also starting to worry her that she hasn't shown up at the studio in almost two weeks.

So what do you do in these yoga classes?" Conor asks. "Is it like aerobics or Tae Bo or something?"

"I think you're just going to have to come to class and find out," Katherine says. She looks across the table at the restaurant and smiles at him, then bites her lower lip. She either hates or loves the fact that she feels so flirty with this guy, in a silly way, almost like she's back in high school. It's got something to do with his combination of burly, towering machismo and shyness.

When he came by the studio to meet her for coffee, he stuck out his hand to shake hers and said, "You've got a great bicycle there," and she said, "I was hoping you were going to compliment my thighs," and he actually blushed, his pale skin flushing almost as red as his hair. Katherine found it so adorable, so sweet, especially on a guy who's easily six foot four, she's been on her best behavior ever since.

"Don't tell me none of your girlfriends back in Boston did yoga," she says.

"How many do you think I had?"

"I'll bet you've broken a few hearts in your time, Mr. Ross."

"Maybe I had my heart broken."

He gazes off over her shoulder as he says this, and Katherine has the feeling this is exactly what happened to him. He looks so wistful, she says more quietly, "Is that why you moved out to L.A.?"

"Let's go with: I got tired of the snow," he says. "I have a buddy who moved out here a few years ago, and I decided to visit for a few weeks." He shrugs. "One thing led to another."

"How do you like it so far?"

"Depends on the day," he says.

"Today, for example?"

"Oh, man," he says and gazes at her with those huge blue eyes. "I'm really *loving* today."

If Katherine had heard this from most of the men she knows, she'd cringe. But coming from Conor, it sounds so sincere, she feels herself go a little limp. There's that funny Boston accent (*Maybe I had my haaht broken*) that makes everything sound sincere, like a haahtfelt declaration, and the innocent look in his blue eyes that makes Katherine think he's probably one of those upstanding guys who's incapable of telling a lie. She can tell he thinks she's out of his league. After dating a bunch of actors and athletes who strutted around as if they were doing her a favor by going out with her—and guys like Phil, another category of ridiculous altogether—it's kind of nice to be with someone who's actually looking at her. Fortunately, there's only so much he can see. She can't be sure how he'd react to her past, so if this has any chances of going anywhere, she'd better keep a few little things quiet. (Like that little five-year period of mistakes and bad choices.)

"You always wanted to be a fireman?" she says.

"I liked the trucks," he says. "I was in the National Guard for a few years and got some training."

"Were you in Iraq?"

"I love being interrogated," he says, "but you haven't told me anything about yourself. I don't even know where you're from."

Most guys wouldn't think to ask, but now that he has asked, Katherine feels cautious and shy.

"Let me take you back to the studio," she says. "I'll show you where I work. If you're a nice guy, I'll give you a back rub."

"A nice guy," he says, "would give *you* one." He reaches across the table and takes her hand in his. He has a big calloused hand that completely envelops hers. "Let's go," he says. "We'll compare technique."

Lee arranged to meet the folks from YogaHappens at her house instead of at the studio. She doesn't want to risk more rumors, especially since she has not made up her mind about this or is even close. It isn't entirely clear what's being offered to her. Alan's been in and out of the house to pick up and drop off the kids and to try to maintain a semblance of normalcy for their sakes, but the two of them haven't been in the house alone together since his disappearing act. The excursion to Garth's opening was the most time they've spent together, and look how that turned out. She's feeling edgy.

She dropped the twins off at the studio, where Barrett is keeping her eyes on them. Barrett frequently proclaims that she "loves children" but her clothes, hairstyle, and voice suggest it's more that she loves pretending to *be* a child. Still, she's reliable and the kids love scrambling around the studio and playing with the Iyengar props, and Barrett promised she'd take them to the playground so they could burn off more energy.

Lee finds herself tidying up the living room, stashing toys and games into drawers and on the bottom shelves of the bookcases on either side of the fireplace. The fireplace that made Lee and Alan feel like they *had* to buy this adorable little bungalow, even though it meant asking Lee's mother for a loan to get together a down payment. She's tidying for the YogaHappens people, of course. Not for Alan.

She tosses a couple of identical backpacks into the closet, and when she turns around, Alan is standing there, surveying the room.

"Looks pretty tidy around here," he says.

"You scared me. Couldn't you have knocked?"

"Sorry, Lee, but it's still my house, too, you know."

"Right. Except it's also your choice not to be living in it now. So I'd really like it if you'd use the bell next time."

He sighs and drops onto the sofa, his arms spread out across the back. He has on a navy T-shirt and the calf-length yoga pants she gave him for his birthday because she knew he'd look hot in them. Her bad. His hair is pulled back into a ponytail and unfortunately, he looks great. As usual. One of her med school friends from a million years ago, the most brilliant, crazy, and gorgeous girl Lee had ever met—Russian—had become engaged to a fat man whose looks were—to be generous—unremarkable. "Marry homely," Irina had said in her thick accent. "They make you look more pretty when you stand next to them, and they are always grateful to have you."

Maybe she wasn't so crazy after all.

"I don't know why you're being so hostile, Lee. I told you, I just need a little space. It's not about *you*."

"Yeah, but since you won't tell me what it *is* about, I can't help but feel a little . . . implicated? I mean, we're only married, Alan. How can it *not* be about me?" This is what she didn't want to do—blow up. It's what she's very carefully been avoiding doing since he walked in. Oh, well. If you get your feet wet, might as well dive in all the way. "And what does that even mean, 'needing space'? It's something my mother would have said in her bra-burning days."

"Okay, listen," he says. "All of a sudden, our lives, *my* life to be more specific, looks nothing like I expected. I just woke up and realized that we're living out of the loop up here, nice as it is. You're running a yoga studio, and it's taking up all *my* time. 'Can you build another closet?' 'Can you redesign the website?' 'The toilet needs to be snaked out.' I'm not singing, I'm not devoting any serious time to music at all. I'm the fucking handyman, Lee. I realized I was on a runaway train, and I had to get off just to catch my breath."

Lee looks at him more closely. Is that all there is to it? She can live with that if it's a temporary pause. Catching his breath. She's come to realize that yoga is her calling, the way to blend her healing instincts into something physical and emotional, even *she* sometimes feels overwhelmed. Still, she notices he isn't looking her in the eyes.

The thing about self-absorbed men like Alan is they think they can get away with anything, so they don't make much of an effort at being good liars. On the other hand, they're good at compartmentalizing their feelings, so they partly believe what they say and can occasionally be pretty convincing.

"People love you at the studio. You know that. The workshops are taking off, and every class where you play music is full. So runaway train or not, it isn't like you're shoveling coal into the engine all day."

"In other words, you're paying the bills, and I ought to be grateful?"

"I didn't say that." And yet, it is true. Alan sold a couple of songs to a series on the WB a few years back, there was that one movie sale, and he still gets residuals. But it's not like it's enough to cover the electric bills.

"Do you mind if I ask when you're thinking about coming back?"

"Let's take it a day at a time, okay?"

"Like I have a real choice."

He gives her one of his smiles. "You look so good in that tank top. What time are these people showing up?"

"Cut it out," she says. But she loves the smile, and it makes her ache to be lying in bed with him right now, and she wishes she didn't hear the footsteps on their front porch.

The YogaHappens people always seem to travel in pairs. Like nuns and Mormon missionaries and the nice ladies who come by the studio (of all places!) trying to hand out *The Watchtower*.

The two men who were in her class are at the door, both shiny clean and fit—one tall and all sinew, with every vein showing on his smooth arms, the other a buff little fireplug of a guy, probably a wrestler as a kid, Lee thinks. The sinewy one couldn't be forty, but has a salt-and-pepper crew cut that draws attention to how handsome and unlined his face is.

"Oh, wow," the sinewy one says as they take their seats in front of the fireplace. "This little place is just great. I wish I could live up here. Silver Lake is the perfect neighborhood, you know?"

This is what people who wouldn't dream of leaving West Hollywood are always saying.

"It's a great community," Lee says.

"You guys want some juice?" Alan asks.

Sinew and Fireplug hold up their hands simultaneously, as if they've rehearsed their act.

"So, Alan," Fireplug says, "I assume your wife has told you what we've been discussing."

"Maybe we should go over it anyway, Chuck," Sinew says.

It's fascinating watching them talk, completing each other's sentences, each knowing exactly when to break in on the other. And they make these rehearsed yoga jokes that aren't really jokes and draw on the most obvious clichés, but which they seem to find consistently amusing.

Sinew: We all know what's been going on in the country for the last few years in terms of yoga, right?

Fireplug: Up, up, up, dog.

Sinew: Yeah, exactly, Chuck. Good one.

Fireplug: And the thing is, the demand is getting so big, the smaller studios . . .

Sinew: . . . which have always been the core (*patting taut abs*) of the industry . . .

Industry? Lee thinks. *Really?*

Fireplug: . . . can't handle the volume.

Sinew: Not to mention the expectations, especially in a place like L.A.

Fireplug: People want more than a class. What they want now is . . .

Sinew: . . . a complete experience.

He says this last word in a fake reverential whisper, as if he's just revealed the secret of life, and that makes Lee wish she'd never let them in the front door. They're probably reasonable guys, and they're just doing their jobs, but there's something about their smarmy and rehearsed presentation that reminds Lee of a Mary Kay demonstration a friend invited her to years ago. They go on for a few more minutes, making a case for themselves and the beauty of what amounts to one more corporate takeover. There are multiple references to Zhannette (they spell it!) and Frank, apparently the owners. She reminds herself that being a purist isn't going to help get the twins into a decent school, and it isn't going to make Alan feel any more appreciated or less overloaded.

Alan seems to have run out of the ability to listen to these guys any longer, and for the first time in weeks, she feels as if the two of them are truly in sync. Maybe it *was* a good thing to invite these two in.

"So how much are you offering for the studio?" Alan asks.

Sinew and Fireplug grind to a sudden halt and look at each other. This, apparently, was not on their script.

"We're not interested in the studio," Fireplug says. "Not one of the YogaHappens Experience Centers is under eight thousand square feet."

"I'm not so sure, Chuck. I think the studio in Santa Monica is only six thousand."

"Could be right. What do I know? I'm just the finance guy."

"What Zhannette and Frank are interested in," Sinew says, "is you, Lee. And *you*, Alan. What we want . . ."

". . . is to offer you an exclusive contract."

Sinew: And you might have heard . . .

Fireplug: . . . that Zhannette and Frank insist that everyone at YogaHappens is very well paid.

Sinew: It's not about their own profits.

Without turning or moving, without even seeing him, Lee can feel Alan stiffening on the sofa beside him.

"But before we get into the details," Fireplug says, "we want to discuss some of the information you gave us. You've got some mighty eccentric bookkeeping there, Lee."

Katherine first came to Lee's studio two years ago and started renting her massage room a year after that. While she loves the feeling of the place and the way *she* feels when she walks in the door—a little protected from the harsher realities of the world—she's lost her ability to actually see it. Which is one of the bonuses of bringing Conor in; seeing it through his eyes, it's almost as if she's looking at it for the first time.

In its previous incarnation, the building was the showroom of a rug dealer. There was lots of open floor space when Lee and Alan bought the storefront—back in the days when Silver Lake was affordable and Alan had sold a song to a movie—and most of it was carpeted. Lee and Alan took it all up (Katherine's seen the before and after photos), revealing hardwood, which Alan refinished. Why he doesn't settle into carpentry and handyman work, something he's really good at and occasionally seems to enjoy, is a mystery to her. The first thing you notice, especially if the sun is shining—and it usually is—is the warm honey color of the floors.

"It's great," Conor says. "My place back in Boston had floors like this. I hate to think what I did to my lungs sanding and laying down the polyurethane."

Flooohz. "I guessed you for a DIY kind of guy."

"I like projects. You have enough projects lined up, you stay out of trouble."

Katherine wonders how to read this. When people talk about staying out of trouble, it usually means they spent a substantial amount of time *in* trouble at some point or other. If Conor follows the stereotype of big Irish guys from Boston, that probably means too many hours spent drinking in sports bars and maybe getting into fights on the sidewalk after closing hours. Although there's something so gentle about him—unbelievably sexy on someone his size—it's easier to imagine him breaking up fights than starting them.

"It's tough for you to stay out of trouble?" she says.

"You ask an awful lot of questions, you know that?"

"I do. It's a bad habit. You avoid answering an awful lot of questions, you know *that*?"

He winks at her and puts his hand on the small of her back. "So where do you do your magic?"

"Let me show you the studio first."

Chloe is behind the reception desk, talking at full volume on her iPhone. Chloe teaches one of the sunrise flow classes at 7:00 a.m., three days a week. She's a bartender on weekends at a club in West Hollywood, and, because her mother runs a boutique agency in Los Feliz, she's studying to get her real estate license. It's such a crazy combination of interests and professions, it all makes sense somehow. She's a terrific teacher with a devoted following of early risers, but her in-class patter tends to be heavy on metaphors that sound connected to her other pursuits. "Bend at the waist and let your body pour down over your legs, like a warm, dark liquid pouring over ice, slowly melting out all the tension and stress." "Pull back your shoulders and open up your chest like you're opening your front door and welcoming in the universe. I call this 'open house pose.'" She had a boyfriend for a while, then a girlfriend. Now she's single, one of those truly bisexual people who fall in love without any apparent preference for gender. That must make life either very easy or extremely complicated.

Odd that she's here at this time of day, but no point in trying to break into what sounds like an intense conversation with her mother. Her mother, who shows up at the studio from time to time, is one of those creepily driven people who seems to calculate how much time you're worth before she's willing to engage with you. Still, you have to admire her for setting up a successful business. She and Chloe act more like sisters, and there are times when Katherine envies the closeness of their relationship. She hasn't talked to her own mother in six years.

In the studio, Conor looks almost comically out of place, slouching a little as if he's intimidated, the way men often do when they walk into a yoga studio for the first time. "Great view," he says. "So show me some of your tricks, lady."

"They're not tricks, Mr. Ross. They're poses. Or *asanas*, if you want to get fancy."

Having said that, she looks him in the eyes and drops down onto the floor. She pops up into a perfect forearm balance, then lowers her feet to the floor behind her and presses up with her hands so she's in a deep back bend. And then, just because she can't resist, she walks her hands in and slowly unfurls to standing.

"Whoa!" Conor is laughing and holding up his hands in front of his eyes. "Don't do that again. You scared the shit out of me!"

"A big guy like you? You're easy to scare!"

And then, payback for showing off, proving that it's the little, unpredictable things that get you in life, she trips over her own feet as she's walking toward him. He's at her side in half a second, holding her by her biceps.

She looks up into his eyes. "I did that on purpose," she says. "Just to see if you'd catch me."

"I have amazing reflexes," he says. "And I'm happy to see

you're human after all. In the middle of that contortion, I was starting to wonder."

Contohtion.

"I am so, so human," she says. "You have no idea."

His hands slide down to her waist, and he leaves them there. "I like human," he says.

It's stupid, really. She doesn't know him at all. Knows almost nothing about him, in fact. But she sees some kind of honesty or trustworthiness or *something* in those beautiful eyes of his that makes her feel more happy and open (*welcome in, universe!*) than she's felt in a long time.

"I really, really hope you mean that," Katherine says.

He bends down and kisses her on the mouth, his arms completely encircling her body, and Katherine feels such gratitude, she hears herself sigh, the way she sighs after doing ten sun salutations in a row.

She's so lost in the moment, she doesn't realize that the little knocking sound she's hearing isn't her heart, but Chloe, tapping lightly on the glass door to the studio. When Katherine makes eye contact with her, Chloe opens the door just a crack.

"Ummm, I hate to break it up," she says, "but I've got a class in half an hour."

Katherine laughs. "Don't worry. We were about to leave anyway. Mr. Ross is a client. This is strictly professional."

"It looks it! What profession?"

"Where's Barrett?" Katherine asks. "I thought she was on the desk this afternoon."

"She's taking care of Lee's kids. They went out to the park, and she called to ask me to fill in. I guess Lee and Alan are having some meeting with their accountants or some businesspeople. They didn't make it clear."

Katherine feels her stomach drop. She's getting a strong feeling this has something to do with YogaHappens.

"Did she say when she'll be back?"

"She said she'd let me know. It all sounded a little mysterious."

Not mysterious enough, as far as Katherine's concerned.

Since Lee has prescribed so much down time, Graciela has been visiting her mother out in Duarte more often. Depending on the time of day, it takes her between an hour and an hour and a half to drive each way. It's not like she loves being in the car, but she's moving, and at least she's not sitting around the apartment bickering with Daryl and putting all her energy into trying not to eat. If she starts gaining weight on top of everything else, she's really going to be miserable.

She tells herself this is the reason she's been spending so much time with her mother, but there's so much more to it than that. Her stepfather died of lung cancer eight months ago, and her mother, never the world's cheeriest person, went into a depression. She spends most of her time sitting in front of the TV watching soap operas on Telemundo or, as she's doing right now, talking back in Spanish to the complainants on *Judge Judy*.

"*¡Tas mintiendo, perra!*" she scoffs.

Graciela has taken it upon herself to clean her mother's little house, one room each visit. She figures that by the time she's worked her way through the whole place, her mother might be feeling better and actually appreciate her efforts. And tendon problems or not, it's a hell of a lot easier than sitting with her mother and listening to her tell Graciela that she hates the way she dresses, that she looks like a *puta*, that she's going to hell. Her mother wants her to get a job, to give up dancing—which she seems to equate with being a stripper—and to get married. Graciela has two brothers who can do no wrong in her mother's eyes. Maybe if they came to visit her once in a while, her mother would cheer up some. Graciela doubts either one of them has been to see her since the funeral. Hardly excusable, since, last she heard, neither one of them has full-time employment.

She puts away the last of the cleaning supplies in the kitchen closet and goes out to the cramped little glassed-in porch where her mother spends almost all of her time.

"I have to get going, Mama," she says. "I don't want to hit traffic."

Her mother nods at the screen and says, *"Esta mujer es una mentirosa."*

According to her mother, everyone on television is a liar. Maybe she has a point, but it's hard not to view this as part of her mother's rejection of everything in life right now and feeling that somehow or other, she's a victim of everyone who crosses her path.

"I cleaned the guest room today," Graciela says. "The closet, too. I'm taking some of Heberto's clothes to a men's shelter downtown."

"I wanted you to clean *my* room," her mother says. "You don't listen to me."

Maybe it's the yoga, but lately Graciela has gotten much better at letting these kinds of comments slide. *You can't control what other people do in life, but you can control your response to it.*

"I'll come back next week and start on your room, okay, Mama? I brought some meals I made for you and put them in the freezer. All you have to do is put them in the microwave."

Her mother turns her eyes to her slowly and says, "You never could cook the way I can cook."

Graciela bends down and kisses her mother on the forehead. "I'll see you next week."

So many streets look identical in Duarte, it's almost impossible not to get lost, even after all this time. Graciela makes a wrong turn getting on the thruway and ends up in a little hard-luck neighborhood that's maybe one of the most depressing places she's ever seen. The sun is too bright, there's trash blowing in the hot wind, and she has no idea how to get out of here. Right behind the houses, she can see yet another mall of big-box stores looming. But she's not giving in to it. She's not giving up and letting the sneer on her mother's face undo everything she's done to get as far as she's gotten.

She takes a deep breath and retraces her steps in her mind, figures out how to get onto the thruway. Once she's speeding back to town, she decides to call Stephanie again. Her phone is still turned off and her voice mail is full. She wishes she knew someone else to call to ask about her, but they're not really close and Stephanie's never even mentioned other friends. Graciela has her address entered somewhere in her phone. The only thing that makes any sense is to stop at her apartment and see what's going on.

Stephanie lives on Sweetzer, right off Melrose. Even though Graciela has spent her entire life in L.A. and therefore should know better, she always assumes that anyone working in the movie business must be doing pretty well and living with

the kind of glamorous frills that are out of her reach. Especially someone like Stephanie, who talks about her connections to People with Names. Not bragging, but just because that's what her life is like.

Graciela Netflixed *Silver Linings* shortly after she met Stephanie. She would have liked more plot and maybe one love story that ended happily, but it had Ellen Page, Jean Smart, Sam Rockwell, and a two-second cameo by Johnny Depp. It was about a WASP family in the Midwest—as far from Graciela's background as you can get—but there was something in the (dysfunctional, of course) relationship between Ellen Page and her mother that Graciela identified with so closely, she couldn't get the movie out of her mind for days. It's how moved she was by it that made her put Stephanie on a pedestal. Not a superhigh one, but even so. Apparently she wrote a lot of it, and you have to admire someone who can create anything that makes you feel that much. It's talent.

So she's surprised when she pulls up at Stephanie's address and sees that it's a pretty ordinary three-story white brick building. There's something a little untamed about the hibiscus and bougainvillea bushes in front. She tries Stephanie's phone one more time, knowing she's not going to pick up, and of course she doesn't.

"Like she's going to answer the door," Graciela mumbles to herself, but gets out of the car anyway.

She rings Stephanie's buzzer and—big surprise—there's no response. Graciela figures that if she were Stephanie, she'd hit the thing a few more times, but even though she's driven all this way, it seems too rude. She stands there for another minute, but she can't make herself do it. For all she knows, Stephanie is out of town or running around arranging meetings. Or maybe she sees Graciela's number pop up and doesn't take the call. But that wouldn't explain the phone being turned off and the messages being full, and on top of that, Graciela is pretty sure the buzzer is not sounding inside an empty apartment. She can feel it. Sometimes she has an extra sense for things, something she really can't explain.

As she's about to leave, Graciela spots through the glass a young, blond woman coming down the staircase from the second floor. The woman opens the door and steps outside and Graciela realizes with a shock that in fact, she's not young at all. Ancient might be more accurate. The blond hair is a brassy gold, combed and teased into a big bubble and sprayed stiff. It could be a wig, but in Graciela's experience, most people try to make wigs more convincing than this. Despite having an unlined face, the exposed skin of the woman's chest and arms (she's wearing a tank top, so there's a lot of exposed flesh) is freckled and as rumpled as a bedsheet. There's a lot of jewelry, too, sort of heaped on in layers, so you can't really tell where one bracelet ends and the next one begins.

"You looking for somebody?" the woman asks. Nice, but at the same time, suspicious.

"I have a friend who lives in the building, but she's not answering her bell."

"Well, maybe that means she's not at home," the woman says, more suspicious than nice this time. She turns around to make sure the door has locked behind her, and that's when Graciela notices that she has a yoga mat slung over her shoulder.

"I love your yoga bag," Graciela says. "I just started doing yoga."

This perks her up, and she instantly turns chatty. "Good for you, honey. Keep it up. I been doing it for twenty years now. It's how I stay in such great shape." She flexes a slack arm. "Bikram, four times a week, one hundred eight degrees. I been the exact same weight since I turned twenty. How much do you think I weigh?"

Graciela is *not* taking that bait. "I'm really bad at that," she says. "It's like guessing the temperature. I never know."

"A hundred and two pounds. A hundred and three if I'm premenstrual."

Premenstrual?

"Nobody can believe it when I tell them I'm forty-seven."

As a matter of fact, Graciela doesn't believe it, either. Reverse the numbers and they might be in the ballpark.

"My friend who lives here got me into yoga," Graciela says. "She does it all the time."

The woman adjusts a tangled mass of gaudy necklaces. "Bikram wants me to get my teacher certification, but who has time? And let me tell you, I have three daughters I been trying to get into it for years. Not interested. They're at boarding school. The bills!"

"My friend is Stephanie Carlson. You don't know her, do you?"

"Stephanie! She lives next door to me. She wants to put me in a movie, but I'm sick of acting. Too much pressure. I love her. I'm glad she got rid of that boyfriend."

"Really?" Graciela has known Stephanie for about four months now and she's never once mentioned an ex to her. Maybe it wasn't a serious relationship.

"Yeah. When he was living here with her, she was so happy all the time, it was depressing. I'm done with men. And believe me, it's not like I don't have opportunities. My girls' father was the last. He left me for an older woman. Imagine that!"

"Have you seen Stephanie around lately? She hasn't been answering my calls or anything."

"I haven't seen her for days."

"Oh. Was she going out of town? On a vacation or something?"

"I believe in minding your own business. I keep to myself; I do my yoga. At forty-two, I've learned to focus on me."

At this rate, she'll be a teenager before the end of the conversation. If you're going to lie about your age, you ought to at least be able to remember the age you claim.

"Do you know any of her friends we could call?" Graciela asks.

"You're nosy," the woman says. "Pretty as hell, but nosy. I don't know anybody. But I'll tell you one thing, if she doesn't show up soon, I'm calling the super. I can't take the smell coming out of her apartment much longer."

Katherine turns on the little scent infuser in her massage room. "Lavender or bergamot?" she asks.

Conor is sitting on the edge of the massage table, watching her closely.

"Lee's the lady who runs the studio?" he asks.

"She is. And I love that you used the word 'lady.' Is that a Boston thing?"

Conor winks at her. Probably he's decided never to answer any of her questions, and it's going to become a running joke between them. Assuming there is any "between them."

"You two get along?" he asks.

"A few minor disagreements. Mostly, I think of her as my

best friend. And since you haven't given an opinion, I'm going with the bergamot."

"Go for it. I have no idea what that is. Anyway, I have a really bad sense of smell."

"Punched in the nose too many times, Mr. Ross? I think you better take off your shirt for the massage."

"Let's start with you. Otherwise I'll feel totally outclassed and intimidated."

"Oh, come on. You just want to see my tits."

"I do. But not right away. This is strictly professional. I'll step outside and you get ready."

Katherine unbuttons her shirt and puts it on the chair, then checks herself out in the mirror on the back of the door. She's had enough therapy to know that she's used men for validation her whole life, to feel attractive, desirable, some version of loved. It's common among women who were sexually abused as kids. Some people take comfort in being part of a larger pattern—misery loves company?—but Katherine has always hated being predictable and having her personal acting out turn out to be exactly what everyone else is doing, almost as if her life and her actions had been determined by the bad behavior some fucking *stepfather* decided to inflict on her. She always liked to think of herself as being so original.

Oddly—or wonderfully—enough, she's never felt more attractive than she has since going into sexual hibernation after the Phil disaster. That's probably what's to be expected, too. She's done so much core work, her stomach has flattened out and her obliques are firm. If Conor likes giant boobs, he's out of luck, but for the first time in her entire life, Katherine has begun to appreciate the fact that she's got a pretty incredibly proportional body. She's *not* flat-chested, *not* wide-hipped, *not* the thousand and one flawed things she's always imagined herself to be. She's just fine. And more to the point, since she's been taking classes with Lee, she's learned to appreciate what her body can *do*—despite all the abuse that's been dumped on it by everyone from her stepfather to herself—instead of focusing on what it looks like.

There's a knock on the door, and she lies on her table, facedown, half wishing they were back at her house, half loving the little game they're about to play. Maybe they'll date a few times before going all the way. That would be a first! Conor comes in and closes the door softly behind him. "Ready for your appointment, Miss . . . I didn't get your last name."

"Brodski," Katherine says.

"Another Irish lady," he says ironically.

"Only on one side of the family. I'll let you guess which."

As soon as his hands touch her back, Katherine feels a warmth rush through her body. He presses his hands into the small of her back and begins kneading along one side of her spine with his big thumbs. Either he's had some formal training or he's the world's most intuitive amateur. "And I'm not sure 'lady' really applies here."

"You let me be the judge of that, okay?"

By the time he's worked his way to her shoulders, she feels so calm and relaxed, she almost doesn't care about anything else. If worse comes to worst, she can always find another place to rent and take Lee's classes wherever she plans to teach them.

When Conor begins working on her neck, she feels his warm breath somewhere in the middle of her back and then, so lightly it's almost like a whisper, the scratch of his beard on her skin. "Who taught you how to do this?" she asks.

He moves his face up her back until she can feel his breath tickling her ear. "I'm just making it up as I go along," he whispers.

"So far, so good, Mr. Ross."

"Glad you approve. You've got some interesting tattoos back here."

"They're not scaring you off, are they?"

"I'm tougher than I look, Brodski. And I bet you're more of a good girl than you like to pretend."

"I wish that were true, Mr. Ross, I really do."

Katherine's phone starts ringing somewhere in her bag. It's Lee's designated ring.

"You want to get that?" Conor asks.

"It's just Lee, my sort-of boss."

"In that case, you should answer it."

"If you're trying to make an honest woman of me, Mr. Ross, you've got your work cut out for you."

"I'm not trying to make you anything," he whispers in her ear. "I'm just trying to get you to sit up so I can see your tits."

"So you're telling us that someone's been embezzling money from the studio?" Alan asks.

The fireplug guy from YogaHappens—his name is Chuck and Dave is his lean cohort, and since things have turned serious all of a sudden, Lee figures she'd better start thinking of him that way—holds up his hands as if he's blocking a punch.

"Whoa. No one said anything about embezzlement."

"We're just saying some things don't add up."

Alan gets up off the sofa and begins pacing. For years he's been after Lee about her practice of letting people in and giving the studio assistants too much independence in collecting the money. The "Post-it Note Brigade" is how he refers to them. For most of her life, Lee has thought of money in terms of big categories—Enough and Not Enough, for example. The specifics have never interested her all that much, never seemed all that important. She knows this is probably an inefficient, immature way to look at finances, but on the other hand, she can't help but believe the world would be a lot more pleasant, congenial, and generous place if everyone had this attitude.

"I'm sloppy about money, I confess," she says. "But in the end, Katherine and I are the only ones who have access to everything."

Alan clearly has a different point of view.

"Jesus Christ, Lee. I told you she was trouble. She's a junkie! You don't give a drug addict the keys to the cash drawer."

Lee wants to leap in with the number of years Katherine has been straight, with the virtues of wiping some slates clean, but she knows that would just lead to nitpicking that would cycle into an argument about petty details.

"Katherine's my friend, Alan, and I don't want you talking about her like that."

"She takes in all these strays," Alan says.

Chuck and sinewy Dave turn toward Alan, nodding, and Lee realizes there's an us-and-them front about to blow in. Or more specifically, an us-and-her.

"Lee does?" Dave asks.

"Lee, right," Alan says. "Any wounded bird she thinks she can put back together. No money? Hey, no problem, the universe—in the form of *our* bottom line—will provide."

" 'She' doesn't take in strays," Lee says. " 'She' has friends and students and sometimes 'she' is a little loose with fees, okay, if people are having a hard time. In the end, it makes for a lot of goodwill and a loyal following. And by the way, 'she' has managed to make ends meet every month, since the first day we opened five years ago."

Lee wonders what her students would think if they had a ringside seat at this performance. She spends time in every class talking about ways to avoid letting people push your buttons, and here she is going into *reacting* mode. But it makes her realize that she's been reacting to the suggestion of a contract, too, without knowing the facts, all to protect Alan's ego, while he seems interested mainly in lashing out at her in this childish way. Come to think of it, under his bravado and his good looks and all that bluster, there's always been a wounded-bird part of him that Lee has been drawn to. In the end, it's probably the most irresistible thing about him. Funny he should be criticizing her for wanting to take care of people.

"Maybe we should get back to the contract," Lee says. "I thought you were interested in buying me out of the studio."

The guys jump back into their rehearsed tag-team mode—Sinew and Fireplug—almost as if they're relieved to be back on solid ground.

Sinew: We have scouts going to studios all around town . . .

Fireplug: . . . who, I'm sorry to say, ha-ha, always end up paying full fare.

Sinew: Ha-ha, right. Some of them look like strays, Lee! Anyway, there's an agreement that you've developed a style that is . . . unique.

Fireplug: Eclectic.

Sinew: Smooth. That goes beyond the merely physical and pulls together a whole range of traditions and techniques, along with a spiritual element.

Fireplug: Delivered in a low-key, *mainstream* way that's rare.

Sinew: In other words, Zhannette and Frank need you, Lee.

Fireplug: And you, too, Alan . . .

Sinew: . . . which we'll get to in a minute. You'd bring something to YogaHappens, Lee, that we don't have. And we'd give
you something *you* don't have—a platform to transform the lives
of thousands of people. Tens of thousands once you begin training other teachers.

Fireplug: And we take care of all the money details. Hey, we
understand it's not everyone's forte. With us, you have a guaranteed salary. Health insurance for the whole family.

Sinew: Zhannette and Frank are committed to health insurance for every employee they're mandated to give it to.

Fireplug: You'd have nothing to do but focus on what you love
and do best. Which is probably what you've always wanted.

Thanks for telling me, Lee thinks. But even so, it is true.

Sinew: We copyright your technique. No one else can teach it
or use the name unless trained and certified by you.

Fireplug: Six-week teacher training program. Seventy-two
hours, total. Forty-eight hundred dollars.

Sinew: We're going to call it "Deep Flow Meditasana."

Bullies, but she does like the name.

"What's the catch?" Lee asks. There's always a catch when
you're dealing with bullies, so she might as well get it out in the
open now.

The guys look at each other and Sinew says, "It's an exclusive
contract. You only teach at YogaHappens."

Fireplug: And naturally, we would own the rights to Deep
Flow Meditasana.

Sinew: But that's obvious, I'm sure. If there was a book or a
tape or any of that.

Fireplug: But let's not get bogged down.

"Rights," like money, are something Lee has never given
much purchase. It's all legal prattle that doesn't have application
in the real world or the details of daily life that she cares about.

While she tries her best to leave ego out of it, she has had a growing sense that there's something unusual, maybe even special about her teaching. So many people show up with injuries from other classes, or do poses in a random fashion they've picked up elsewhere that does more damage than good. She has thought about labeling what she does but never took the idea too seriously.

She looks over at Alan. He's sunk back into his corner of the sofa, arms folded across his chest. For some reason, the sexy clothes and the shiny hair look a little silly now. All style and no substance. But she's never been able to resist the urge to take care of him and, silly or not, she can't stand the thought of abandoning him.

"What about Alan?" she asks. "You said you're interested in him as well."

"Naturally," Sinew says, "we've been following the work you've been doing at the studio, Alan. You're a brilliant musician."

"Amazing," says Fireplug.

"The classes with his live music are always full," Lee says.

"Exactly. And Zhannette and Frank have been trying to find the right person to play live music in selected classes. And they feel they've found him in you."

"Have they been to the studio?" Alan asks.

"No, of course not."

Of course not? "Then . . . ?"

"We prefer not to discuss their personal lives with employees," Sinew says and gives a little laugh. "I'm sure you feel the same way."

Fireplug: The point is, we have a very, very nice offer for Alan as well.

Sinew: Once we've secured your position, Lee.

Lee's cell phone rings and she glances down at the screen. She doesn't recognize the number. "I'm sorry," she says, "but I have to get this. We have two kids and they're with a babysitter."

"The twins," Sinew says. "Go right ahead."

"Lee, I'm so sorry to bother you." A harsh, slightly panicked whisper. A familiar voice she can't immediately place. "They gave me your number at the studio. It's Graciela."

"Hi, Graciela. I'm in the middle of something right now, so if—"

"I'm sorry, Lee, but I didn't know who else to call. I'm at Stephanie's apartment."

"Is everything all right?"

"No, no, it isn't. Not at all. I need help."

Smell?" Graciela asks the older woman. "What kind of smell?"

"Like I told you," she says, "I don't get involved in other people's business. But it's not what I would consider pleasant or healthy. She's got those cats. Maybe that's it. But something's gotta be done."

Cats, something else that Stephanie has never mentioned to Graciela. Graciela had two cats herself, but Daryl is allergic, so she had to find homes for them when he moved in. The family they ended up going to seemed loving and kind, and they'd get to go outside, but driving Martha and Chita up to Pasadena was so sad, Graciela doesn't even like to let the memory of it cross her mind.

"Does the super live in the building?" Graciela asks.

"He used to, but we've had to make some cutbacks, like everyone else. He comes in three times a week now. I had a chance to invest with Bernie Madoff, but I took one look at the numbers, and I knew enough to run in the opposite direction."

"Ummm . . . good for you."

Graciela knows that the only way to get through to a person like this is to appeal to her vanity. The woman might be a little batty, but at the moment, she's Graciela's only chance at getting into the building.

"Something I've always wondered," Graciela says, "is whether it's okay to leave your jewelry on when you're doing hot yoga. I mean, those bracelets alone must get broiling hot against your skin. But since they're obviously worth a fortune, where would you leave them if you took them off?"

"I'm glad you like them. You've got taste. My daughters tell me I look like a hooker. The mouths on those girls! I never take this stuff off. Bikram won't let me. He says I add a touch of glamour to the class."

"I'm sure you do."

There *is* something glamorous about the woman, in her eccentric and extreme way. Graciela makes out a few details from the tangle of chains and bangles on the woman's thin wrists and compliments them. This has the desired effect, and after a few more minutes of chatting, Graciela asks the woman if she'd let her into the building so she can knock on Stephanie's door. She surveys Graciela, almost as if she's trying to decide if she has a concealed weapon, and then agrees.

"But I'm coming with you. I don't want to be responsible for any break-ins."

"I'm Graciela, by the way."

The woman is bent over, fiddling with a massive set of keys.

The bracelets, necklaces, and dozens of keys form a musical accompaniment to her every gesture. If she even heard Graciela, she's not remotely interested in her name. The jangling is making Graciela even more nervous.

"You do have a lot of keys there."

"I'm a collector. They bring me good luck even if they make it hell trying to get into the building."

Once inside, Graciela notices the smells of garlic and incense in the hallway and the woman says, "Hmm, smells like Henrietta's having that baked chicken dish of hers again. Here's Stephanie's door."

There is a strong, unpleasant odor near the door, partly disguised by Henrietta's garlicky chicken. It smells to Graciela like some bad combination of rotting food and old kitty litter. She raps lightly on Stephanie's door and puts her ear to the metal. There's no response and no sound from within. She tries again, a little more firmly this time. Still nothing. The woman comes up behind Graciela and nudges her aside.

"You're not going to get anywhere like that," she says. She raps on the door so loudly and insistently that someone down the hall pokes out his head and then retreats.

"Stephanie," she brays. "Stephanie! It's Billie. Open up. I need to talk to you."

No response. Undeterred, she tries again. "It's Billie, Stephanie! Open up or I'm getting the super out here."

Miraculously, there's a rattle of chains from inside, and the door swings open. Before Graciela has a chance to register on Stephanie, she's greeted by a wave of warm, stale air that carries with it a stronger version of the kitty litter odor and the unmistakable smell of alcohol. A skinny little orange and black cat struts out into the hallway, and then Stephanie, acting as if everything is totally fine, stands in the doorway and says, "Graciela. What are you doing here?"

Except her mouth is so dry, it's hard for her to pronounce consonants, and the words are garbled.

"She's worried about you, that's what she's doing here," Billie says. "And looking at you, I don't blame her."

"I hadn't heard from you in a few days," Graciela says, "so I got worried."

Stephanie's short hair is matted to her head, and her eyes are so red and swollen, Graciela can almost feel an ache in her own eyes when she looks at them. She's wearing a sweatshirt that's dirty in ways Graciela doesn't want to speculate on and a pair of nubby black sweatpants covered in a layer of cat hair and crumbs.

"I've been working," Stephanie drawls, the least convincing thing Graciela's heard in a long time.

"I figured it was something like that. I know you've had a lot on your plate. Mind if we come in?"

But before Stephanie can answer, Billie has pushed her way into the apartment and, emboldened, Graciela follows. The apartment doesn't look any better than Stephanie herself—newspapers and take-out food containers are scattered everywhere, and on a coffee table near the sofa, there are more empty wine bottles than Graciela cares to see. There's a pile of blankets and rumpled sheets on top of the sofa, meaning Stephanie has been sleeping there. The TV is playing with the sound off, and after a minute, Graciela realizes it's *Silver Linings*.

Most unsettling of all is a big pile of kitty litter in the middle of the room, as if Stephanie was too out of it to fill the box and just dumped it out of the bag onto the floor.

A little gray cat scoots out from under the sofa and rubs

against Graciela's leg. She bends down and picks up the sweet little thing.

"Oh, Marlene, there you are," Stephanie says. "I've been looking for her. I'm sorry I haven't had a chance to tidy up today. I was on the phone, and I was just about to do a yoga tape."

Graciela thinks about the last time she saw Stephanie. It doesn't seem possible that it was only about two weeks ago. She's suffered such a steep decline, and it's so visible, Graciela feels sick to her stomach. She holds the little cat up near her shoulder and rubs her face against its fur for comfort.

"Stephanie," she says, "I don't . . . what happened? How did you . . . ?"

But Stephanie has such a far-off look in her eyes, seems so clearly to be *not there* that Graciela knows she isn't going to answer. Even if she herself could formulate a coherent question. Billie has installed herself in the one chair in the room that's relatively uncluttered. "I love this chair," she says, patting the arms. "Did you get it at Ikea?"

What are you supposed to do in a situation like this? It would almost be simpler if Stephanie were passed out; then Graciela could at least call an ambulance. What Graciela really wants to do is run away and forget she saw any of this. But she can't do that. She owes Stephanie. She drops the kitty down onto the floor and walks slowly toward a glass door. She slides it open, and there's a rush of air into the room that's so cool and sweet, it makes Graciela think she's never fully appreciated the air quality in L.A. She steps out onto a little balcony, takes out her phone, and calls the only person she can think of right now.

After many years of some pretty heavy life experience, Katherine thought she was way past shyness and modesty. The list of "Things She *Hasn't* Done" would be as short as the list of "Mistakes She *Hasn't* Made." But right at the top of the roster of new experiences would be: "Date a decent, honest guy." So maybe that explains why she feels so oddly shy about sitting up in front of Conor, half naked and, after twenty minutes of his massage, flushed and blissed out.

"Turn around, Mr. Ross," she says. "It's a professional courtesy. I'm teaching you the tricks of the trade."

He runs his hand down her spine, right to where the curve of her butt begins, gives her a crooked smile, and sits on the edge of the massage table, his back to her. She props herself up and leans against him, so he's supporting her weight. Katherine can imagine lots worse ways to spend the rest of the day than closing her eyes and staying in exactly this position. And frankly, she can't think of too many nicer ways. *Please don't fuck this up,* she thinks. But she isn't sure if she's directing the thought to Conor or to herself, and she's not sure if there even *is* a "this" yet.

"I'm so glad you picked up," Lee says. "I'm up at the house."

"I know," Katherine tells her. "Chloe said you're having some kind of meeting."

"I was, but I don't have time to talk about that. I just got a call from Graciela. She's at Stephanie's apartment, and it sounds as if Stephanie's in trouble. Possibly serious."

As soon as Lee gives her the news, Katherine realizes she's

been waiting to hear something like this for a long time now. Stephanie has the unmistakably fractured energy of someone who's abusing something and headed for a fall.

"Alcohol?" Katherine asks.

"That and maybe pills, too. Graciela isn't too familiar with this kind of thing."

No surprise there, either. Whatever Graciela's demons might be—and everyone has their own resident devils—they clearly do not live in the neighborhood of drugs and booze.

"She wants me to meet her down there. It's not great timing, but she sounded pretty worked up."

"What can I do?" Katherine asks.

Conor, sensing the mood apparently, turns around and starts massaging her shoulders and gently rubbing his cheek along her neck as Lee fills her in. Lee would like her to call Barrett and have her bring the twins back to the studio. Make sure everyone's settled in for a few hours and give Barrett thirty bucks, in case she ends up having to take the kids out for dinner. Then walk down to the reservoir, where Lee will pick her up. She's not sure she's prepared to face this alone.

"I've got a little experience in this area," Katherine says, hoping there's no follow-up question from Conor later. "I'll be there as soon as I can," she says. "I'm with a friend right now."

Conor takes this as a cue to kiss her neck.

"Oh, the fireman!" Lee says. "I forgot. Never mind, Kat, you stay there. I'll be fine."

"No, I don't want you to go alone. I'll meet you down at the reservoir." She flips her phone shut.

"Problem?" Conor asks.

Reluctantly, Katherine slides off the table and pulls her shirt on. "One of Lee's students," she says. "Sounds like she's been on a binge or something. I'm going out to West Hollywood with

Lee to see if I can help. Good Samaritan and all that." She turns around and Conor is standing, arms across his chest, still grinning. "Can't you be at least a little disappointed I'm leaving, Mr. Ross?"

"I would be if I weren't coming with you. Don't forget I'm a professional Good Samaritan, Brodski."

Barrett is twenty years old and a senior in college. She's a short, small woman who, like a lot of girls who trained to be professional gymnasts, looks as if she's never quite got past age fourteen. She wears her hair in a ponytail, and she talks in a high voice with a slight lisp.

She comes skipping into the studio with the twins and, if she didn't know better, Katherine would have guessed she was their slightly older sibling. Which, all things considered, is a pretty creepy thought. The twins' faces are smeared with chocolate, but, knowing Barrett, it's probably from one of the cocoa puddings they sell at the raw food café down the street. Barrett opens the door to the yoga room and Michael and Marcus dash in.

"Cute," Conor says. "They remind me of my sister's kids."

"Your poor sister," Katherine says.

"Don't say that!" Barrett says. "They were better today! Only one fight. Well, only one *major* fight. They're really upset about what's going on with their parents."

Well, who isn't?

Marcus is stacking up the yoga blocks in the careful way he tends to do everything. Architect is Katherine's guess for his future, but in truth, she doesn't really know a whole lot about kids. As soon as he has a stack nearly as high as his head, Michael makes a beeline from the opposite side of the room and knocks it down. Marcus screams at him and launches into a futile defense of his territory.

"I spoke too soon," Barrett lisps. She effortlessly pops herself up onto the counter at the front desk.

Barrett teaches a yoga class for kids on Saturday mornings. Half price because she's not fully certified yet. She's developing a pretty loyal following of mothers who want to get their kids into something that helps them focus. Katherine observed the class once and couldn't get past her voice. But there's room for a little of everything.

Conor walks into the yoga room and the glass doors swing closed behind him. Like most bullies, Michael responds well to a more physically imposing presence. He begins a wary and quiet retreat from his brother as soon as he gets a good glimpse at Conor's size. Conor kneels down on the floor in front of Marcus and begins helping him stack the blocks. "Hey," he calls out to Michael, "come over here for a minute. We need your help."

"Smart," Barrett says. "That's exactly what you're supposed to do—enlist his help. That way, he won't want to knock it down. It's just he doesn't listen when I tell him."

"It helps to be six-four," Katherine says. "And have red hair. And a dick." She looks at Barrett. "Sorry."

"I'm *not* a kid," Barrett says. "I know what those are." She pulls both legs up on the counter and bends at the waist toward her feet in the most perfect forward fold Katherine has ever seen. "I've even sucked one."

"Too much information," Katherine says.

Katherine tells Barrett the new plan of action, without mentioning the real reasons. The fewer people who know about

Stephanie's problem, the less likely a lot of rumors are going to start spreading.

Conor comes out of the yoga room and slips his hand around Katherine's waist. Why is this all so easy so quickly? "You handled that pretty well," Katherine says.

"Speaking as someone who's never done an up dog in his life, don't you think someone ought to get those kids into a yoga class?"

Talking to her knees, Barrett says, "Alan tried to get them to go, but *Lee* doesn't want to force them into anything just because it's her field or whatever."

"Well, it sounds like that's where you come in," Conor says. "You're the resident kid expert, no?"

Barrett pops up and vaults off the counter. "I could give it a shot," she says. "Even though I don't have a dick."

A few minutes later, Katherine and Conor are walking down to the reservoir to meet Lee. It's a warm late afternoon, and the houses are glowing in the sun. "Are you good at everything?" Katherine asks. "Are you one of those really nice guys who's just good at *everything*?"

"I've got my fair share of weak points and fuckups, Brodski."

"I'm not sure I believe you. Like you had some drunken, drug-ridden past?"

"I've had a few beers in my life. But no drugs. My brother fucked up his life on that shit. I spent years trying to keep him clean, he'd get better, and then he'd go right back."

"I'm sorry. How is he now?"

"Let's talk about something else," he says.

Yes, that suddenly seems like a very good idea. "How long are you stationed at the firehouse?" she asks.

"I'm doing rotations of different neighborhoods. I'll probably end up being here for a couple of months, total. Lucky we met when we did."

Katherine hopes that's true. She does want to believe it was lucky.

L
ate in a long, emotional roller coaster of a day, the sight of Katherine and her fireman sitting on a bench beside the reservoir is a welcome relief. He's sprawled across the seat with his arms spread along the back, showing off a singularly impressive wingspan. He's saying something to Katherine, and she's laughing, really laughing, in a way that Lee rarely sees. It would be nice if something finally worked out for Katherine in this area. It's the missing piece in the puzzle of her life after all the disappointments and disasters. She can see the two of them glowing when they come over to the car. "I'm sorry to break up your day like this," Lee says. She almost used the word "date," but she has a feeling Katherine would bristle.

"Conor's professionally obliged to have his day broken up by crises," Katherine says and makes introductions.

"I'd love to come and help if I can," Conor says. "But if that's awkward . . ."

"Of course not. It might be helpful to have you there."

There's something so reassuring about Conor, the big solid presence of him, Lee agrees to let him drive to West Hollywood. Anyway, he's much too tall to fit into the backseat comfortably, and she likes the idea of stretching out herself back there. She fills him and Katherine in on what she knows about the situation, and Conor assures them he's pretty good at handling such things. "I know a lot of people who've fucked themselves up over and over again."

Katherine casts a worried glance in Lee's direction.

Despite all the progress Katherine's made in the past two years, and her appealing tough-girl routine, she still tends to take things personally, mostly because she feels so bad about the mistakes she's made over the years. She feels she should be criticized and punished, and so she's always ready to spot criticism, even when none is intended. It's all that good old Catholic guilt that was drummed into her from birth about how unworthy she is of being loved, even though, from the sounds of it, it's everyone around her who was unworthy of her.

"What do you think of the studio?" Lee asks.

"It's great," Conor says. "Very low-key. I like that."

"Conor's coming to your advanced inversions workshop next week," Katherine says.

"Careful what you joke about," he says. "I just might. I've never minded making a fool of myself."

Lee calls Graciela, and by the time they pull up in front of Stephanie's building, she's standing on the sidewalk, her arms wrapped around her, visibly shaken. When Lee goes to hug her, Graciela melts against her shoulder and starts to cry.

"I'm sorry," she says. "I'm really, really sorry. I probably shouldn't have had you come all the way out here. It's just been a long day, and . . ."

"Don't even think of it," Lee says. "What's going on in there?"

"I don't even know. She seems out of it and the place is a mess. It seems like she's dehydrated, and she keeps drifting off. There's this crazy neighbor of hers. . . . Anyway, as soon as I told her I thought we should go to the hospital, she started getting hostile." She looks over at Katherine and Conor. "I didn't mean for everybody . . ."

"It's all right," Katherine says. "We wanted to come. This is Conor, by the way."

"Hi. Sorry to get you down here."

"Did she hit you?" Conor asks.

Graciela shakes her head no.

"How'd you get that . . ." He points to a small cut on Graciela's forehead.

"She threw a few things around, but it didn't seem like she was aiming or anything. It was just an accident."

"I know a lot of EMTs," Conor says. "I can call one and have an ambulance down here in no time, if that's best. We'll make sure they don't have the lights on and that the whole thing is done very quietly."

Lee can see that Graciela is more comforted by the presence of this big capable guy than she is by either Katherine or her. With her thick, tangled hair and her dark features and perfect complexion, Graciela looks even more beautiful in her exhaustion and weariness than she usually does.

"You don't think that will make things worse?"

"I'll take responsibility if it does," Conor says. "Let's go in. There's someone else in there now?"

"Billie, her neighbor. But she can pretty much take care of herself."

Graciela starts walking toward the apartment building, and Katherine nudges Conor and says, "Go in with her. She's a mess right now."

"Come with us."

"Maybe we shouldn't overwhelm her with too many people. We'll call in a few minutes and you can let us in."

Lee watches them heading into the building, checks out the look of sad resignation on Katherine's face, and wishes she hadn't interrupted the date by asking Katherine to come down here.

"Great guy you've got there," she says.

"Yeah. Probably too great for me."

"No one's too great for you, Kat."

Katherine starts laughing. "That's such a line, Lee. And so not true. He really deserves someone like Graciela—sweet, no past."

Lee puts her hand on Katherine's arm. "Don't do this," Lee says.

"I don't know what you're talking about."

"Please? For me? Don't. Now let's go in and see what we can do."

PART TWO

E very Tuesday and Thursday morning for the past three weeks, Becky has been picking up Imani and driving her to a yoga class at a different studio somewhere in L.A. While Imani knew it was a big trend and "everyone" was doing it, she had no idea there were so many available options. Becky told her she knows of about 120 studios scattered around the city, and that doesn't include the private places and the out-of-the-way classes taught in community centers and schools and gyms and the YMCA.

"How do you *know* all this?" Imani asked her.

"The old-fashioned way: Internet. I subscribe to about three dozen websites where they review studios and update classes and post gossip about teachers. Pictures, too, in case that's your thing. And Twitter has been *amazing*. Every afternoon at five I get a tweet about the best classes and workshops going on the next day. Everyone fights for a spot, so you have to register in advance or try to bribe your way in. It's worse than getting tickets for concerts."

It doesn't sound very *om shanti* to Imani, but she's the novice here and, yoga or not, it's still L.A.

"Can't you just use your name?" Imani asks. "That ought to be enough to get you in."

"Are you kidding? *Everyone* goes. If I won an Oscar, maybe I'd get moved up the list. Anyway, it's embarrassing using my name like that. My screen name on these sites is 'yoga roommate,' which I thought was kind of clever."

"Cute."

Becky is officially between projects and trying to get in shape for a movie that starts shooting in a few weeks. She has to do a sex scene and there's nudity involved, so she wants to be in perfect shape.

"No body double?" Imani asks.

"Of course there's a body double. That's in all my contracts. But I don't want anyone on the set to think I'm using one because I'm out of shape. I actually have to look *better* than the double to save face, so it would be easier if I just did the scene myself."

Imani feels lucky nudity was never an option on network TV. If yoga helps Imani get Becky's thighs and obliques, she's willing to put up with gazing off into infinity for a couple of seconds at the beginning of class and pretending she's visualizing world peace. At first she thought Becky was calling her because she happened to be available (most of Becky's friends work nonstop) or because she felt bad for her. But it's brought them a lot closer, and now she feels like a real friend.

The names of the places are what Imani loves the most. Yoga Bind, Yoga Bend, Yoga Hop, Yoga House. A few dozen clever uses of "mat" and "dog" and "down" and endless plays on branches and trees and limbs. A lot of dharma and karma. The names remind her of hair salons and how they're always coming up with some new, nearly witty pun on hair, just when you thought they'd all been used up.

This Tuesday, Becky calls Imani at 8:00 a.m. and tells her she's texting her the address of a studio in Santa Monica and she expects to see her there at eleven o'clock.

"Come on, Becky," Imani says. "Can't you find something a little closer?"

"Oh, my God, girl. This is Taylor *Kendall*."

"I'm waiting to be impressed."

"Honey, I was online at the dot of midnight when they opened the website to reserve places in his class. I got the last two spots, and according to my clock, it was twelve oh two. He is the *best* yoga teacher in the country. I mean, he trained with . . ."

This comment spurs another list of names Imani has never heard of, some of them unpronounceable ones with an Indian inflection, others those weirdly androgynous, soap opera names so common among yoga teachers, she's discovering. Campbell Dylan. Chrysler Marks. Rand Bryce. And people criticize black women for the Africanish names they give their kids! (Imani was her manager's choice; her mother had gone for Loretta, a fact not even Becky knows.)

What Imani is also discovering is that there are about six hundred teachers in the country who are, unquestionably, *the best*. Funny how they all happen to be *gorgeous*.

But, long ride or not, Imani agrees to meet her. She feels as if bumping into Becky in the cupcake bakery was fate. She's had more fun over the past few weeks with Becky than she's had since . . . well, for a long time. It's all the driving around to parts of the city she's never been to before, the hopping and jumping that she's getting quite good at, even the fun new clothes that make her feel sexy and athletic. She's always been fit, but she's never felt athletic before. There's always a moment in these classes when she finds herself rolling her eyes ("Take a few deep, poignant breaths and direct them toward that little storage space in your body where you keep your sadness"), but she does it anyway. And no matter how silly it sounds, it's having some kind of effect. She doesn't believe for one second that twisting her spine is helping to "wring out toxins" or whatever it's supposed to be doing, but it is true that she's started to feel as if a dark mood is being wrung out of her. Maybe she's emptying out her "storage space." Glenn has noticed a difference, too.

For months after the miscarriage, she couldn't stand having him touch her. She felt betrayed by her body and detached from it, as if it had rejected her baby. She'd never felt quite so disconnected from herself. When she and Glenn started having sex again, she'd pretty much gone through the motions to please him. He was so good to her and always had been. If he knew she was using her acting skills more than her passion, he never said anything. But for the past couple of weeks, she's felt connected again and in control. All that balancing on one leg has made her believe that she's capable of mastering her stability, physically and in other ways, too. When Glenn put his arms around her a couple of nights ago, she felt as if she was responding in a way she hadn't in far too long.

She goes to her closet and puts on a gray tank top edged in yellow and made out of a clingy material that absorbs sweat like a dream. Best of all, the deep V shows off her cleavage without looking as if that's the point. How'd that happen? She tries on a few different pants (she's been back to the store Becky took her to five times!) and goes with a pair of black crops. She can unzip them from the cuffs and show off her calves. Even the name of the company, which she initially found too cute for words, has begun to appeal to her. Lululemon. It's kind of bright and whimsical, and in addition to everything else, that's usually how she feels when she puts the clothes on.

The yoga studio is in a big white building a couple of blocks from the beach, and at 11:15 when Imani gets there, there's a line around the corner. It's kind of the way it used to be going to movie theaters in Texas when she was growing up, back when people went to movies. On top of that, there's a line of paparazzi in the street, snapping pictures. It almost feels like a premiere. Goddamned bunch of vultures, but on the other hand, she *does* love the way she looks in this outfit, and she slings her yoga bag over her shoulder and does a little hop up to the sidewalk.

Becky's near the front of the line, chatting with Sue Holland, child star turned alcoholic turned beloved teen idol turned serious actress, and Faith, one of the other leads from *Roommates*. They all greet with big, sisterly hugs, the unmistakable waiting-for-the-doors-to-open energy in the air. Imani can hear the paparazzi snapping pictures. "Imani, over here! Becky, how's it going?" Her manager will be thrilled if these photos show up on the Internet. She knows she's looking gorgeous.

"You didn't tell me Johnny Depp was teaching," Imani says, nodding toward the long line.

"I took a workshop with Taylor in Kauai," Sue says, "and he kicked my *ass!*"

This starts a competition between Becky and Sue about who has taken the most difficult and exhausting classes and workshops and how close to passing out each came how many times. Imani thought the whole point of yoga was a lack of competition, but she's definitely seen a lot of that over the last few weeks. She's been surprisingly good at rising above it, though. Although come to think of it, maybe being a purist about not competing is just another form of competition.

"I kind of feel as if we're dinosaurs," Becky's costar says, "and these guys are the real celebrities."

Someone in the line behind them says, "On Taylor's website, he said his agent is negotiating for a workshop in the Staples Center."

"Agent?" Imani says. "Really?"

"It's a big thing now," Becky says. "They can negotiate amazing contracts with studios and for workshops at retreats all over the world. I was talking with Yram Tild a few months ago—"

"Yram?!" Sue screams. "She is incredible. I've been trying to get into one of her workshops for months. You *know* her?"

"A little. Anyway, she said her agent got it in her contracts she has to fly first class, which makes sense because she has to start teaching as soon as she lands. And a lot of teachers get TV and video deals so—"

"I cannot believe you actually *talked* to Yram!" Sue says.

Imani has a vague sense that once upon a time, fitness teachers crowed about knowing movie and TV stars as a way to make themselves seem more important. Crazy world.

"The really cool thing," Becky says, "is that I got *three* adjustments last workshop!"

"From *Yram?*" Sue shrieks. "Oh, my *God!*"

"How are you spelling that?" Imani asks.

"Y-r-a-m," says Sue. "She's so ethereal and gorgeous, it's unreal. She's like a magic princess. She has American parents, but she was raised at a monastery in the Himalayas by monks who gave her her name and training."

Imani is tempted to point out that "Yram" is "Mary" spelled

backward but doesn't want to burst anyone's bubble. "I'd love to take her class," she says, hoping it sounds convincing.

The inside of the studio is unexpectedly gorgeous, a lot of rose-colored wood and ivory walls. The room itself is heated, nearly hot, and there's a lot of polite but tense jostling for position. Imani's noticed this look people get when they're claiming their territory with their mats. They plant their equipment with focused intensity, no looking side to side, no acknowledging anyone else's presence even though the whole point of the intensity seems to be to keep everyone else away from them. They ought to just post a sign.

But today there are so many people, the mats are nearly on top of each other and half the people are sitting upright with their legs folded in lotus, looking as if they'll explode if anyone suggests they move. Someone does. A perky little woman in a unitard.

"Sorry, folks, but I'm going to have to ask everyone to reposition a little. We have thirty more people coming in. There's plenty of room in here if we line up properly. We'll start in the left-hand corner and skootch everyone together."

"I hope you're not claustrophobic," Becky whispers. "I'm so glad I took a hit of pot before I got in line."

When Taylor Kendall comes into the room, there's a round of applause and the kind of cheers that Mick Jagger would envy. He's shirtless and wearing a pair of loose cotton drawstring pants that reveal a provocative hint of butt cleavage. He's not tall, and he's definitely not a bodybuilder, but there's something undeniably sexy about his lean, perfectly proportioned torso and his confident ballet dancer's strut, back arched and chest thrust out, as if he's showing off a tattoo somewhere above his nipple. His arms are topographical maps of musculature and the circulatory system.

"Okay, folks. There are eighty-six people in this room. But do you know how many are on the wait list? One hundred and twenty-five. And how many were turned away completely? At least two hundred more."

Inexplicably, this provokes another round of applause.

"So I hope you're going to make good use of your time here and the *gift* of having gotten in." This is the first time Imani has paid three hundred dollars for a *gift*. "You ready to begin?"

More applause, and this time Imani joins in—Taylor's wandering the room and is now right next to her.

"Okay, before we start, I want to tell you one thing. I know I look like a big dummy, okay. But I am not as stupid as I look, okay?"

There's a roar of laughter and applause, but in fact, Imani is relieved by the comment. You wouldn't mistake him for a brain surgeon.

"I know a lot of you came here today because someone said to you, 'You have to go out to Santa Monica and take this class. This guy is a pretty good teacher.' Am I right?"

A lot of heads start bobbing. He lays a hand on Imani's shoulder. "Am I right, girlfriend?"

For the record, Imani wants to say, *not every black woman in America wants to be called "girlfriend," especially by some scrawny white guy she's never met before.*

Instead she says, maybe a little too loudly, "Yeah, you right, *girlfriend.*"

Imani gets a big laugh, and he moves away from her quickly.

"The important thing to remember is that the class is not about *me*. It's about *you*. Okay? It doesn't matter how many people were trying to get in for my class today. It doesn't matter how many times I've been on *Larry King Live*. (Three, okay?)

It doesn't matter that I've been on the *Today* show and that *People* magazine voted me 'Sexiest whatever.' Who *cares*? Maybe you heard that I sold more DVDs on QVC than any other yoga teacher. Ever! Big effing deal. It's all about *you*. This class is only as good as you make it for *yourself*. And hey, you can buy the DVDs out front after the class anyway! I'm going to be signing them for an extra twenty-five dollars, three percent of which will go to the Taylor Kendall Foundation."

Maybe she's imagining it, but Imani could swear he's giving her a cold, hard stare. He looks away and rubs his hands together.

"Are you ready?" he shouts. "I said, are you *ready*? Okay, that's more like it. I'm going to make you wet today. I'm going to stretch you open, and we're going to go *deep*. You're gonna need to make noise, so make some noise. Let go and let it out. Let's *go*! Are you ready? Are you *ready*? Awesome. Now, everybody sit back down for a minute while I do a demonstration."

By the middle of the class, Imani is indeed wet. Soaking, in fact, with sweat dripping down her face and even off of her fingertips. The fact that she's sweating as much as she is makes her care a little less about the people on all sides of her who are dripping onto their own mats and, when they stagger their bodies and extend their arms, onto hers as well. Taylor has long curly hair that comes down past his shoulders. He started off class with it in a ponytail, and in the past fifty minutes, he's had it up in a clip, wound into a goofy little topknot, and flowing freely around his shoulders. Imani wants to dismiss him as one more annoying narcissist, but he's a great showman, and at least to some extent, this is show biz.

The students are mostly thin women in their twenties who've somehow or other perfected the skill of silently drawing attention to themselves while looking as if they're completely absorbed in what they're doing. The men mostly bear a striking resemblance to Taylor, same types of bodies from what she can see, and either long-haired or completely bald.

While Taylor has given Becky two adjustments already (funny how you catch on to this kind of thing quickly) and one to Sue, he hasn't so much as touched Imani since their little exchange before class began.

Unfortunately, that's about to change.

As far as Imani can tell, he's putting the class through the same paces she's been put through in almost every class Becky has taken her to. The big innovation is that he's renamed every pose in a way that emphasizes parts of the anatomy. Not "down dog" ("too negative and demeaning") but "up butt." Not "child's pose" ("children go into a million poses every hour") but "knees spread." Not "plow," the pose they're in now, but "crotch in face pose."

"Drop your knees on either side of your ears and get your junk closer to your face," he says. "You're sweaty, you're loose, here's your chance."

Imani doesn't want a chance. Her back is starting to hurt and the combination of the heat, the sweat, and the imagery Taylor is using is beginning to make her feel a little ill. She stays in plow, legs straight. Plenty deep for her.

That's when he comes over to her and kneels on her mat with the front of his body pressed against her back and his face practically between her legs. This feels like the closest she's come to cheating on Glenn since she stopped doing love scenes on X.C.I.A.

"Lower the knees," he says.

She shakes her head, too contorted to say anything. Plus he's looking at her with more hostility in his gaze. Let him. She's not budging. He takes his hands and puts them on the backs of her thighs and applies pressure. When she doesn't move, he gives a little push.

That's when Imani feels something pop in her lower back.

Lee's Pose of the Month: April
Marichyasana

I've chosen marichyasana as pose of the month because, like all spinal twists, it's detoxifying. And because there are a million variations on this one, there's a version to suit every need. And let's face it, who among us doesn't need a little dextoxification every once in a while?

If you're trying to manage a chemical addiction, this pose can help the liver and the spleen wash out all poisons you've built up in your system, making it look like an untended litter box.

But drugs and alcohol are not the only things we need to detox from. There are relationships that leave us so full of emotional and spiritual poison we need to purify on the deep level we get from really twisting and squeezing them out of our spines. (Kind of like the way we sometimes wanted to "wring someone's neck," back before doing yoga, when we still dabbled in violent metaphors.)

And sometimes we need to wring out whatever self-destructive patterns of behavior are making it impossible for us to accept that we do deserve a good relationship or a steady job or just a plain old *break* every once in a while.

But here's the thing about twisting and detoxing— it isn't as much about *wringing out* as it is about *lifting up.* Your head, your heart, your spirit. Because you can't get into marichyasana, or any of the twisting poses, unless you have your chest lifted and your heart open and are ready to move into it.

And believe me, you can't start clearing all that emotional and spiritual litter out of your life unless you're first ready to hold your head high and open your heart and *lift* yourself out of the old patterns and the rehearsed reactions and expectations of failure.

Lift, open, twist. Shampoo, rinse, repeat. Don't overthink it. Just do it. Don't get bent out of shape.

Namaste
Lee

P.S. Barrett's Saturday morning "Good Doggie" classes have really started to take off. Tell your friends. And don't forget: It's not *just* for girls! My twins are having a great time!

Lee clicks the "post" button on her page and closes her laptop. Even though she'd hate to count up the number of hours she spends online—by necessity, for work, mostly—Lee has never been a big one for the computer. The "Pose of the Month" usually turns out to be the "Pose of Every Third Month if I'm Lucky." It's weird to think that as a yoga teacher she has to keep up an active online life, just to stay in touch with students and build her business. It seems counterintuitive. Still, there's something kind of cozy about lying in bed and checking e-mail and ordering a delivery of groceries, as she's started doing since Alan moved out. Adapting.

In the past month, life has settled into a groove of some kind. Lee can't say she doesn't miss having Alan around the house, because she does. She wouldn't admit that to many people because as humiliating as it is to have someone walk out on you (with only vague plans for reuniting in the future) it's even worse to feel their absence as strongly as she does. The whole incident with him has made her question the validity of working so hard to not feel angry all the time. Maybe a little righteous anger would help. Maybe she really *should* visualize wringing his neck. Or, more to the point, maybe she should not feel so guilty when she *does* visualize wringing his neck.

She always worries that she's betraying her students in those moments. She feels like a hypocrite.

Last week, she lay in bed and thought about punching him, really laying into him and screaming at him. But those were extenuating circumstances.

He had come over to discuss the contract with YogaHappens and ask her if she'd come to a decision yet. Ever since the meeting with "the guys" at their house three weeks earlier, he's been pressuring her into going ahead with it. There are still a few questions about the amount of money they'd actually be making, but one thing is certain: it will be a *lot* more than she's making now, with Alan's salary being a complete bonus.

"I'm thinking it over," she told him.

"Yeah, I know. But they're not going to give you forever to answer. It would be good for you, Lee, a real opportunity."

She doesn't mind that Alan is so behind this plan, and it isn't as if she is dead against it, but it bothers her that instead of coming right out and being honest about his motives, about the advantages to *him*, he's spending all this energy trying to convince her it's about the benefits to her and her career. Why can't he just tell her the straight-out truth for once? Is it really that hard?

"I'm thinking it over, Alan."

They were sitting at the table in the dining room at the time, and the kids were at Barrett's "Good Doggie" class. Alan had looked across the table at her, a little sad, a little pleading. And then a familiar gleam had come into his eyes, and Lee knew exactly what he was thinking. For a minute, she forgot that everything was different in their lives. All of a sudden, she felt that direct line between the two of them that they'd always used to communicate nonverbally. His obvious desire for her started to heat up her body, without a word being exchanged. She realized how much she had missed his touch and how much she missed the release she always felt from having sex with him, and she looked over at his dark, full lips and just *wanted* him. When she talked about it with Katherine later—and Katherine was the only person she discussed it with—she told her she'd been horny, which was easier than getting into the longing and loneliness.

She'd looked back at Alan that day and held his gaze for about one second too long, and next thing she knew, he had her backed up against the sofa in the living room and was running his hands all over her thighs. She hopped up and wrapped her legs around his waist and he carried her like that to their bedroom. Both of them seemed to be driven by so much more intensity and hunger than usual, and when their mouths came together, Lee heard herself sighing and felt her body melt in a way that she hadn't felt in a long time. A little pulse somewhere in the back of her head kept repeating *He's back, he's back,* over and over, almost as if she needed to convince herself. Even her concerns that there could be someone else started to dissolve: he wouldn't be like this with her if he was seeing another woman.

But afterward, he popped up off the bed and started pulling on his clothes. "That was fun, babe," he said.

Fun? A sweaty ninety minutes of power yoga can be "fun" but that isn't the word she would have used to describe what they'd just done.

"Think about the contract, okay?"

Two minutes later, he was gone. Not back after all, but gone again. That's when she started thinking about slugging the guy.

Her cell phone on the table beside the bed rings, and she sees that it's her mother. This is a call she isn't ready for at this hour of the morning on a Saturday. But out of a sense of obligation, she reaches for it anyway. Except it isn't only obligation. Lee feels a complicated combination of love and pity for her mother and is always hoping, with an explosive mix of optimism and magical thinking, that during one of their conversations, her mother will stop projecting her own doubts about herself onto Lee, and they'll get to the love they feel for each other somewhere under the surface resentments.

In her youth, Ellen had aspired to be a writer. She'd taken an entry-level job in publishing right out of college and lived with a roommate on Bank Street in the West Village in one of those cheap sublets that were easy to find in the late sixties. If you believed Ellen's version of her own story, it was one of the happiest times of her life. She liked her job, wrote on the kitchen table at night, and was receiving "promising rejections" from the *New Yorker*, *McCall's*, and every other publication she sent her stories to. She'd felt with certainty that something was about to happen and her life was about to open up for her.

What happened was that she met Lee's dad. He was twenty

years older than Ellen and a legendary editor at Random House. Tall, handsome, intelligent—how could she say no when he asked her to marry him? She'd have that much more time to write once she quit her job and moved up to his place in Darien.

Except that isn't how it had worked out. Probably that isn't how it ever works out for anyone. Ellen just got lost in her husband's life. Compared with all the famous writers her husband worked with, many of whom visited them and spent the weekend, her ambitions seemed ridiculous and all those "promising rejections" just reminders of what she lacked in terms of talent. She became a mom, a housewife.

"Oh, Lee-lee, I'm sorry, it sounds like I woke you up, honey. I'm never sure what your teaching schedule is."

"It's okay, Mom. I've been awake for a while now. How's everything going?"

"It's going great, honey. It really is, I haven't been this happy in *years*."

"I'm so glad, Mom."

This is true. When her mother is depressed, she tends to be self-pitying and angry, lashing out at Lee and anyone else within earshot, excoriating them for not understanding her problems, not appreciating the *sacrifices* she made for her family, and sounding personally affronted by every piece of good news, even about her own grandsons. When she's happy, there's less lashing out, or at least it's all done in a cheerier tone.

"Aren't you going to ask me why, honey?"

I was hoping you'd ask about the twins, Lee doesn't say. "I was just about to, Mom."

"Oh, Lee. You are going to love this news so much. It makes sense on so many levels. It really pulls together so many of my interests."

Her mother's voice has that tone she uses when she's

imagining criticism and is trying to head it off at the pass. "I can't wait to hear it, Mom."

"I know you're going to think it's a little crazy, but really, I think this is going to make us even closer, honey. You know that's what I've always wanted."

"I know, Mom." *It's what I've always wanted, too,* Lee knows better than to say. If she did, her mother would interpret it as criticism of her, and there would go another half hour of her life.

"Well, you know that based on *your inspiration,* I've started taking yoga classes at the Y."

"You told me. I think it's great, Mom." Last she heard, her mother had attended two classes and then decided that it was a waste of money. Maybe she started going again. A little wave of uneasiness is beginning to wash over Lee, and she really wishes she hadn't taken the call.

"I'm sure you don't believe me, but I'm really quite *good.* I'm able to do almost all those things where you bend over and whatever else it is."

"You always were flexible."

"You're just saying that, but it's *true.* Anyway, I made friends with the yoga teacher there, Laurence, this lovely young man who always smells so nice. And *don't* call him Larry! Anyway, I invited him out here for dinner one night, because I wanted him to see the house. He showed up with his 'friend'—Corey or something like that—very nice. And Bob didn't mind at all about it being two men. I know you think Bob's a big Republican, but he's a supporter of Lieberman."

Lee is having a familiar feeling, the one where she feels as if her mother just walked into her house with a huge trunk and told her she's staying for six months. *Oh, Mom,* she wants to say, *don't tell me what I think you're going to tell me.*

When Lee was a kid and her flute teacher told Ellen that Lee had "promise," Ellen went out and bought herself a tenor recorder and took two lessons. That was before the divorce, back when Ellen and Lee's father had money. Ellen had never been supportive of Lee's premed ambitions, but once she got into medical school, Ellen began researching nursing programs. When Lee's sister got into Juilliard, Ellen began taking piano lessons. You could say it was all a flattering way for her mother to be closer to her kids and to find some common ground, but what it always boiled down to was her mother being disappointed in her own abilities and then willfully making everyone feel guilty about their own talents. *It all comes so easy for you. You think you're all so much better than me. You're all* laughing *at me and don't try to pretend you're not.*

So now it was happening again.

"Laurence thinks I would make an excellent teacher. Not on *your* level, honey. Don't worry about me trying to compete. And anyway, since I'm back east, it's not like we'd be going after the same students. Laurence says there's a huge market for what he calls 'old-lady yoga,' which is apparently a much more affectionate and positive term than it sounds."

It's true that there is a need for more compassionate teachers to instruct older students who have different physical requirements. Her mother isn't especially athletic, but she is fit. She'd benefit from a good mentor.

"Does Laurence offer teacher training?" Lee asks.

"In other words, you think he's just flattering me to get some money out of me for the training. Reeling in some foolish old woman. Next thing I know, you'll be accusing me of having a crush on him. As if I don't know that he's gay and, even if he weren't, it's highly unlikely he'd be attracted to me. Have a little more faith in me than that, Lee!"

"I didn't say that, Mom. I was just wondering . . ."

"Anyway, that's not the main thing. The main thing is, he fell in love with the house. He's been looking for a place to use as a yoga retreat center, and he thinks this would be perfect. Can't you imagine it, honey?"

"I guess I hadn't thought about it much, to be honest."

"Oh, now you're trying to discourage me, but I think he's *right*. We could have people put those mats out on the side porch in summer. And he thinks the barn could be converted into a big yoga studio or whatever for under a hundred thousand. We'll have to get another mortgage to put in extra bathrooms, anyway."

"I thought Bob was feeling pinched during the recession." Bob was an ineffectual man who retired from the insurance business at exactly the wrong moment. Lee had been hoping that he had invested at least some of his portfolio wisely and had a good portion of it locked away.

"When you decided to go into this yoga business, Lee, I didn't discourage you."

True, assuming you don't consider "Yoga is a freak thing. You'd be better off joining the circus" discouraging.

"Honestly, Mom, if you've thought it through and you really think it would be a good idea, then I'm behind you, one hundred percent."

"That's all I wanted to hear, honey. All I want is your support. I don't want or need or expect anything else but that. Oh, one more thing: Laurence wants to do a little benefit weekend here to get things off the ground and help raise some money for the blocks and belts or straps or whatever it is. And he asked me if you and Alan could help him launch it. It would be such a huge, huge boost to us if you did—a big yoga instructor and her rock star husband from Hollywood. We could use the names of some of the celebrities you teach. Who's going to know if it isn't true? It would be incredible. He tried to get that Asian one with the long hair? I forget his name, but he wanted to be *paid*! Can you believe it? The whole point is it's a *benefit*. And he wanted us to pay for his plane ticket! Even after I told his 'agent' he could have our bedroom and we'd sleep in the guest room. I told him I'd make him breakfast, too."

"I'll think it over, Mom, but to be honest, now isn't the best time."

"I know I'm completely insignificant in your lives, honey, but I helped you out when you needed money. You'll be coming east to visit us anyway, no?"

"I've been meaning to talk with you about that." She had hoped Alan would be back home before it ever became necessary to discuss any of this with her mother.

"Is something wrong?" Ellen asks. "It's not the twins, is it? I know you don't believe me, but I have a sixth sense about these things."

"It's not about the twins, Mom. They're fine."

"Thank God. I knew it couldn't be. I would have had an intuition."

But Lee still can't bring herself to mention it, so she tells her mother that she's been given a very nice offer to work at a big yoga studio, health benefits and all, and she probably shouldn't leave L.A. for a while.

"In other words, you're saying my little retreat center is too rinky-dink for you now. Well, I never pretended it was a big deal like *your* life. Give me credit for *something*, Lee."

"Please don't, Mom. It isn't that. It's just . . . Alan temporarily moved out, Mom."

There is a long moment of silence from the other end of the phone, and then, in a different tone of voice, one full of warmth and the kind of compassion that Lee knows—has always known—her mother to be capable of: "I'm so, so sorry, honey."

It's almost as if the petulant, insecure child she was talking to a few minutes ago passed the phone to an adult. "What happened?"

Lee tells her a version of the story that almost makes sense to her as she's saying it. She emphasizes that no one's planning any drastic moves for the moment, but everything's a little complicated now. It's not as if they're breaking up, it's just a little breather. Her mother sobs audibly. She mumbles something about the twins, and Lee is happy that she's told her, and, in this moment of shared sadness, she feels closer to her mother than she's felt in a long time.

Ellen blows her nose. "I'm so happy you felt you could tell me, honey. It makes me feel so much closer to you. So . . . maybe Alan would come play at the benefit alone while you take care of the kids out there."

Stephanie is nursing her second Diet Coke and finishing her pitch of *Above the Las Vegas Sands* to Sybille Brent. Sybille appears to be listening in a vague, wine-soaked way, sprawled back into the cushions of a banquette in the Sky Bar at the Mondrian Hotel, her very thin legs wound together tightly. It's nearly dusk, and from where she's sitting, Stephanie can see miles of Los Angeles down below, bathed in the faint golds and yellows of twilight, the sickly hues of the unhealthy air pretty, soft, and languid. Like something from a fever dream, which is how the sprawling, overstuffed city often looks to Stephanie at this aching in-between time of day. Stephanie can't decide if Sybille's little nods and eye-widening gestures in reaction to what she's saying represent genuine interest or condescending detachment. The bar is one big outdoor room, and a cool but pleasant breeze blows through the bougainvillea and Sybille's soft white hair moves slightly.

Stephanie's manager set up the meeting. Sybille, a woman of a certain age—although no one's certain what age that is—recently made a vast fortune in a spectacularly ugly divorce from her husband, a high-profile real estate developer in New York. She's spending a few months at the Mondrian to get away from New York, and she's looking for projects to invest in. At one time, she apparently had acting ambitions, and this is a way to connect with the business later in life without looking ridiculous. It would give her something to do, a hand in movies, and a screen credit her friends can applaud at the premiere.

It's a fairly common way to raise money for a project, but it's not the easiest way. In some respects, it cheapens the project—everyone knows this is no one's first choice for funding—and usually these folks expect something in return—a role for a friend or a hand in the shooting. Over the past few weeks, Stephanie has had four such meetings with four such people, all pretty discouraging. No one has read the book; no one seems especially interested in the story. They all want to talk about casting (without really knowing the roles) and dropping the names of people they allegedly know or supposedly worked with or hope she knows. One guy even asked her if it could be shot in 3-D.

"I hadn't considered it," she said.

All the mutual pretending makes her feel a little crazy at times, although certainly less crazy than she was before the shameful intervention at her apartment. And since nothing else has worked out for Stephanie, it's worth a shot. Claiming she's raised a certain percentage of the budget will make it more likely for others to invest, and in any case, it beats lying around her apartment with a bunch of empty bottles and used kitty litter. But she's not going to go *there* right now.

"I like the way you describe the plot," Sybille says.

"It's an amazing novel, and the author is incredibly talented."

"I read the book last week, as soon as we had the meeting arranged. I found it interesting and passionate but overwritten in places. A young writer using language like a new toy and a little too in love with the sound of his own voice."

"There's some of that," Stephanie says. She's always felt this way, but it was never discussed in any of the reviews, so she's kept her reservations to herself. Stephanie is impressed that Sybille read the novel and that she's put her finger on a stylistic weakness. She has a velvety voice, a little smoky, like Lauren Bacall's, and one of those carefully trained and modulated ways of articulating every word.

"It sounds as if you read a lot," Stephanie says.

"Yes, but don't tell anyone. It makes you look out of touch these days. I studied literature at Vassar, another piece of information I don't toss around since I look enough like a dilettante already. Your description of the book makes more sense to me structurally than the book itself," Sybille goes on. "I like the way you emphasized the sister's wedding. I think that could be a frame for the whole piece. Set it up as the place the story is going, right from the first scene."

When Stephanie mentioned this very idea to the author, he was insulted and refused to talk with Stephanie for two weeks. "I've always thought that's how it should be done, but the author didn't agree with me." Stephanie finishes the Diet Coke, and a waiter materializes at her side and asks if she'd like another. "Please," she says.

Sybille observes this over the rim of her wineglass, and Stephanie has the feeling she's attaching exactly the right significance to it. One of the worst things about *not* drinking is that everyone immediately assumes you're a drunk. A few weeks ago, she would have been on her third glass of wine by now, and Sybille wouldn't have batted an eye. But "I'll have a Diet Coke" is treated as if it's synonymous with "I'm an alcoholic." Well, if the shoe fits. And after struggling with this escalating drinking problem for the past year, she's willing to admit that it does fit. As bad as it all was, the worst for her was realizing afterward that she had *Silver Linings* playing on the TV with the sound turned off. Oops, not going *there*, either!

Sybille has that sleek, carefully tended rich-lady hair and the figure of a one-time trophy wife. Someone named Anderson, a much younger man with beautiful eyes, occasionally appears and hands her a message or discreetly asks a question. Stephanie is guessing he's a gay assistant, but hasn't entirely ruled out the possibility that his duties include more than arranging her calendar. Sybille gives off an air of intelligence and genuine compassion, but there's also the aura of refined decadence that sometimes surrounds people with lots of money and equal amounts of free time. She's wearing a subtle, intoxicating perfume that isn't quite like anything Stephanie has ever smelled before. Probably made with the glands of an endangered animal and costs in the five-hundred-dollar-an-ounce range.

"Have you thought about writing the screenplay yourself?" Sybille asks. "You have good ideas, and you'd have more control over the project. I think you have integrity."

"The author wants to write it. Although I'm not sure that's working out very well. Promising him he could is how I got the option, and it's in his contract."

"You could buy him out, I'm sure."

No doubt she could, assuming she had the money. The Diet Coke arrives, and Stephanie can feel Sybille's eyes on her as she sips.

"You don't drink?" she asks.

"Not today," she says. "I've been to a yoga class and might attend a second one later tonight." Nothing untruthful in that.

"There's lots of that here, I'm told. Yoga. New York as well."

"Everywhere these days."

Sybille shrugs. "Everywhere" is not of great interest to her. Her sleek, aging body indicates pretty clearly that she works with a private trainer, probably at home. Pilates, no doubt.

"You know a lot about it?" Sybille asks. "Yoga?"

"I've been doing it for a while," Stephanie says.

"Well, that is perfect. I'm interested in putting a yoga element into the script."

"Really?"

"Yes. Your expertise would undoubtedly be useful."

"To be honest," Stephanie says, "I'm not sure how much I know about anything these days."

Sybille leans forward, puts down her wineglass, and pats Stephanie's knee. "Sometimes you need to feel that way. I suspect you know more about a lot of things than you give yourself credit for."

Stephanie is suddenly overwhelmed with gratitude and looks off into the sweet melancholy of the dusk, the fading sunlight, the twinkling buildings. What was it Dorothy Parker said? If you can make it through the twilight, you can make it through the night? Something like that. Well, she's almost made it through the twilight of one more day. Three cheers.

"I like you," Sybille says. "You have smarts and courage.

Vulnerability, which always helps balance things out. I watched *Silver Linings*. Anderson told me you're rumored to have done a lot of the writing on it."

"The screenwriter had a breakdown during rewrites, and I took over." It's a relief to finally admit this to someone since, for years, she's been protecting the writer's interests.

"Let's be blunt with each other, shall we? I want a project, and I like the sounds of this one. I like you. I feel I can push you a little bit, although I count on you to call me on it if I go overboard. Basically, I don't know much about the business, but I'm ready to start writing checks."

"All right." The advantage of working with people who are new to this is that they haven't yet figured out how much they can get away with and get for free, since everyone is so desperate to get something under way.

"I'm impatient, though. I don't want to invest ten years in this. We can have my lawyer deal with the author. But I'd like you to start on the screenplay immediately."

"I'm ready to do that." The idea of having something concrete to do is hugely appealing to her.

"I have a request, however," Sybille says.

"Of course." *Here it comes*, Stephanie thinks.

"The father is divorced, correct?"

"He is."

"I think it would be interesting if we could beef up that role a little. Give him more money and stature and make him more the villain of the piece. I'm all for subtlety, but everyone loves a villain. We can have him starting to do yoga, in a completely humiliating and age-inappropriate way. The tight little pants, the claptrap, the whole thing. I think we'd want to make him look especially foolish. The piece needs comic relief in moments, and he can supply that, too."

"I suppose it wouldn't hurt."

"We can show him trying to get in touch with his 'spiritual side,' which amounts to nothing more than accepting the fact, after forty years of deceit, that he's attracted to men. We don't need to hit it over the head or offend anyone, but perhaps he can show up at the wedding at the end with his new boyfriend, a frail thing in his twenties who teaches yoga, a complete embarrassment to the older man, although he doesn't realize it and even seems proud of his little friend."

"We might want to make the young boyfriend somewhat likable," Stephanie says. "Give him a few redeeming qualities."

Sybille thinks this over, sips her wine. "We'll give him eyeglasses. It's a walk-on role."

This is not as bad as Stephanie feared. The father, she convinces herself, is an underdeveloped character anyway, and the whole thing could be a good treacle-cutter if done properly.

"I can work with that," Stephanie says.

Graciela is woken up by the sunlight streaming in the windows of the loft in downtown L.A. she shares with Daryl. She keeps meaning to get blinds or curtains or something to keep out the light, but the windows in the converted office building are huge, and from a practical and financial point of view, the whole process seems a little daunting. She buries her head under the covers and curls up against Daryl's back. He was deejaying at a private party last night and didn't get in until almost four this morning, only a few hours ago. He's in a deep stage of sleep, his breath sonorous and his knees pulled up toward his chest like a child. If she saw that he was sucking his thumb, it wouldn't be a complete shock. This, she is certain, is the true Daryl, sweet, childlike, innocent. Because he's such a lean, handsome man— half African American, half Dominican, with perfect smooth brown skin—Graciela was surprised when they first made love at how inexperienced he seemed. Not suave and practiced, despite the many girlfriends he'd had and the way his looks might suggest, but eager and hungry, like a teenager. And almost in disbelief that he was in her bed and she was in his arms. Even after all this time, he looks at her when they're fucking and he's getting close to coming and says, "Oh, my God, you're so beautiful. You're so *fucking* beautiful!"

Despite everything, how can she resist that? Something in his intensity is so real, so genuine, it takes her to a place where there's nothing but the two of them and the overpowering passion of the moment. There's no modesty or shame between them, nothing that's taboo, no need to hide anything.

She can feel the sun on the back of her neck. One day, one of them will have a big break, and they'll hire someone to come in and deal with the windows.

That's when it hits her. The big break. Today's the day that could open a door to everything she's been waiting for. Her audition for the Beyoncé video. She feels a kick of panic and excitement in her stomach and slithers out of bed without waking up Daryl.

Under Lee's ministrations, her injury is about eighty-five percent healed. She was hoping she'd be even further along, but in most ways, she's in much better shape than she feared she would be back when it happened. Not perfect, but she can work around that. She's promised herself she's going to give it everything, but without blowing out her injury again. She feels more acceptance of the fact that she's genuinely good, and all she has to do is show her real self, without being crazy and desperate.

She's worked up an audition piece with her friend Lindsay and has the choreography down pat. Lindsay spliced together clips from YouTube of Jody Watley in her *Soul Train* prime, and they studied them for hours and put together a routine that's got elements of hip-hop and popping, mixed in with classic funk and even disco, so the routine should be surprising and different from whatever everyone else is doing. For music, she's using Marilyn Monroe's version of "Diamonds Are a Girl's Best Friend" remixed with a deep funky groove prowling underneath that Daryl helped her put together. It's a subtle nod to the fact that Beyoncé recorded a version of the song for a commercial—referencing her without using one of her tracks.

After she's showered and dressed, she notices that her phone is blinking. She checks it out and sees it's another text message from Conor. This is the third time he's tried to get in touch with her in the past two weeks. She was grateful to him the day he showed up at Stephanie's with Lee and Katherine. He confirmed Graciela's opinion that Stephanie was severely dehydrated, in addition to everything else, and convinced her to go to the hospital. He and Katherine had gone to the hospital with Stephanie, and she'd called later in the day to make sure everything was okay. She didn't expect he'd keep her phone number, and she certainly isn't going to call back. Nice as he is, she's not interested. That's number one. Number two is that he's Katherine's boyfriend or possible boyfriend, depending on how far that's gone. And number three, if Daryl ever got wind of it, he'd be furious, especially if she told him she'd returned the call, or the text message, even to tell him to stop getting in touch.

As she's deleting the message, Daryl silently comes up behind her and wraps his arms around her. "Who's that from?" he asks sleepily.

"Lindsay. She's coming in an hour to pick me up for the audition."

"I'm gonna drive you," he says, his face buried in her wet hair.

"No, you're not. You'll make me too nervous. I have to get completely focused."

He accepts this, probably because he's still exhausted and wants to go back to sleep. "Use some of your yoga. I'll come pick you up afterwards."

She isn't going to refuse this. It's one way to satisfy him, and if she screws up in the audition, he'll be there to scrape her back together.

"You'd better not come before four," she says. "These always take longer than they're supposed to."

"You'll be amazing," he says. He spins her around, and it looks as if he has tears in eyes although it might just be sleepiness. "I want you to be great," he says.

"Thanks," she says. "I'll do my best."

He gazes into her eyes. "Look at me, baby. I want you to get this!"

This isn't exactly an apology for *what happened*, but at least it's an acknowledgment that for a moment there was some doubt about how completely he was supporting her success.

"I know that," she says. "And you know what?"

"What?"

"If I do get it, I'm going to buy us some blinds!"

As Lee is about to go into the studio to start teaching, one of the assistants calls her over to the desk. Lee has a pretty good idea of what's coming. Standing in front of the desk is Evelyn, a woman in her thirties who comes somewhat erratically. She has a fairly advanced practice, although she tends to treat classes more like endurance workouts and goes into certain postures with thrusting moves, almost as if she's bench-pressing a barbell when she's reaching up into warrior 1 or a crescent lunge.

What Lee finds annoying is that Evelyn *always* has an issue with paying for class. Either she's forgotten her credit card or lost her wallet or has an elaborate story about having walked out of a class halfway and therefore is eligible (she believes) for a freebie.

Today, according to the studio assistant, the problem is a ten-class card that expired back in January. It still has three unused classes on it, and Evelyn feels she should be allowed to continue to use it. Lee is willing to go the distance for anyone who can't afford classes or is in a temporary financial fix, but in Evelyn's case it feels more like a game. Evelyn is a lawyer and is wearing a pair of designer yoga pants that Lee knows for a fact cost close to two hundred dollars.

After the assistant has explained the matter, Lee says, "Okay, Evelyn. I see what you mean, but I remember talking about the terms and expiration date of the pass when you bought it. You said the expiration would help motivate you to come to class more often."

"It's possible we said that, but that's not how it worked out.

So I really think the responsible thing to do is to let me use it up, Lee. There are three classes left on it. I mean, I hate that *yoga* is now all about *money*."

It's so unappealingly manipulative to try to guilt-trip Lee with this line, especially given the expensive pants. A surprising number of students insist that yoga should *not* be about money, which usually boils down to yoga not being about them spending money on classes. Although the whole thing feels like a game, there's a little pleading in Evelyn's voice that makes Lee think she partly just wants to be taken care of. It's probably why she started coming to yoga in the first place, and while it isn't exactly appealing, it's a lot more forgivable than anything else.

"How about we compromise," Lee says. "Use it today, and then we start fresh next time you come."

"You're a champ," Evelyn says. "I knew you'd do the right thing. I'll just hang on to the card as a souvenir."

Certainly the card will reappear at the studio sometime in the near future.

There are about twenty-five people in class today, a good group, although Shane is at the front of the room. He's a tall, hippieish guy with a bit of a paunch who seems to be allergic to deodorant. Other students have complained about him, but Lee hasn't figured out how to address the issue without being insulting. It's probably best to just come out and say something, but the thought of it fills her with embarrassment and dread. An anonymous letter would be convenient. Of course, Lee does wonder if there'd be so much objection to his hygiene issues if he were twenty years younger and had a six-pack.

Money and body odor—it would undoubtedly be nice to have someone else deal with things like this.

No Katherine in class today. *Again.* She hasn't been practicing at the studio since Alan confronted her and suggested she'd been tampering with the books. Lee can understand why she's upset, but the truth is, she misses her presence in class, and Katherine is an anchor for Lee, someone she knows is into the deeper connections of mind and body than a lot of the students. It's because Katherine is completely immersed in the breathing.

There's a great split Lee has noticed among students in any given class. There are the ones who actually make an effort at breathing and understand that it's the center of yoga and others who ignore it completely and complain that they find the discussion of breath "irritating." *I know how to breathe!* students will sometimes complain. But of course, they don't really.

"Let's make it all about breathing today," she says. "The harmonizing music of your body, the element that can balance out your emotions in a matter of minutes, no matter where you are or what you're doing. So let's all sit comfortably and begin there. A long, slow, steady breath in through your nose."

At this suggestion, she sees the woman sitting beside Shane move her mat a few feet back.

Lee has arranged a date for a tour of the YogaHappens Experience Center in Beverly Hills and to give a class. They told her they would promote the class on their website and promised she would have a large group of students. After class, she logs on to the YogaHappens website in her office at the studio. It's an elaborate site with music and animated images and, underneath it all, the sound of soft rain. On the Upcoming Events page, there's a picture of her taken by a photographer they sent out to

Edendale last week. It's probably the most flattering picture of herself Lee has ever seen. There's some kind of perfection to her complexion and teeth that probably means the picture's been retouched. It would be nice to believe it didn't require a seriously heavy hand, but she suspects otherwise. In the last year or so, she's begun to notice lines and dark shadows and maybe a little bit of hardness that's been etched into her face by trying to manage everything all at once. Aging, she keeps reminding herself, is not a disease. She knows that the key is finding something to love in the new creases and to view the circles under her eyes as signs of character, but as she stares at the soft, smooth face on the YogaHappens web page, she can't help but want to see *that* when she looks into the mirror each morning.

Deep Flow Meditasana is described as "a unique blend of poses and yogic traditions that defy conventions and expectations and take you on a strange and beautiful journey far from the stresses and pressures of your daily life. Like a soft breeze that caresses your face and brings with it the scent of something exotic yet strangely familiar. Allow yourself to take the trip, to be carried away, to be transported to the heart of your yoga practice and, very possibly, to the depths your soul."

Purple, that's for sure, and not very specific, but it does sound appealing, and oddly enough it does capture something true about the way Lee thinks of her classes as journeys, with a beginning and a destination.

Lee herself is described as "one of the hidden gems of the L.A. yoga scene, a teacher of unparalleled talent and uncompromising integrity, with a background in medicine and credentials as a one-time fashion model." At least it doesn't claim that she was a brain surgeon. And she did pose for some photographs for a designer friend *one time*, making the model claim technically accurate, she supposes. Still, it's a little worrisome they feel they need to promote her with hype. The description she provided emphasized her experience as a mother and founder of a studio.

Alan is mentioned briefly in a corner of the page as Lee's husband and described as "a rising star on the L.A. folk scene and one of the emerging voices in the spiritual music movement, which he partly founded." It continues, "Alan will be playing live at select classes to create an aural ambience that will open up new doors of perception and feeling in those lucky enough to reserve a space. Extra fees will apply."

Lee sees Katherine talking to a client and ushering him out to the sidewalk. In many ways, she thinks of Katherine as one of her best friends. She stands in the doorway to her office and waits for Katherine to come back into the building.

"Busy day?" she asks.

Katherine smiles. "I can't complain. Tomorrow's a little slow, so it balances out."

Lee follows her back to her massage room and watches as Katherine strips the sheet off the massage table.

"Can I help you with that?"

"I'm fine," Katherine says.

Lee wants to believe this, but she finds herself saying, "If that's true, why do I feel as if you're dodging me or trying to get away from me? I'm sorry Alan talked to you about the books. He just flies off the handle sometimes."

"I'd rather not get into it. I know I don't have the cleanest record in the world, so when something comes up, it doesn't surprise me if someone like Alan questions me."

"It has nothing to do with your 'record,' Kat."

"Really? It never crossed Alan's mind that I might have started using again and dipped into his pocket to pay for my habit?"

"You've never liked Alan."

"I'm not sure how my opinion matters one way or the other.

Besides, that really isn't the point. We were talking about how he feels about me."

"He likes you, you know that. He's been spending more time at the house lately."

Katherine nods and turns away, begins to line up her bottles of oils and creams. "By 'lately,' you mean since you agreed to the YogaHappens thing?"

Lee is stung by the comment, especially since it's true. But she understands that Katherine is threatened by the possible changes. She decides to let it pass. Their friendship is strong enough to withstand a few bumps.

"Today is Graciela's big day," Lee says. "I told her to call me after her audition, but I haven't heard anything yet."

"Let me know when you do," Katherine says. "Sorry, Lee, but I have a client in five minutes."

What Lee really wants to ask her is how things are going with Conor. Katherine hasn't mentioned him in days, and he hasn't been at the studio. With her history of self-sabotage, Katherine's track record for this sort of thing isn't great. But that gets back to "records," a topic best avoided. She goes back into the office and checks her phone for a message from Graciela. Nothing yet.

I'll admit," Becky says, "that Taylor Kendall was a little extreme. I don't remember him being so self-centered, but you can't help him for having an ego with that kind of success."

"Honey, I met Barack and Michelle at one of the inaugural

balls, and they have less ego. Plus all he talked about was how we were supposed to *let go* of ego."

"That's true. 'Stop thinking about yourself and spend more time thinking about *me!*' "

The good thing about Becky is that she has a sense of humor about all this. It's one of her many saving graces. It's what got her through her divorce and the assorted ups and downs of her career. She keeps her head down and does her job, enjoys the perks, but doesn't take herself too seriously. She once described herself as "a female Hugh Grant—not exactly great range, but appealing and unthreatening." And she is completely fine with that. Versatility can make you a great actor, but Julia Roberts didn't get where she is doing accents.

They're driving downtown in Becky's Prius. Imani's all for saving the planet, but the way the car goes silent without any warning gives her the creeps. It's like being with a friend who all of a sudden stops breathing. Imani didn't have any major back pain after the incident with Taylor Kendall—just a few days of a dull ache every time she moved a certain way. She played it up in front of Becky, but Becky didn't seem to be impressed.

"The truth is," she said, "I'm a little addicted to a few aches and twinges somewhere in my body after a class. I figure if I don't feel that, I haven't worked hard enough."

Imani is tempted to tell her about the class she took up in Silver Lake. Maybe it's just because it was the first class she ever took, but Imani still thinks she felt better afterward than after any of the classes she's been taking with Becky. More centered, if that's the word. But Becky would probably consider the class too "easy" or low-key, and she'd end up feeling like a lightweight and a wimp for suggesting it. Maybe one day she'll head back up there solo and check it out again.

Today they're headed to a studio that Becky promises has been around *forever* (whatever that means) and offers a style of yoga people swear by to cure a variety of joint and muscle problems. Supposedly it's another heated class. Imani's not thrilled about that, but it can't be any worse than that sweat lodge workshop with whatshisname, the Narcissus de Sade.

As they're about to get out of the car, Becky turns to Imani and says, with more seriousness than usual, "What are you doing about work?"

It's a sore subject, and one Imani has been avoiding for months now. Somewhere back in the middle of her *X.C.I.A.* days, Imani felt almost invincible. Everything was going so well, it was hard to believe sometimes. She had a great role on a hit TV series; she was married to a guy who was kind, gorgeous, and completely supportive. Offers were coming in for other series and there was a buzz building about movie offers. Even if TV is definitely where all the energy is today, the prestige is still in movies. There's still the feeling that you're not a "real" actor unless you're on the big screen. Getting pregnant was the final event in what felt to her like the world's longest winning streak. She sometimes worried that she didn't deserve to be this happy, but every day she woke up and did her best to enjoy it. Taking a break from the show was the right thing to have done, especially since the writers had figured out a way to explain her character's absence and eventual return.

And then it all began to come apart. She has only a vague memory of the morning she lost the baby, one that's somehow connected to the scent of the geranium oil in the moisturizer she was using when it happened. Every time even a fragment of memory gets triggered, she hears a faint ringing in her ears and feels herself beginning to shut down. She remembers Glenn cradling her head in the hospital and trying to help her stop crying. She threw out the moisturizer a long time ago.

In addition to the sadness of losing the baby, she felt a weird vulnerability she'd never known before. For a while she didn't want to leave the house, couldn't get behind the wheel of a car, was terrified of loud noises. If she could lose the baby, just like that, suddenly, without any warning, what else could happen? The thought of standing in front of a camera, something that had always felt so natural to her, something that made her feel most like herself, was intolerable, like being in front of a firing squad.

Becky's question about work is like a metal probe hitting the nerve in a tooth. A jolt runs through Imani's body. But this is something she's begun to worry about herself. She left the show almost ten months ago now, and in this business, that's the equivalent of five years.

"Some days I think I'm ready to get back to work," Imani says. "But some days, it still terrifies me. I think I need more time, but I wonder if the longer I stay out of it, the more afraid I get."

"After the breakup," Becky says, "I just wanted to run away. I didn't care where I went or what I did, as long as no one knew me. What I really wanted was to be invisible. But we can't ever have that again, honey. Anonymity's like virginity—when it's gone, it's gone. This is what helped me the most." She nods toward the yoga mat flung across the backseat. "I just kept coming, because I couldn't think of anything else to do. And it helped."

"Why?" Imani asks. "How?"

"I have no fucking idea," Becky says. "And you know what? I don't care. As long as it does. Let's go. This place is notoriously harsh if you're late."

The studio is on the second floor of a yellow brick building downtown, and Becky, who has a phobia about elevators, races Imani up the staircase. They're laughing when they open the door to the studio and panting a little bit. That's when the smell hits Imani.

"Something's not right," she whispers to Becky. It smells as if someone is marinating dirty laundry in a vat of warm vinegar.

"It's just the carpet," Becky tells her. "There's a lot of sweat, and I guess it gets ground in. Someone told me to expect this."

"Oh, okay. Did they also tell you to expect me to run in the other direction?"

"It's not about the carpet, Miss Lang. Just focus on the benefits."

"If they supplied a gas mask, I might be able to. And we're not even in the room yet."

The man behind the desk is so cheerful and welcoming, Imani feels a little relieved. He recognizes them—not virgins and not anonymous—but he's being equally nice to everyone. Probably has to be to compensate for the stench.

Imani nearly swoons as soon as she walks into the yoga room. It's a big, open space with an industrial feel to it, and it's crowded with people, pretty much all of them wearing what look like bathing suits. Surely the heat can't be as bad as it seems. She must be imagining it. Or maybe there's some system malfunction, because if it *is* as bad as it seems, it surely can't be intentional. She and Glenn went to Egypt, and the temperature in Aswan was almost 110 degrees. That's what it feels like.

As for the smell, she isn't going to think about it. If all these people can stand it, she supposes she can, too.

It starts out easily enough, some waving of the elbows and the usual loud breathing, but about fifteen minutes in, Imani is drenched in her own sweat and beginning to feel irritable. The instructor is standing on a little podium, and even though there are maybe fifty people in the room, he seems to know everyone's name. There's something a little creepy about that.

"Hold it, hold it, hold it, Thomas. Higher, higher, higher.

If you can you *must,* Barry. Thirty more seconds on the clock. Higher, Amy."

She's all for encouragement, but the combination of the extreme heat and the smell and the militaristic monologue of the instructor is making her want to shout out a big fat *Shut up!*

But maybe the worst part of it is that the walls are covered in mirrors. The problem is that they make the room seem like a locked little ecosystem and, worse still, make it impossible for her to look away from her body, dripping in sweat and teetering through half the poses.

Every time she thinks she really is going to lose it completely, she thinks about what Becky said to her: It works. No idea why. All she has to do is believe it. Show up. Do it. Pose by pose. One drop of sweat after the next.

But she tries to imagine that there's a little reservoir of fear inside of her, a pool of it, a finite amount, and that every time more sweat runs down her limbs, she's getting closer to draining it dry. Let the carpet seep it all up. As long as she leaves some of it behind when she walks out of here, she's going to consider it a win.

When the music stops, Graciela is, as choreographed, suspended in midair. Only for a half second, of course, but long enough to make the point that she is capable of some breathtaking leaps that make it look as if she's able to float through the air in slow motion. In the silence, she lands back on the floor as softly as a cat.

There are three people watching her: the choreographer, the director of the video, and a small woman who looks as if the skin of her face has been pulled back and tucked into the elastic of the big flying saucer beret she's wearing.

"Thank you," the choreographer says, dry as sand. "Interesting choice of music."

"Especially for *this* decade," the woman with the hat says, and the choreographer gives a little snort.

Graciela never has a clear idea of how she's done at any audition. There's too much tension in the moment and she's so focused on what she's doing and, at the same time, so inside the music, it's never entirely clear what she looks like. She didn't miss anything she had planned today, didn't pull any muscles, and for the most part, was perfectly relaxed. They let her dance for the full two minutes, usually a good sign.

But the current reception, bland and slightly sarcastic, isn't very reassuring.

"We'll be in touch," the director says.

"You have my—"

"Yes, yes, yes. We have everything."

The whole thing feels like a massive anticlimax, after all the preparation, the injury, the weeks she's put into taking it easy, trying to heal. All for this. *Yes, yes, yes, we have everything, see you later. Don't call us.*

"Thank you for the opportunity."

"She's polite, anyway," the little woman says, as if Graciela isn't standing right there. The woman reaches up to her beret and really does look as if she's tucking her skin under her hat.

Crossing the floor to the exit feels like a classic walk of shame, but she does it with as much dignity as she can muster. As she is about to leave, someone's cell phone rings, and the director calls out to Graciela, "Hold on."

She doesn't stop so much as freeze, her hand reaching for the door, unable to turn around. She can see the three of them in the mirror on the wall in front of her, huddling over the table, chatting into the phone, and looking over the notes they took. The director finishes the call.

"Graciela, isn't it?"

She turns. "Yes."

"She'd like to see you perform that again."

Graciela looks around the room. None of the mirrors looks suspicious, but you never know. There's no question about who "she" is.

"Can you do that for us? Run through it again?"

"Of course."

"If you were cast in the video, would you agree to cut your hair?"

"I would," she says.

The little woman wags her head in a sassy sort of way. "Right answer. We're planning on long hair anyway."

When she steps out of the building and onto the street, Graciela has the distinct impression that her life has changed. She wasn't given any assurances, but after her second run-through, the phone rang again, and this time they asked her if she knew how to do the Charleston. "We're using a lot of surprise elements," the choreographer said.

When Graciela was a girl, she was obsessed with Josephine Baker—her elegance and glamour and that crazy dance style of hers that wasn't like anything anyone else did before or since. She had only a faint memory of a grainy black-and-white video she saw of Josephine Baker doing a Charleston in a documentary, but, filled with hopefulness and optimism and a touch of pure joy, she launched into twenty seconds of what she hoped was a close approximation.

Now that "she" had given her nod of approval, "they" were downright friendly.

You've got such great spirit.

Doesn't she? I saw that immediately.

And the smile! Of course, we won't use that, but it's priceless.

Lindsay is waiting in the lobby of the building. She silently asks Graciela the inevitable question. Graciela shrugs and then can't help but burst into a huge grin. Lindsay screams and runs toward her, arms open.

"You got it?"

"It wasn't a 'no' anyway. I'm pretty sure it was a solid 'maybe.' "

"Did they love the routine?"

" 'She' did."

"*She* was there?"

"Not exactly. In another room, I guess. Anyway, she saw it. And called them." And then, Graciela can't help but scream: "*She* thought I was great! Is Daryl here?"

"He called. He's on his way. I can't believe your feet are actually touching the ground. Why aren't you floating?"

They step out onto the sidewalk, arm in arm, and that's when Graciela sees the big hulking frame of Conor, leaning against the building. He nods and smiles at her and starts walking toward them.

"Hey, Graciela," he says.

Graciela smiles at him. She has done nothing wrong, she

reminds herself, has not encouraged him in any way. Maybe she should have just talked to him when he first started calling, but that's past, and she has to let go of it.

"Hi, Conor," she says, trying to make it sound cool but not unfriendly. "What are you doing down here?"

"I've been trying to get in touch with you for a while now."

"I just had this audition and . . ."

"I know."

"Katherine told you?"

"No. Chloe, up at the studio. How did it go?"

Lindsay has stepped aside in a discreet sort of way, pretending to do something with her cell phone. It makes Graciela feel even more uneasy, as if she's picked up some vibe between them.

"It went okay," Graciela says. "I'm sorry about the calls, but I've been really busy . . ."

She lets her voice trail off. There's no good way to finish the sentence. *I didn't want to encourage you? What made you think I was interested?*

"Yeah, you yoga girls are pretty bad about returning phone calls, I gotta say."

Graciela looks him straight in the eyes. It's always best to just get it said. In the end, it makes things easier, doesn't it?

"I live with someone," Graciela says. "On top of that, Katherine's become a good friend of mine."

"I know you're Katherine's friend," Conor says. "I didn't know about the boyfriend, but . . ."

"But now you do know." It's Daryl, standing behind Graciela. He puts his hands on her waist. "Now you do know, okay?"

If there's an upside to not having taken any of Lee's classes since Alan's insulting comments about the money, it's that Katherine has been spending way more time on her pink bicycle. She's been working off her stress and anxiety by pedaling it up and down the streets of Silver Lake until her thighs are aching, and then around and around the reservoir until she feels some of the emotional release she usually feels after taking a class. And these days, there's a lot she needs to release.

Today, as she pedals around the reservoir for the second time, she starts to feel a little giddy. Probably the bad air she's sucking into her lungs, or maybe just an overwhelming sense that things aren't going the way she'd like. The funny thing is, she can't really blame Alan for questioning her about the accounting. As much as she resents, maybe even loathes, Alan for his assumption that she's a weak person who, based on her past actions, is destined always to fuck up, she can't help but think he's got a point. Maybe all the fucked-up shit that happened to her as a kid really did mess up her brain chemistry forever.

As she's rounding the north side of the reservoir, a hot wind kicks up a storm of dust, and she decides to take a break and sit on one of the benches that look up toward the hills. She opens up the little leather pack strapped in under the bicycle seat and takes out her eyeglass case. Too bad she doesn't wear eyeglasses. She takes out the joint she put in there this morning and lights up. One good hit of it, and the rough edges of the day start to smooth out. The idea that pot is a gateway drug is a joke; with her, *life* was the damned gateway drug.

By the third or fourth hit, the sky has turned an amazing shade of yellow, and she's feeling so lazy and languid, she can't imagine getting on the bike again without first dozing off for a second with her face turned up to the sun. Nothing much strikes her as all that important, not even the thing with Conor. She takes her phone out of the pocket of her skirt. No calls. Well, she can't really blame him for giving up after she told him she didn't think they should pursue a relationship. "Pursue a relationship" are the exact words she used. Nice and technical and void of all emotion. He'd admitted to her that he'd left Boston because his previous girlfriend had ended things suddenly, for reasons that didn't make a lot of sense to him. After two years of living together, she came to the conclusion that their backgrounds were just too different—a polite way of saying she wanted someone with a college degree and a tidy, well-heeled WASP family. The last thing he needed now, when he was trying to get over her, was to get involved with someone with her own history of instability and problems committing.

Selfishly, she admits it's too bad. She can still taste his mouth—spicy with the good-boy tastes of toothpaste and Juicy Fruit chewing gum—and she can still feel his big hands all over her, warm and tender. As soon as she saw him with Graciela—sweet, pretty Graciela—she understood that that was the kind of relationship that made sense for Conor. Not Graciela herself, of course, but someone like that, instead of a world-class fuckup like her.

She dozes off and has a vivid dream that a tall, red-headed guy is burying his face in her neck, murmuring something about how she's perfect as she is. She wakes with a jolt and realizes that someone *is* sitting beside her on the bench, brushing her neck with his fingers.

Not a tall redhead: Phil Simone.

"Scared you, didn't I?" he asks.

"You know I don't scare easily, Phil." Phil is one of those guys who seems to materialize and disappear into thin air with equal ease. And half the time, you can't be sure how present he is, even when he's standing in front of you. "I thought you moved to Seattle."

"Yeah, I was there for a while. I had a job with Boeing, but it didn't really work out. I decided to come back down here. Fucking rain and clouds got to me."

"That can happen." In the six months or so Katherine dated Phil, she came to realize that about one-quarter of what he said was true. The rest was an elaborate web of exaggerations and lies that he spun together for no discernible reason. She was long past the point of caring one way or the other. Now it was more amusing than anything else.

"You back in that apartment?"

"Nah. I gave that up. I'm crashing with a buddy of mine."

"Lucky guy."

He shakes his head. "Still there with the sarcasm, huh? You better be careful, Kat—nobody likes a bitch."

"You know what's surprising, Phil? That isn't true—a lot of men love bitches."

"Yeah, well, I'm not one of them."

"Better find another bench then. As I recall, you told me I was 'born a bitch' and would 'die a bitch' once every couple of weeks."

This conversation pretty much sums up the tenor of their relationship for the whole time they were seeing each other. A lot of snarky back-and-forth that went around in circles until they got sick of the game and wandered into the bedroom.

Phil Simone is one of those smarmy, skinny guys incapable of honesty, fidelity, and sobriety for more than twelve hours at a stretch. Not fully employable, not handsome, with bad teeth and questionable hygiene. And yet, no one ever asked Katherine what she was doing with him. The answer was written all over his long face and wiry body: amazing fuck. He has one redeeming quality, and even though he's childishly proud of it, he does know how to use it.

Eventually that gets tiresome, too, and when Katherine stopped answering his calls or letting him in when he knocked at her door at midnight, she saw it as the cornerstone of the self-esteem she was trying to build up. It was over a year ago that she broke it off and she's been happily chaste since. It can't be a good sign that she's finding his greasy hair and mocking tone just a tiny bit exciting. She made a vow to herself that she'd never fall for Phil again or any of his brothers of spirit—the boozers, the users, the losers.

"You still giving back rubs?" he asks.

"Only to the paying customers, Phil. And I'm not cheap."

"Wasn't always the case, as I remember."

"I wouldn't trust my memory if I were you. It might be a little impaired."

"Probably not as impaired as yours, though, right?"

Of course he's right. Who's she trying to kid? She figured she was too good for guys like Phil, but it turns out she can't quite bring herself to believe she's good enough for someone like . . . the fireman. That doesn't leave much. She fires up what's left of the joint and takes a hit. "You got a point there," she says and passes the roach to him. "Interest you in a little more impairment?"

He takes it from her and finishes it off. "You still living up off Dexter?" he asks.

"I haven't been evicted yet."

"You should invite me up. I miss that little house."

"I've got my bike," she says.

"Yeah. I noticed. Gone all outdoorsy and athletic, huh?"

"Nah. I just use it to pick up guys."

"Oh, yeah? How's it working out?"

"Better than I planned," she says. She stands up, feeling more sad and defeated than she's felt in a long time. *Let's get this over with,* she thinks and gives him an inviting nod.

Graciela feels the incredible high of the audition melt away. What is Conor doing here? And how much trouble is his presence—not her doing, not her desire—going to cost her? He looks completely unruffled by Daryl and keeps grinning in that boyish way of his. He sticks out his hand to Daryl.

"I'm Conor," he says. "I know your girlfriend from up in Silver Lake."

"Yeah, okay," Daryl says, "so what are you doing down here?"

"I wanted to ask Graciela a couple of questions."

He looks so relaxed and nonplussed as he says this, Graciela starts to wonder if maybe she has it all wrong, and she should have answered his calls in the first place. But Daryl is beginning to puff his chest out in that way he gets when he feels threatened. Can he really think she'd cheat on him or even flirt behind his back? If this gets ugly, she gives Conor the advantage; he towers over Daryl and has that brick wall kind of stance you see on bouncers.

Lindsay sprints over and says, "You won't believe it, Daryl—Graciela made it through!"

Daryl spins Graciela around. He looks a little stunned, but genuinely happy. Hopefully all this other nonsense will blow over. "You did? They liked you?"

"They loved her. *Beyoncé* loved her!"

"You *met* her?"

Daryl looks so genuinely excited and happy, Graciela decides not to completely contradict Lindsay. "I sort of met her. I mean, they all said she liked what I did, so . . ."

"Graciela, that is fantastic news. Congratulations."

This is Conor and, happy as Graciela is for the vote of confidence, she wishes he hadn't said anything. Daryl turns around and puts a hand on his chest. Daryl has that temper, size difference or not. *But please,* she thinks, *let me enjoy the moment. Don't let it get ugly.*

"So these questions you want to ask?" Daryl says. "Why don't you ask me?"

"I'm not sure it concerns you, my friend, but if you'd rather I ask you, I have no problem with that. In fact, if you'd all like, I'd be happy to buy you a drink, help Graciela celebrate her good news."

"You know, I think I can buy her a drink myself," Daryl says.

"Fair enough. How about I buy this lady a drink, and we'll all be happy."

"I'm Lindsay."

Perfect, Graciela thinks. She can tell from the tone in her friend's voice that she's a little smitten already. Lindsay hasn't been dating anyone since her last boyfriend revealed he was married with two kids.

There's a bar Lindsay knows about a couple of blocks away, and as they're walking, Conor asks a lot of questions: Was she happy with her performance? Did she get nervous before? Does she think when she's dancing or is it mostly muscle memory? He has a way of asking that makes him sound genuinely interested, not only in her, but in the whole topic. It shows a genuine concern for and curiosity about other people that's pretty rare. Daryl, to be honest, rarely asks questions like that. She wants to believe it's because he's polite and a little shy, but it's probably true that there are so many things about other people that make him feel envious or threatened, he prefers to skim along the surface.

"What about you, Daryl?" he asks. "What do you do?" And when Daryl tells him, Conor says, "It's kind of perfect then, isn't it? The two of you? You probably give her a lot of musical inspiration."

"He does," Graciela says. And it's true.

It isn't until they're seated in the bar and have toasted Graciela's success that Conor brings up Katherine. He turns a little serious and melancholy when he does.

"It's not that I'm expecting you to have any answers," he says. "I'm just looking for a few clues or a little insight. I'm not the world's greatest catch, but she and I had a real connection, and then, boom, she slams the door shut in my face. Maybe she said something to you? Or she's got someone else?"

Graciela doesn't really know Katherine all that well. It's not like they share a lot of personal information. But because she's got that pretty, funky style and radiates a lot of sexual energy, people do talk about her. Stephanie has filled Graciela in on a few surprising facts about Katherine's past, although how much of it is true and how much is rumor is not clear. It's probably best to say nothing. But in the dim light of the bar, there's so much genuine disappointment on Conor's face, Graciela says a little more than she probably should.

"What I heard," she says, "is that she thinks you're too good for her."

"Me? Funny thing is, my last girlfriend thought I wasn't good enough."

"I guess she's got kind of a rocky past."

"And she thinks someone from a housing project in South Boston has been clean and squeaky his whole life?"

"I don't know," Graciela says. "But she knows you've been hurt and doesn't want to disappoint you. And as far as I know, there isn't anyone else."

Lindsay has been keeping quiet the whole time. She's one of the more generous people Graciela knows, and, once she got wind of Conor's feelings, she bowed out. Graciela is going to work on finding her someone, but it certainly isn't going to be Conor.

"Have you gone and knocked on her door?" Lindsay asks.

"Not really my style," Conor says.

"Aw, come on. Maybe you need a new one."

"Plus I don't have her address."

Lindsay sighs and pulls out her iPhone. "You technophobes," she says. "What's the spelling of the last name?"

As soon as Katherine saw her little Craftsman cottage on Redcliff Street, tucked away, high in the hills above the reservoir, she fell in love. Head over heels. The first time she crossed the long wooden walkway that leads from the street to the front door, she felt as if she was coming home. Sort of a ridiculous thing, really, since she'd never spent a lot of time thinking about where she lived or where she wanted to live. It was just a reaction deep in her gut to this particular place. The reaction most people have when they see it is: *Oh, my God! You* live *here? How did you find it?* When they say that, what she hears underneath is: *I figured you'd live in some shabby studio above a restaurant.* Sorry to disappoint, but no, she lives here.

By the time she and Phil walk up to the house, it's dark out, and the lights of the city down below are spread out like a glowing blanket. She always leaves a light on, so when she comes home, the shingled cottage has the same magical welcoming feel it did when she first saw it. She pushes her bike across the walkway, with Phil behind, and locks it to the railing. She should probably bring it inside, but it's hidden from the street by the leaves of an overgrown bird of paradise, and it's just easier.

"I forgot how sweet this place is," Phil says, peering over the side of the walkway to the steep hillside below.

"It is that," Katherine tells him.

Technically, there's no way she should be able to afford the rent on a place like this. But the house was owned by a divorced woman in her late fifties who died of breast cancer, and it's tangled up in the messy settlement of her estate. The woman's son is renting it to her and gave her a deal because he thinks she's hot (he lives in Los Feliz and comes around unannounced every once in a while to check up on her in the hopes, she suspects, of catching her sunbathing) and, more to the point, because she agreed to rent it without a lease, furnished, with the understanding that she might have to move out with no more than a week or two notice.

Despite falling in love, Katherine came close to not renting it. She didn't want to fall in love with a place she was destined to lose, and on top of that, it seemed a little too spacious and wonderful for . . . well, for her. The kind of place that probably ought to go to a nice couple, maybe with a kid. Or maybe two gay guys with great taste and a well-behaved dog. Not to *her*, in any case.

Lee was the one who talked her into taking it, and for the past two years, the house has been one of the great sources of consolation in Katherine's life.

"Yo," Phil says when she turns on the light in the living room. "You've done some big cleaning in here."

"Not really. Just no boyfriends coming around to mess things up."

After she kicked Phil out of her life, she *did* do some cleaning. Some *big* cleaning. She actually unpacked more than she had in all the time she'd been in the house until then. She rearranged the furniture and put some of the pieces she didn't like into storage. She uncluttered it and made it feel like home. Her home. She even bought a sewing machine (thirty-seven dollars on Craigslist) and made curtains for her bedroom. Who knew she hadn't completely obliterated everything her grandmother had taught her about sewing back in that previous life of hers? Once she decided to stop courting disaster with a series of bad boyfriends—Phil, for example?—she discovered she loved having everything orderly and clean, the counters spotless and the huge windows with a view of the reservoir sparkling. And not because she's expecting anyone to show up to inspect the place, but because that's how *she* likes it.

"Have anything to drink?" Phil asks.

"Water, juice, and, if you make it yourself, coffee."

"That's it?"

"Sorry. I finished the last of the milk with my Cheerios this morning."

"Oh, I get it. Still on the wagon."

"I'm an addict, Phil, and yeah, aside from the very occasional joint, I'm happy to say I've been sober for two years now. Your move to Seattle didn't send me rushing for bad stuff."

"Jesus, Katherine," Phil says. "I know you think I'm a big loser, but don't pretend you're not happy to see me. Just a little bit?" He sidles over to her and presses himself against her suggestively. "Just a little bit? Not Romeo and Juliet, but we had a few good times, didn't we?"

For her, the "good times" they had together served pretty much the same function as the drugs—a way to numb out any thoughts or feelings she didn't care to deal with. And one or two hours of Phil's lean and hungry charms, if you could call them charms, certainly did make it near impossible to think of anything else. It was when she realized she actually could deal with the feelings, live through them and get past them, without any substances or distractions, that she stopped returning Phil's calls.

So what does it mean that she actually invited him here tonight?

"You look so fucking good in this skirt," he says, sliding it up higher and running his hands up her thighs. "Oh, man, I forgot how smooth your legs are. Silk," he whispers into her ear.

Katherine's a big girl and she knew what she was getting into, but she didn't exactly know how she'd feel about it when she got it. She backs away from him a little and says, "Speaking of cleaning up, Phil, I've got some towels in the closet outside the bathroom just in case you want a shower."

He lifts his arm up and sniffs. "Got a little sweaty walking up here, huh? I thought you liked that."

"Sometimes I do and sometimes I don't."

She leads him toward the bathroom, past the guest room that she's emptied of furniture altogether and made into a little yoga and meditation room. Her mat is in the middle of the room and there are some pillows against the wall. She's in here every morning when the sun comes through the windows and warms up the floor.

Phil struts into the room and stands on the mat, folds his hands into an approximation of prayer. "*Namaste*, baby," he says.

"Don't, Phil. Just don't."

"Hey, what? Am I insulting your spiritual trip? I thought fucking was your religion."

He lifts up his right foot, trying for something like tree pose, and falls out. Not pretty. It looks kind of pathetic, really.

"To hell with it," he says.

When he's in the shower, Katherine faces it head-on. Having him come to the house is more or less the same thing as using again. Go numb, don't deal with it, block it out. She shouldn't have lit up the joint, either. It was all part of the little pity party she's been throwing for herself the past couple of weeks. Poor Katherine can't deal with a little accusation of financial misdemeanor. Can't deal with a decent, respectable guy showing some interest. Can't face the possibility that he might disappoint her or, way, way worse, that she might disappoint him. She didn't really think he'd hook up with Graciela, but seeing them together made her realize he belonged with someone like her, some sweet girl he could bring home to his family, someone who was guaranteed not to have any skeletons popping out of her closet or showing up in her shower at the most inconvenient times.

Except really, brushing off Conor is just the coward's way out. The *old* Katherine's way of dealing with things. Or not dealing. Trying to control everything when in fact she's just being out of control in a different way. And it isn't as if she's been able to get him out of her mind anyway.

She goes into her meditation room and looks out at the lights of the city, benign and gentle from up here. All those people going about their lives, making their own mistakes, angry or happy or lonely. Funny how there's really only one person she wants to be with right now, and he isn't in the shower. She pulls her phone out of the pocket of her skirt. At least she didn't delete his number. She'll call. She'll be a grown-up. As soon as she gets rid of Phil.

He comes out into the living room, conspicuously naked except for the towel he's using to dry his hair. "Great shampoo. Tea tree or some shit like that?"

"Phil," she says. She takes the towel out of his hands and wraps it around his waist. "I don't know how to say this to you, but . . ."

"Aw, fuck me! Are you gonna tell me I came all the way up here for nothing?"

"I'm sorry. It's been kind of a strange year for me, and I'm trying to keep myself together."

"Spare me the therapy session, okay? You really are messed up, Kat, you know that?"

"I do know that, Phil. But I'm working on it."

"Whoopee shit."

"Your clothes in the bathroom?"

"Yeah. 'Here's the door, what's your hurry.' You could at least suggest we watch TV."

"I don't have one."

"What a bitch."

She knew they'd get back to that sooner or later.

"You owe me, Kat. I'm taking the rest of that fucking shampoo. It's the least you can do."

When he goes back into the bathroom, Katherine hears footsteps on the walkway outside. And then her bell. Lee sometimes drops over at this hour, on her way from the studio.

Except it isn't Lee, it's Conor. Not his usual grinning self, but stern in the yellow glow of the light beside the door. Katherine feels a wave of calm disappointment wash over her. She has the worst timing in the world. It's always been this way. Maybe she could dash out of the house with Conor. But no, that wouldn't work.

"Mr. Ross," Katherine says, resigned to the disaster about to occur. "Passing through the neighborhood?"

"I just saw Graciela," he says. "Since you wouldn't return my calls. To try and figure out what happened here. Are you going to let me in?"

"Let me call you tomorrow," Katherine says. "It's not the best moment."

"Come on, Brodski. Let's get this settled."

That's when Phil walks up behind her, hair wet, shirtless, holding the bottle of shampoo. "Not tea tree," he says. "It's black fucking walnuts. Who's this guy?"

"I rang the wrong bell," Conor says.

Lee has never had the teaching equivalent of stage fright. She's never lost her place in front of a class or found herself wondering what it was she wanted to say. Still, she feels a mild, low-grade anxiety about her upcoming class at YogaHappens. It will be the first time in a long time she's given a class off her own turf and the first time in a very long time when she will be, she knows, evaluated as she goes along.

She's made detailed notes on the flow she wants to use, the physical focus of the class, and the way she wants to introduce a short, deep meditation. But somehow it all feels forced and false to her, and sitting at the table in her dining room, with the kids wrestling in front of the television, she keeps tearing up her notes.

Lee was twenty-four the very first time she took a yoga class. She was living on the Upper West Side of Manhattan in a rambling prewar apartment that was officially rented to someone who hadn't lived there in almost a decade. There were four bedrooms—five if you included the little maid's room in back that was about the size of a closet—and eight people sharing the place. They deposited their rent checks into the account of a woman who, rumor had it, was living in Berlin and was supporting herself largely on the profits of the sublet. One bedroom was shared by a girl whose name Lee can't remember and a guy the girl barely knew. He worked nights and she worked days and the two roommates rarely crossed paths, even in the kitchen. Someone lived on the sofa in the living room, and there were usually two or three people visiting from out of town who overstayed their welcomes and had to be asked to leave.

Initially, none of the discomforts of the place (there were only two bathrooms, for starters) had mattered to Lee. Her life, her real life, was lived in the lecture halls and on the floor of the hospital where she had labs and volunteered so she would get more exposure to patients. Everything else she did was preparation and study for those classes or recovery from the rigors of sleepless nights related to them. What did she care about how long she had to wait to get into the bathroom or how little room there was in the refrigerator? She had never felt quite so alive or quite so clear about where she was heading. She'd been dreaming of becoming a doctor since she was a kid, and she had buried herself in premed classes for most of the time she was an undergrad at Wesleyan University. Even the constant headaches and the stomach problems related to all the studying she was doing in med school didn't bother her. It was all in the service of something that mattered deeply to future goals.

But somewhere in her second year at Columbia Medical, something began to change. All the praise she'd received her whole life for her studies began to be meaningless to her. She was turned off, nearly repulsed, at the way the human body seemed to be reduced more and more to chemistry and science, with less emphasis on human beings, on whole human beings, on *people*. Healing was a completely fragmented study here, in which specialties had to be chosen and referrals made to other specialists, until all sense of a person and a life was lost. The doctors she met kept talking about the pressure to reduce their time with patients, to run the minimum number of tests, prescribe something, and be done with it.

It all seemed so far removed from what she'd been planning

for her whole life, she began to feel completely lost. The magical world of the classes and rounds began to feel like protracted torment. For the first time in her life, she began skipping lectures. She started smoking, and, with a combination of confusion and despair, more or less stopped eating. What was the point?

Lee tries not to think about that period very often, but when she does, she thinks mainly about the horrible cold she always felt. Even when she was in the big, overheated, overpopulated apartment. When her weight dropped below one hundred pounds, it was as if there was nothing between the raw wind and her insides, and no matter what she did or how many clothes she piled on, how many cups of chamomile tea she sipped, she could never get warm. The more she felt herself slipping away, the less she cared what happened to her. If anyone commented on her pallor or weight, she'd turn on them with the ugly defensiveness of someone who understands she's in the wrong. And yet, underneath that, she had an inchoate longing to be rescued.

Rescue came in the form of Jane Benson. Plain Jane, as the roommates in the apartment called her, a Columbia Law student who was so ordinary and unmemorable, people pretended to forget she actually lived there. One Thursday afternoon when Lee was folded into a ball on the living room sofa nursing a cup of tea, Jane asked her if she'd like to go to a yoga class with her. Lee had known some dancers who did yoga, or claimed to, but the word still had a slightly exotic and esoteric sound. When she thinks about it now, Lee can hardly believe that she went with Jane, and she doesn't know what motivated her to do so. It seems as if fate lifted her up off the sofa and pushed her toward the door.

There were yoga studios in the city in those days, although nothing compared with the number and variety that have arisen since Madonna and Gwyneth made yoga mats and sun salutations trendy. But the class she went to with Jane was held in the

drafty meeting room of a Presbyterian church off Amsterdam
Avenue. There were maybe six or eight students sitting on blankets on the floor, none of them especially fit looking, and Lee felt
too young and physically out of place, gaunt and drained. The
teacher herself looked like a glamorous former dancer with long
gray hair she had woven into a braid draped across her shoulder.
She had beautiful blue eyes that Lee still remembers to this day,
and when she first cast eyes on Lee, Lee felt as if she was seeing
right through all of her defenses, as if there was no point in trying
to hide from her. Lee let her vulnerabilities show.

She had had no idea what to really expect, but somewhere in
the middle of class she felt more challenged than she'd felt in a
long time, not because the physical demands were so great but
because for the first time in a long time, no one was demanding
anything of her, no one was judging her. The teacher saw through
her, all right, probably knew exactly what she was feeling, how
cold and numb she felt, but she neither pitied her for that nor
condemned her. She only asked her to sit and experience herself
in the moment. She only asked her to be still and—and here was
the most difficult piece—to have compassion for herself.

It would have been nice if Lee's life had turned around right
there and then. It would have saved a lot of time and a lot of
anguish. It was a slow and gradual change, so slow Lee didn't
even realize it was happening until she woke one morning and
understood that she had let go of one dream and had started to
pursue another.

She'd studied enough to know that the chemistry and science behind a lot of the claims made by yoga teachers was
shaky and insupportable. According to the textbooks, the body
and the inner organs just did not respond the way the instruc-
tors said. And yet, she herself was experiencing a transformation, born of the connections she was beginning to feel between

body and mind and spirit that simply could not be denied. If the holistic attitude toward the body expounded by her yoga teachers made no sense to her brain, it made complete sense to her gut. She felt it.

And this, she realized, was what she'd been looking for all along—not a science to help people cure their diseases, but a system to help them live their lives in a way that made sense.

The foundation of everything she does in classes, the core of everything she teaches, is what she learned from that very first yoga teacher—compassion for self, flaws and all. Flaws *especially*. Everything she has to teach starts there.

She hears a shriek from the next room and runs in. But it's just the twins playing in a gleeful way with a big balancing ball. Michael actually helped his brother get up on it and is pressing into his back so he doesn't fall. Unnervingly atypical, but best to leave well enough alone.

Plain Jane never commented on how bad Lee looked at the start or how she began to improve, but Lee knew she witnessed it. She went on to finish law school and moved to New Orleans, and then Lee lost track of her. Two years ago, Lee started to look for her online, to thank her for what she did for her. Eventually she learned that she'd been in a car accident and had died after a long struggle. She wished then that she'd hunted her down sooner, so she could tell her how she'd helped her.

She goes back to the dining room table and takes out a fresh index card and starts all over. She'll begin with love and compassion as guiding principles. She'll start with that simple, clear feeling she had at the beginning of that very first class in the church basement. She'll begin with Jane.

When Imani first started going to yoga classes with Becky, she was a little turned off by the conversations. "Conversasanas," as she called them.

I felt incredibly open in dancer's pose this afternoon.

Fascinating!

I loved when she had us open our arms wide in tree pose.

Me, too! Only I think those were "branches" we were opening.

My ardha chandrasana was off tonight.

Honey, my ardha chandrasana's been off for years!

It reminded her of how she feels when people sit around a dinner table and discuss their dogs for thirty minutes. Or when she hears traffic reports in a distant city. Dogs? Love 'em! But what the hell is a follow-up question to a report that Dippy was a little moody this morning? And sorry to hear that the I-95 connector in Denver is backed up. And that's relevant to my life *how*?

And so Imani surprises herself when, over coffee, she hears herself telling Becky, "You know, I really loved the way I felt in utkatasana today." (What? Who said that?)

"You're kidding," Becky says. "I have never liked that pose. I always feel so cramped and boxed in somehow. And I hate sticking out your butt like that. My knees go out of alignment, and I feel as if I'm going to tip forward onto my nose *and* land on my ass at the same time."

"I know, but when I tucked my pelvis and dropped my shoulders, I felt my whole back straighten out." She keeps thinking of how Lee, in that very first class, kept telling her to "knit her pelvis and her lower rib cage together." It made no sense at the time, but she keeps coming back to the image as a way to better align her body.

"It was wonderful," she goes on. "Like when you're listening to a piece of music and it ends with this chord that pulls everything together. Just . . . click, and . . . ahhhh. It all made perfect sense."

"I always feel that way in trikonasana. I love it when I reach, reach, reach and then just lower my arm down. Everything feels as if it falls into exactly the right place. And your thighs feel great!"

"That's the triangle one? I could use a little more practice there." Okay, she really *is* having this conversation. These words really *are* coming out of her mouth. And she even means them!

"Not that I was noticing, but your crow is just getting so freaking good, I might have to kill you," Becky says. "Not that there's any competition."

"Hell, no. None. And just FYI, I held that damned stick thing, warrior three, for the entire time. Arms straight out in front of me."

"Uh-oh," Becky says. "You are officially hooked! I can so tell!"

"No way! Or maybe just a little. If you promise not to tell anyone . . . I dreamed I was doing poses last night. How sick is that? I used to dream about Hugh Jackman. And the worst thing is, when I woke up, I felt all off balance because I hadn't done them on both sides."

"Oh, my God. I've created a monster. I have never dreamed about yoga. Or about Hugh Jackman. Those tiny little eyes? No, thank you."

For an awful long time now, Imani has been using her

cynicism and irony as a shield. She's been in enough therapy to know that. So it's a little strange to her to be talking about this in such an earnest way. Not that she objects. A couple of days ago, she was in a class in which the teacher was talking about "letting go." Nothing unusual there, since they all seem to talk about "letting go" at some point or other in class, at which point, Imani usually expects to hear a chorus of farts.

But that day, her defenses were so broken down from fifty minutes of going into poses, the words sank in in some way they hadn't before. And she did let herself drop the tension in her muscles and sink into the floor, and she did think that if she could take this feeling with her somehow ("off the mat," as they were always saying, another expression that had initially set her teeth on edge and now makes a lot of sense to her) her life would be better in some small but significant way.

"When does that movie start shooting?" Imani asks.

"Two weeks," Becky tells her. "But there are a few read-throughs next week."

"I'm losing my yoga friend!" Imani says. "What am I going to do?"

"It's a temporary loss. Why don't you start reading some scripts? You have the time. You don't know when you might find one that's really good. You have to get back on track."

"Before I'm forgotten, you mean."

"Look, we all run that risk. If you're out of the public eye for more than ten minutes, you start to grow mold. It happens to everyone. Just *begin*. Don't have any expectations; do as much as you can do."

"It's beginning to sound like conversasana."

"Right. And you're the one who started singing the praises of your chair pose. So use it. And listen, you don't need me hauling you into yoga classes. I got a tweet last night about a class at the YogaHappens in Beverly Hills. Some hot teacher is giving a 'Deep Flow' Something or Other class. Everyone's talking about it. You should go."

"I'll take it into consideration," Imani says. "As long as I don't get my back knocked out of joint."

"The teacher is a woman. And the whole thing is described as a journey . . . oh, I don't know . . just go. I'll send you the link. And remember to book it in advance. It's definitely going to sell out. There's a huge amount of buzz."

Stephanie heard about Lee's class at YogaHappens from Graciela. Graciela and Katherine are going together to support Lee since she's a little nervous about the class. New studio, high stakes, Beverly Hills, all that. It strikes Stephanie as a little odd that Lee never mentioned it during any of the classes she's been attending at Edendale, but then, she might not want to give business to a competing studio.

Ever since *that day*, Graciela has been calling Stephanie pretty much on a daily basis, usually with some little piece of news or some question that is clearly an excuse to check up on her. Not that Stephanie minds. She appreciates the attention, and in a way, it makes her feel less ostracized by the events of *that day*, as if it's just one more mistake that no one is going to forget but everyone is going to get past.

On the whole, Stephanie has been doing amazingly well at

getting past things in the last few weeks. Past the shame, past the anxiety, and past the little waves of desire for a drink that occasionally wash over her. True to her word, Sybille Brent cut her a check for writing a draft of the screenplay, and so, for the moment, Stephanie's life has fallen into a nice, simple, well-funded rhythm. Up at dawn, write for two hours at the table in her newly spotless living room, yoga class at her gym, writing and lunch in a funky hamburger joint around the corner from her apartment, drive up to Silver Lake and take another yoga class with Lee. Coffee and a little more writing, if she has the drive. And then, turning in early with a book.

She has a rough draft of the first act of the screenplay, and she's ready to dig into the second. Within a month, she should have the whole thing completed, assuming she can keep everything together. As for buying the author out of the option to do the screenplay himself, Stephanie is letting Sybille's lawyers handle that. At the start of every yoga class, Lee advises her students to "choose an intention." In the past, Stephanie pretty much skipped over this one. Her intention was always to get through the class with a minimum number of times taking child's pose and not too many memories of Preston and how pissed off she still was at him. But now, she breathes into a few new mantras: *It is what it is. . . . One day at a time. . . .* and *Don't micromanage.* Nothing terribly original, but all surprisingly effective.

She meets Graciela and Katherine at a juice bar down the street from the YogaHappens studio. She has the same reaction to seeing them she always has—a muted happiness that feels real and consistent (she's never *not* happy to see them, even on *that day*) but is somehow limited to their shared experience of yoga classes. It's not as if she has a whole lot in common with either one of them, and it's hard to imagine she'd be friends with someone like Katherine under any other circumstances. But there's something about being in a room with these women and breathing in unison with them and struggling with the same shared physical challenges that makes her feel connected. It doesn't matter that both of them are more skilled practitioners. There are at least a couple of poses she knows she does as well as anyone else, and the rest she's working on. *Everyone has at least one pose,* as Lee often reminds them, meaning that in a ninety-minute class, there's at least one moment of expertise, even if it's corpse pose.

She gets her juice and joins them at their table and decides to ask Katherine a question that's been bothering her since she first heard about this.

"Why is Lee teaching a class here? What I heard is that everybody gets exclusive contracts at this studio. So is she thinking about giving up Edendale?"

"Oh, come on," Graciela says. "Lee wouldn't do that. It's her place. I mean, look how full her classes are. She's got to be doing okay."

They both look at Katherine, who, Stephanie thinks, is keeping suspiciously quiet. Katherine has on a vintage yellow sundress that would look totally ridiculous on anyone but her, with her big, round eyes and the notes of irony and hard experience implicit in the punky haircut and the tattoos.

"Well?" Graciela says.

"It's not so simple," Katherine says. "Lee has a big following, but there's a lot of overhead. If a couple of classes are light, it hurts. And she's always offering a sliding scale or coming up with some way to let someone take classes for free."

"Now I'm feeling guilty," Graciela says. "All that help she gave me leading up to the audition."

"Don't feel guilty, honey. That's what she loves. It's what

gives her the most pleasure. It just doesn't pay the bills. Two kids? Alan off doing whatever."

Stephanie lets this new information sink in and then says, "So it sounds to me like she *is* thinking about closing Edendale. We're going to find out anyway, Kat."

"You have to ask her. But do you know how much health insurance costs? For four of them? And let's say you're right. It's just a change of venue."

Stephanie is getting a bad feeling about this. She's never been great with change and the thought of losing the anchor of Lee's classes at the homey studio in Silver Lake makes her feel slightly ill. On the other hand, if Lee has always been there for her, she owes it to her to keep her best interests in mind rather than her own selfish interests. Maybe she'll stay open until she's finished the screenplay and landed on completely solid sobriety.

"True. We could always come to her classes here," Graciela says.

"It's a little steep," Katherine warns.

"I have to admit," Stephanie says, "that I hate chains. Bookstores, grocery stores, pet stores, movie theaters. Now yoga studios? A few years ago, it would have been a joke—a chain of yoga studios running the little guys out of business." It's partly what's happening in the movie business, too—all the money going to the top and less and less for the independents and the middle rung. Even all those supposedly independent and small production companies are now just subsidiaries of the big guys. But everyone has a right to make their own deal, and if she'd gotten an offer from Paramount, it isn't like she'd have had to sleep on it before snatching it.

When it's time to hit the road, they hitch their mats up to their shoulders and head out. Katherine seems quieter than usual, and Stephanie's tempted to ask. But she's one of those people who have a low privacy fence built around themselves, and there are a lot of subjects you don't bring up and questions you don't pose. It's easier to gossip about Graciela's good news and speculate on how close she is to getting the role in the video.

When they get to the YogaHappens Experience Center, all conversation stops.

"Jesus," Stephanie says.

The building is set impossibly far from the street, with a rosewood walkway leading to it, covered by a trellis with an orange trumpet vine woven into it. Stepping under the trellis feels like entering a magic kingdom. By the time you get to the front door, you already feel as if the traffic and noise of the street are fading into irrelevance. There's a soft sound of trickling water that Stephanie assumes is piped in on speakers, until she sees that the wall of the building beside the front door has been covered with what appears to be corrugated copper with water trickling down over it. Impressive, even if you're determined not to be impressed.

The inside of the studio feels even more serene, with faint chanting sounding from an invisible speaker system. It looks like a cosseted, wood-paneled spa, and there's a smell in the air like . . . she's not sure; honey and lavender are what come to mind immediately.

Graciela is clearly wowed, and even Stephanie has to admit it's spectacular. Katherine, on the other hand, seems mostly focused on finding Lee among the crowd of people lined up at the front desk. So far, no sign.

"Do you think that can be right?" Graciela asks, reading from a pamphlet. "Individual classes are thirty-five dollars?"

"That's what it costs," Katherine tells her. "But it includes unlimited use of the sauna, in case you have unlimited time on your hands, which you probably do if you have unlimited funds and can pay thirty-five dollars for a single yoga class."

They get checked in and go to change in the glass and marble locker rooms, which look like something out of a Roman bath as reimagined by a Vegas decorator. Stephanie would love to see the balance sheet on this place. It doesn't seem possible that they could be turning a real profit, despite the mob of attractive young women wandering from the sauna to the showers draped in terry cloth robes supplied by the studio. The Italian bath gels and moisturizers are from a company Stephanie has read about in style magazines but has never felt self-indulgent enough to actually purchase. Too bad she didn't bring a little travel bottle she could pump a sample into before leaving.

The receptionist proudly told them that there are between five and six classes going on simultaneously from six in the morning until ten at night, so maybe it's purely an issue of volume.

"And on Fridays we have a midnight 'Hour of Power Chill'— a heated class done to ambient chill and deep house music. And soon we'll be having live music supplied by a master harmonium player—Panjit Alan. After the Chill class, there's a champagne bar in the Karma Lounge."

"I quit drinking at just the wrong moment," Stephanie said to Graciela.

"Sparkling cider is also available," the receptionist, paid to be helpful no matter what, put in.

It all sounds too silly to be believed, even if there's something appealing, too, about all the pampering.

When the three of them step out of the locker room, Katherine puts her hand on Stephanie's arm and says, "Isn't that Imani Lang?"

The mention of the name, which Stephanie had been bandying

about a few weeks ago when she was pitching her movie, gives her a little pang of regret mixed with excitement. She's been hoping Imani would turn up again at a yoga class, but she never appeared. Now here she is, curled up in the corner of an orange cushioned banquette built into the wall, talking quietly into her cell phone, dressed in the creamy V-necked yoga top Stephanie was coveting at Lululemon only last week.

"Has she ever come back to Lee's studio?" Stephanie asks.

"Not that I know of," Katherine says. "Come over with me."

Imani puts away her phone as soon as she sees Katherine, springs up off the banquette, and gives her a hug. "My Silver Lake savior," she says. Like a lot of successful actresses Stephanie has met, Imani has a way of sounding sincere while at the same time seeming to project loudly enough to be heard by the small audience of adoring fans she knows are watching.

"Savior's a little exaggerated," Katherine says, "but I'll take it. You remember Stephanie?"

Imani gives Stephanie a relatively cool hello, and Stephanie reminds herself that, sometimes, coming on too strong too quickly can backfire. She's been getting better at holding back a little and not trying to impress or make an impact right out of the gate. *Don't force it,* Lee tells them in class. *Let the pose blossom.*

Stephanie introduces Graciela, and then says, "You never came back to Edendale. We've missed you."

"I keep meaning to. I've been making the rounds of a lot of studios with a friend."

"I saw a picture of you and Becky Antrim on TMZ," Graciela says. She's just sweet and innocent enough to get away with making this kind of comment about a gossip site and not have it sound insulting or invasive. "You both looked gorgeous. At a workshop in Santa Monica, I guess it was."

"The less said about that the better," Imani tells her. "Becky's the one who told me about a class here today. Deep Flow Something." She shrugs. "I'm way better than I used to be, I can tell you that."

"It's Lee's class," Katherine says. "That's why we came. You didn't know? You'll see how good she is, now that you have other teachers to compare her with."

At the door to the studio, they're stopped by an attendant, a slim man with a ponytail, gorgeous shoulders, and a smile that's somewhere between beatific and *Jaws*. "You'll be happy to hear," he says, "that you won't need your mats. Everything's supplied!"

Stephanie peers over his shoulder, and indeed, there are mats spread out across the floor of the vast studio, a few different shades of orange arranged in a carefully composed pattern, like a rubber mosaic. The lighting is low, with little bulbs twinkling on the ceiling, a constellation of distant stars. How pretty and how irritatingly perfect.

"When you say we'll be happy to hear we won't need our mats," Stephanie says, "I assume that means we can't use them?"

"It is a policy," the attendant says.

"How do I know who's used the mat before me?" Imani asks.

"They're individually sanitized every night," he says, "with organic witch hazel and orange peel extract. And then treated with ultraviolet light. And by the way, I'm a big fan, Miss Lang. Oh, and we'd like to encourage you not to bring plastic water bottles into the studio. We sell reusable metal YogaHappens containers out front. They're coordinated with the color scheme of the studios."

"Maybe next time," Imani says.

"Certainly," the attendant says. "And if you don't want to use them today, I'll be happy to keep your plastic bottles here until after the class. We can label them with your names."

Stephanie would find the whole thing less annoying if they

just came right out and confiscated their forbidden supplies and tossed them in a barrel, as they do at airport security. The rehearsed quality of this polite phrasing is insulting. And she hates being told what will make her happy, especially since using her own mat and drinking from her own plastic (!) water bottle is what would please her *most* right now.

"How much are the bottles?" Graciela asks.

"Forty-two dollars," he says. "But there's unlimited filtered water throughout the Experience Center at no charge, and you get a coupon for a complimentary organic Himalayan kombucha tea—or a cappuccino—in the Karma Lounge."

Between the champagne and the cappuccino, the Karma Lounge is starting to sound like a pretty spicy spot. Next they'll be crowing about their ice cream sundaes and roast beef sandwiches.

"We're expecting a full class today, so you ladies might want to go in and choose your practice zone."

"Is Lee here yet?" Katherine asks. "The teacher?"

The attendant gives her a grin that's supposed to be friendly, but looks to Stephanie as if he's letting Katherine know she's just one of the insignificant little people and shouldn't even be asking about the star.

"I'm sure she's in the greenroom, focusing. If you'd like to send her a message, I'd be happy to find someone to deliver it."

"That's okay," Katherine says. "I've got my eye on a particular mat and I don't want to get zoned out of my zone."

"Greenroom?" Imani says as they walk in. "I am so in the wrong profession."

The greenroom is not, of course, green but a faint shade of salmon that goes with the burnished orange tones of the rest of the studio. Lee finds all the coordinated colors incredibly restful, which is probably the point. She and Alan decorated their studio using intuition and, it's true, some flooring and discontinued paint colors they got a good deal on. It hadn't occurred to her that they might hire a decorator or a feng shui consultant, not that that would have been an option anyway. But everything here is planned down to the smallest detail. It feels a little manufactured, but there's something reassuring about it, too.

The greenroom is sectioned off in a clever way with low screens and soft cushions scattered over the floor. There's a woman in an immaculately white leotard meditating in lotus in one corner and on the other side of the screen behind her, two men are talking about the fact that there were eight hundred applicants for an open position in their West Hollywood location. Lee is dumbfounded by the number. How can she feel anything other than grateful and flattered that she was actually sought out by YogaHappens and has been given this incredible offer? The corporate ambience is a little off-putting—many of the details scream "focus group"—but it's all about what happens between her and the students.

Alan was supposed to come today, but he called her at the last minute to say that he was closing in on some final arrangements of a song they're about to send off to their agent. Lee's pretty sure he could have come, but in some ways, it's a relief he's not here.

When she thought about him being in the class, she was excited that he'd see her at her best, teaching a group of new students. But then it occurred to her that that might make him feel competitive with her. She wonders how many times and in what ways she's held back in the past, just so she wouldn't make Alan unhappy. And it's possible she would have held back today if she'd known he was in the room.

A young woman with bright eyes comes over to her and asks if she'd like anything before class—water, coffee, a chair massage? There's only so much pampering she can take and the chair massage idea, appealing as it is, definitely crosses the line.

"I'm fine. But thanks."

"Okay. My name's Diandra and if there's anything you need, ask for me."

"Do you teach here?"

"No, I wish. I get one hour of class time free for every three hours of service I donate. Zhannette and Frank are so generous with everyone, it's really beautiful."

"Have you met them?"

Diandra's eyes pop open. "No! My God, I would love to, but there are only a few people who've met them. They're very reclusive."

Fifteen minutes later, Diandra returns and tells Lee it's time to start class. How ridiculous that after all these years and hundreds of classes, Lee feels a new nervousness about standing in front of students. The most logical interpretation is that she must really want to impress the studio, that she must really want the job.

Diandra leads her to the back of the greenroom and then through a narrow door that opens directly into the studio where she's teaching. They certainly thought of everything. The room is full, maybe a hundred people, but the mats are laid out in such a tidy arrangement that there are aisles between them for her to walk through as she teaches and plenty of space in front to demonstrate.

Having spent several days thinking about ways in which she can make the class a little more elaborate, perhaps more suited to the upscale demands of this studio, she spots Katherine and Stephanie and has a realization, just before she starts speaking, that she can't change anything without throwing off the balance of what she does and why she loves to teach in the first place.

"Let's start seated," she says, "eyes closed. This class has been described as a journey. But before we embark, how about doing a little *un*packing? Your expectations, your desire to do ten sun salutations, your plans for later in the day, the argument you had this morning, your safety net. Leave them all behind. Start off feeling light and liberated, no fears, no assumptions, nothing to knock you off balance or distract you. Just you and me and a beautiful empty slate to play with. Once you see it and feel it, open your eyes, and we'll begin."

As Imani is driving home, she calls Becky and leaves a message. "I can't believe you missed the class today at Yoga-Happens. Of all the ones we've taken, I have to say, it was the best. The teacher has a studio up in Silver Lake. Turns out I already took a class with her. I never mentioned it because I was afraid you wouldn't love her and then I'd feel like an ass. But she's amazing. Anyway, that's not why I'm calling. I'm going to take your advice and call my agent and let her know I'm ready to start reading scripts. So thank you. Call me later. Let's figure out a time to go to Silver Lake together."

It isn't until after Imani has clicked off her phone that she takes account of what she's just said. She's ready to move ahead, ready to *get on with her life*. Maybe she unpacked her bags of all her fears and expectations at the start of that class. And now she's free. But as soon as she absorbs that image, really allows herself to believe it, she feels an ache inside her. Getting on with it means letting go of something, of the past. Of the baby she carried for four and a half months but wasn't able to carry to term. Her daughter. Ellie. *Don't name the baby until the third trimester,* a friend back in Texas had told her. But Imani was never superstitious. And some-time in the beginning of the fourth month, she started feeling as if she knew the baby, her moods and her personality. It was impossible to describe, even to Glenn. Just a powerful understanding and connection that she'd never experienced before. Maybe it was all crazy, hormonal projection. How could she say for sure? She talked to her when she was alone—to Ellie—except, when she was pregnant, she never felt she *was* alone. She felt her soft heaviness in her arms, such a real, true feeling, it was eerie.

In all the months since losing her, she still feels that weight in her arms sometimes. It's been a comfort in some ways. She knew she shouldn't dwell on it or (and this is probably the true part) *indulge in it*, but letting go of the feeling just so she could "move on" always struck her as cruel abandonment. Leaving behind her baby. Who would care for her? Who would love her? How *could* she do that?

As she's about to turn onto Los Feliz Boulevard, she starts crying, crying so hard she almost can't see the road. She makes a quick detour into Griffith Park and parks the car and shuts down the engine and falls against the steering wheel.

When she looks up, she sees that the sky is a rare bright blue above the green of the park. It's surprisingly quiet. A woman is reading on a bench right near her, and on the grass, a little girl in a yellow dress is chasing after a dog, laughing and shrieking.

It all starts to go blurry through Imani's renewed tears.

"I'm sorry," she says, barely able to get the words out. "I'm sorry, baby, I'm sorry, I'm sorry." The little girl is farther away now, chasing the dog, laughing hysterically. And she knows this is the moment, this is how it has to be. *I just have to, baby. I just have to let you be. You have to forgive me, Ellie. I tried so hard. I did my best, baby girl. You have to believe me. I wanted you with my whole heart and soul. I wanted to be with you and take care of you and love you. It just wasn't meant to be. So I have to let you go now.*

I just have to let you go.

All right, she thinks, and she starts to calm down. This is the moment and the way it's going to happen. She starts up the engine and mops her tears. No more crying. No more. She slowly backs out of the parking space and then drives onto the road and into the flow of traffic, ready to begin.

PART THREE

Amid compliments from Diandra and a few other studio employees in the greenroom, Lee acknowledges that she had a wonderful time teaching. There is something exhilarating about the energy created in a room with so many people, many more than the studio in Silver Lake could ever hope to hold, all doing the same things, more or less in unison. From her perspective, the class looked at times like a wonderful dance that she was choreographing as it went along. Everyone moving and breathing together, so that at times it felt as if the collective spirit really could effect change in the world. She often has this feeling in front of her classes, but today, the bigger group just made it feel that much more powerful.

As she's gathering up her things to leave, her two old friends—Sinewy Dave and Fireplug Chuck—come in through another mysterious door, all smiles and good cheer. This is the first time she's seen them in the studio, and they're dressed in the orange T-shirts everyone who works here is apparently obliged to wear. They're both amazingly fit, albeit in entirely different ways, tall and lean and short and pumped, like a pair put together for the ways their bodies complement each other and contrast.

"You were awesome!" Dave says.

"Totally amazing," Chuck tells her. "And more to the point . . ."

". . . exactly what we were hoping for."

Fireplug: Exactly the kind of creative class we need to round out our offerings.

Sinew: And the feedback from students has been incredible. They are ecstatic.

Fireplug: As are . . .

Sinew: . . . Zhannette and Frank!

All Lee can do is tell them sincerely that she appreciates hearing that and that she herself had a great time.

The men bob their heads in unison and simultaneously lower the clipboards they have pressed to their chests.

"A few notes we made as we observed," Sinew says.

"I didn't see you in the room," Lee tells them. She had been expecting them to attend, and for some reason she was relieved when she saw they weren't there. They laugh together at her comment.

Sinew: We have our ways. . . .

Fireplug: Video cameras. Very discreetly placed. They help maintain quality control.

Sinew: Which is becoming a surprisingly big problem . . .

Sinew: . . . in our industry.

Fireplug: Most of what we've got here is just stuff to be addressed at a later date.

Sinew: And not anything we expected you to realize first time out.

Fireplug: We noticed that there were about six people who got in with their own water bottles.

Sinew: I have eight, Chuck, but same ballpark. Ordinarily, the welcomer at the door talks to the guests about this as they're coming in, but because it was so crowded today, he obviously missed a few.

Fireplug: No big deal. In the future, you go over and remove the bottles and put them outside the door. All very discreet and supportive.

Sinew: You very softly say: "Don't let that happen again."

Fireplug: We prefer you use those words. All teachers do.

Sinew: Reinforces the same message.

Fireplug: Very effective.

This issue strikes Lee as so petty and inconsequential she's embarrassed even to respond to it, one way or the other. Diandra had mentioned the water bottles to her before the class, but it was the kind of thing she couldn't take seriously. Apparently, it's an obsession with everyone who works here. The guys tell her there are just a few other small items: she didn't start off the class making sure everyone had signed a waiver, she didn't promote the upcoming studio events, and she didn't suggest that students replenish with fresh juice or a blender drink at the Karma Lounge. Oh, and one other thing, it would be great if she'd put in one or two advanced poses that she advises the students *not* to try but that she demonstrates anyway. Maybe a pose that involves her foot behind her head or a complicated arm balance.

"The students feel more comfortable and safe," Sinewy Dave says, "if they're reminded that the teacher can do things they can't."

"And you might tell them," Chuck puts in, "that if they want to do the more complicated and sexy poses . . ."

"We prefer you use that word. Very effective."

". . . that they should think about private lessons. One hundred and twenty an hour."

Sinew: Other than that . . .

Fireplug: . . . it was brilliant. Beyond even . . .

Sinew: . . . our expectations. We'd love to celebrate by having you join us for lunch in the Karma Lounge.

Fireplug: It encourages students to hang out there if they see the teachers going in.

"I'm not terribly hungry," Lee says.

"A small beverage would suffice."

"Absolutely. It's in the staff handbook."

Katherine's massage client has booked a ninety-minute appointment and explains to Katherine when she comes in that she would like a detoxifying massage.

"I've just come out of a two-week rehab where I was treated for addiction, and I'm still feeling a little fragile. I need special attention paid to my kidneys and adrenals."

"I understand completely," Katherine says.

Naturally, she does, but the client, Cecily, is a tall, slim woman who has been coming to Edendale for massage and yoga classes for over a year now. She is fit and agile, has perfect balance in classes, and follows a strict diet of raw foods. With all the work Katherine has done on Cecily's body she has never noticed any signs of the marks, scarring, and sensitivity that she's used to seeing with drug abusers and drinkers. She might have believed some esoteric form of disordered eating, but this revelation comes as a shock.

Cecily is lying facedown on Katherine's table, and as Katherine is about to press her hands into her perfect back, she lifts her head up and says, "What kind of oil are you using on me?"

"It's organic almond oil."

"Anything in it?"

"I was going to use one with a light scent of lavender, which a lot of people find to be purifying. But if you'd rather . . ."

"Oh, my God," she says. "I'm so glad I asked. Nothing with floral or herbal extracts or oils. It's *completely* off-limits for me."

"I have unscented. Or a plain lotion, if that's better."

"Unscented oil is fine. I'm sorry, I don't mean to be demanding, but I can't let anything throw me off."

Katherine was never one to talk about her addictions and drug issues to people. She was always humiliated by what she saw as her own weaknesses and has found that in general, she deals with her problems best when she keeps her head down and focuses on them in privacy. It's one of the reasons she's never gotten into twelve-step programs. But she's noticed over the years that this is not the norm, and that most people can't stop talking about their dependencies and addictions once they step or are pushed out of denial. She's tempted to ask Cecily what she was using, but she knows that all she has to do is keep quiet long enough, and that will be revealed.

And sure enough, after half an hour, Cecily says, "I think for me, the hardest things to give up were the tinctures. And naturally I used the nonalcoholic varieties."

"Tinctures?"

"It started off with echinacea and goldenseal, for immune system support. It turns out they're gateway extracts for a lot of people. You feel a cold coming on and you go buy some echinacea tincture, and you feel a little bit better. It's totally acceptable and unregulated. We're surrounded by advertisements for them in every yoga magazine and health food store. The next time you're in Whole Foods, you happen to notice that there's an entire aisle of tinctures. So you think you'll try Saint-John's-wort for your mood, and then valerian to help you sleep. And then yerba extract to help you wake up. And that's not even scratching the surface. Something for your eyesight, something for your joints, something for your hair." Katherine can feel Cecily's body shudder a little beneath her hands. "And then there are the capsules and the mineral extracts and the homeopathic cures and the Bach flower remedies."

It's clear that Cecily is crying now with the addict's combination of regret and self-pity. Katherine puts a piece of tissue into her limp hand, and she brings it up under her face rest and blows her nose. "I was spending a few hundred a week on remedies. I'd sometimes chew a whole vial of homeopathic medicine as if it were candy. I'd shop at different stores so the clerks wouldn't be able to tell how much I was buying. I was isolating more and more. It's not social the way drinking or heroin is."

"I guess not."

"One Saturday morning, I found myself at a GNC in the mall surrounded by a lot of bloated guys buying protein powder in plastic drums. That was my bottom. That's when I knew I had to confront the fact that I had a problem."

"Were you doing . . . vitamins?" Katherine asks.

Cecily shakes her head, crinkling the paper covering the headrest. "I never *touched* vitamins," she says proudly.

At the end of their session, Cecily gives Katherine a thirty-dollar tip and asks her for her discretion.

"Of course," Katherine says. "You just have to believe in yourself and trust that you can get through it."

"I do. I never want to go back there, believe me. It was a very, very dark place. I've started taking Xanax, which really lowers my anxiety when I go food shopping. Which reminds me, I should take half of one now. I pass a Whole Foods on the way home. Actually, there's a health food store, too. What the heck, I'll take a whole."

Katherine walks Cecily out to the sidewalk and stands in the warm air, drinking in the buzz of the street life at this time of day. She loves this about Silver Lake—the way there's more of a community and small-town feel than in other neighborhoods in L.A. The downside is that you bump into a lot of the same people all the time. Like, let's say you were trying to hook up with some wonderful guy who works just down the street and then, when you finally do, you freak out because he's *too nice* and then, when you decide you maybe won't sabotage a potentially good thing before it even gets going, you resort to your fucked-up old ways and completely blow it. She can still see the look of hurt and anger on Conor's face when Phil came up behind her that night. The whole incident was so embarrassing and misguided, she can't stand to focus on it. The good news is that she kicked Phil out when she did (one point for sanity, anyway) and that instead of spiraling out of control, she just got herself back into a routine with Lee's classes. So there's that. One of the guys who works at the station house with Conor told her Conor was going to get rotated to another neighborhood soon. Always that way with new guys.

Maybe he's mulling over the next step. Or maybe his silence means he's already decided his next step, and it's away from her.

She spots Stephanie sitting at a sidewalk table at Café Crème across the street, working on her computer and waiting for Lee's afternoon class to begin. She waves, and Stephanie beckons to her. Katherine sprints across the street and joins her at her table.

"I like the shoes," Stephanie says.

Katherine looks down and realizes that she's barefoot. She likes to work without shoes sometimes; everyone is so used to seeing people barefoot in the studio, no one even notices.

"Glad you approve," Katherine says. "They were reasonable. How's the work coming?"

"It's coming. I won't know if it's any good until I'm done."

"When will that be?"

"Soon. I give it to the producer . . . we'll see."

She's scrutinizing Katherine in a way that makes Katherine feel she has something she wants to ask her. "Is everything all right?"

"Look," Stephanie says, "I know you and Lee are good friends, and I don't want to get in the middle of that, but how serious is she about this YogaHappens thing?"

It's always best to mind your own business and let people make their own decisions, even if you think they're mistakes. She doesn't really believe the move will make Lee happy, but on the other hand, she's not in a position to judge. Maybe she feels Lee is abandoning her and doesn't *want* her to be happy.

"I'd guess she's pretty serious."

"It's a big mistake. We have to talk her out of it."

"I don't know, Stephanie. I'm trying to focus on avoiding my own mistakes."

"Me, too. But don't you wish you had a little help sometimes?"

When she has had help, it's usually come from Lee. "When you say 'we have to talk her out of it,' I assume you mean I do."

"I think you have to try."

Graciela is scrubbing out the storage space beneath her mother's kitchen sink when she gets the call. Heberto, her mother's late husband, was a do-it-yourself kind of guy and, like most do-it-yourselfers, he had lots of ambition and limited skills. Graciela's discovered that there are half-finished electrical and plumbing repairs all over the house. Almost every room contains some evidence of good intentions gone astray—a little box of building materials, half-filled tubes of caulking, pieces of tile, sections of drywall. At some point, he obviously tried to do something about a leak in the drain of the kitchen sink, but he either lost patience or faith in his abilities to complete the job. When she opened the cabinet, she was greeted by the sight and smell of mildewed sponges, damp rags, and boxes of Brillo pads and dishwasher detergent that had partly disintegrated.

One thing she's learned from helping her mother out is that the bigger the mess she tackles, the greater the satisfaction in getting the job done.

She replaced a washer, tightened a few loose nuts (Heberto had, of course, left the wrenches under the sink), and began throwing things out. Boxes of unusable cleaning supplies, containers of ammonia and floor wax covered with slime or rust or both. She stripped down to one of Daryl's tight T-shirts she'd thrown on that morning. When she hears her phone ringing on the kitchen table, she's covered in sweat and soap scum, and she decides to let it go to voice mail. A few minutes later, she slides out from under the sink and surveys the job. Spotless. One of the lesser accomplishments of her life, but still one that offers her a great deal of pleasure. She can't fix her mother's life; she can't change her attitude; she can't make her happy. But she can clean her house up so that when she's ready to make some of the other changes herself, everything will be in place.

She can hear the shrill voices of the Telemundo soap opera coming from the TV in the room out back and her mother's laughter and curses at the characters. No matter what she says, no matter how dismissive her mother is to her, somewhere inside, surely she appreciates what Graciela has been doing for her.

The message on her phone starts out slow and solemn. It's Mickey Michaelson, the little woman with her face tucked up into her beret. It turns out she is the assistant to the choreographer and an indispensable part of the team assembled for the video shoot.

"Graciela," she says and then pauses. She has one of those peculiar accents that have a little Britain, a little France, a bit of the South, and a whole lot of affectation. A common accent in the sovereign country of the Entertainment Industry. "I'm sorry to have to be the one to tell you, but someone has to do it, right? Starting next week, you're going to be working your *ass* off, young lady. You're Dancer Number Five, baby. Call me."

Graciela catches sight of her reflection in the window above the kitchen sink. If Mickey could see her now, she'd probably retract the offer. Her hair is matted, and her T-shirt is filthy. Well, nothing like a little reality check to bring her down to earth, just in case she was at risk of getting a swollen ego.

She goes out to the glassed-in room where her mother is ensconced in front of the TV. There's a loud commercial on, some kind of antacid represented by a cartoon character routing out the digestive system of a poor overindulgent soul.

"Mama," she says. "*¿Puedo bajar el volumen, Mama?*"

Her mother frowns, but mutes the TV.

"I fixed the leak under the sink, and I threw out all the mess down there."

"*¿Sacaste el moho?*"

"I got rid of as much mildew as I could. I think it's all gone."

"*Buena chica,*" her mother says.

It's not that it's such a great compliment, really. It's the kind of thing you might say to someone you hired to clean for you. Probably something her mother heard from her employers when she *was* cleaning houses. *Good girl.* But it's something. And at the moment, Graciela is so happy for even this small bit of praise, she feels her cheeks getting warm with happiness.

"I just got a call, Mama. You won't believe it. I'm going to be in a new video. With Beyoncé, Mama. The one from *Dreamgirls,* you remember?"

"*¿La gorda?*"

"No, the one who looks like Diana Ross. She's gorgeous. It's a really big break for me, Mama. There were about a thousand girls who auditioned."

Her mother smiles and nods her head, although not with any particular happiness. The commercial finishes up and she turns on the sound again.

"Make sure you wash your hair before your 'big break.' You look like a witch. And wear a different shirt. I can see your nipples. Big. *Como una animala.*"

Graciela feels as if the wind has been knocked out of her. A witch? An animal? Did her mother just say that? She walks out of the glassed-in room, goes back into the kitchen, ties up the trash bags she's filled with junk, and puts them in a barrel outside the kitchen door. She's about to put her blouse back on, when she spots her phone on the table. She should call Daryl; she probably should have called him first. But what if she hears that little catch in his voice, that tone that she knows means he feels threatened and worried that any success of hers will threaten their relationship somehow or make her love him less? What she needs right now is some unqualified enthusiasm. She picks up the phone and dials.

"Lee," she says, "it's Graciela. I wanted to tell you. . . . I got the job. I just got a message and—"

Lee screams so loudly and with so much excitement, Graciela thinks for a minute that her mother might hear, TV or not. "I am so happy for you, sweetheart! I'm so proud of you! We have to celebrate."

"Honestly, it wouldn't have happened if you hadn't—"

"It's *you*. It's your talent. Your hard work. *You* did it. You earned it. You deserve it."

A few minutes later, she drapes her shirt over her arm and goes out into the glassed-in room. The sun has come out again, and the room is stifling. There's an air conditioner, but her mother never uses it while Graciela is there, claiming she doesn't want to use the electricity. But more than once, Graciela has heard her switch it on as she's walking out of the house.

"I'm leaving, Mama," she says.

"What about the kitchen closet?"

"What about it, Mama?"

"You said you were doing that today, too."

"The next time . . . ," she begins. But no, she can't keep coming back like this and putting her whole self on the line. "You can do it yourself, Mama. You can do it yourself or you can hire someone to do it or you can call your sons. Call Manuel or Eddie. Tell them to come clean your closets."

"Too good to help me out now? *Eso es todo?*"

"I've never once disrespected you. I've never done anything but love you and try to help. I won't let you insult me anymore. I can't. Okay, Mama? When you want to call and apologize, you have my number. Until then, don't bother."

Outside, Graciela puts on her blouse, but her hands are shaking too badly to do up the buttons. She looks back at her mother's house and half expects to see her mother racing out the front door, chasing her in anger. But of course, the house is quiet, except for the sudden clatter of the air conditioner being turned on and the sunlight glinting off the windows. She takes a deep breath and starts down the walk, realizing that her hands have stopped shaking. She buttons up her blouse partway. She feels a little buzzing in the back of her head that isn't anger or anxiety or nervousness or guilt: it's the thrill of excitement. She did it. *She* made it happen. She got her dream job. It doesn't matter if her mother calls her and apologizes or not. She'll always be there for her mother, but she doesn't need her. Her mother's opinion of her own daughter doesn't alter the fact that Graciela's life is in a very different place than it was an hour ago.

When Lee met Alan, he'd recently graduated from NYU with a degree in American studies, one of those vague majors that incorporates literature and pop culture, a bit of politics, and a whole lot of personal opinion. "*Me* studies," as some of their friends called it. He'd wanted to study music, but he'd been forbidden by his parents in Chicago. After school, he'd had an entry-level job at Fidelity and an internship at a law firm, but nothing really suited him professionally. He was not, he explained to Lee, the kind of guy who could work under other people. "I'm too rebellious," he'd explained. "Too independent. I'm too creative to be tied down to an office." She admired his spirit.

He was living in Brooklyn and working as an assistant to a handyman, a job that paid pretty well and left him plenty of time to pursue his real love.

The first time Lee heard Alan play and sing was at his place in Brooklyn. They'd had dinner together, had several glasses of wine, had made love, and then he'd pulled out his guitar and sang to her. "If I Had You," a song from the 1920s with a sweet, simple melody that he sang in a soft voice, accompanied by plucking a few basic chords on the guitar. *There is nothing I couldn't do, if I had you.*

It was a warm night; the peeling paint on Alan's bedroom walls was hidden by the flickering candlelight. He was naked, and his summer-colored skin was glowing. A single lock of dark hair hung down over his forehead as he sang to her. *If I had you.* He was smiling, sweetly, the whole time.

By the end of the song, he *had* her. Body and soul.

That performance was what convinced her he had genius. So clear, so pure, so effortless.

It was a shock when she saw him perform in front of an audience at a small restaurant in the East Village. The effortlessness was gone, replaced by a hard-edged drive that made his voice sound raw and his playing a little too assertive. But she was crazy in love with him then, and any doubts she felt were quickly banished by her infatuation. The stakes were so different when they were in their twenties. Everyone she knew was casting about for something, chasing a dream, and it was understood, even if unexpressed, that eventually they'd put aside their unrealistic, unrealizable fantasies and find a career that would at least pay the bills.

A lot of her early relationship with Alan was assuring him that he had the talent and only needed the right opportunities. That's what you did when you loved someone. You believed in them and you supported them. Right? And when Alan said that the opportunities for *his kind of music* and *his kind of song-writing* were better in L.A., she'd believed him and supported him and packed up and moved. She never regretted that part of it.

When they first met in New York, she'd billed herself as a waitress, which was true at the time. She only revealed that she was learning about yoga when she was sure he wouldn't laugh at her or think she was a flake.

Lee started seriously studying (versus practicing) yoga with Rosa Gianelli, an older woman who'd moved to Paris in the six-ties to study with B. K. S. Iyengar. Iyengar had been brought to Europe by Yehudi Menuhin to spread the gospel of yoga. And Rosa had uprooted herself and left her family for months to train with him. Lee had been sent to Rosa by one of her earliest teach-ers, and Rosa had seen something in Lee that she felt Iyengar would approve of—her compassion, her sincerity, and her eye for detail. She took it upon herself to train her, free of charge, as she'd been taught, step by step. Rosa instructed Lee in the asa-nas with a meticulousness that was at times maddening. They'd work for hours, sometimes days, on one pose, just as Iyengar had done with her. Rosa taught by positioning Lee's body, but also through language, beautiful, precise metaphors to describe every movement that made each gesture come alive—the "dome" at the arch of her foot, the "head of the cobra" when she pulled back her shoulders. Rosa's language and intensity made Lee forget that she was in the most ordinary of ordinary suburban houses on Long Island. She'd take the train from the city and walk to Rosa's house each morning, have a cup of Folgers instant coffee and a Stella D'oro anisette toast with her, and then allow herself to be transported to a different world. Rosa made Lee study the yoga sutras, too, so thoroughly that at times Lee thought it might have been easier to finish medical school. Sometimes they fought. Rosa pushed too hard, could be mean, and was stingy with praise. Still . . .

Lee has a great deal of respect for the training that a lot of the teachers she knows have received, but she can't help thinking at times that their workshops and crowded seminars are like skimmed milk compared with the heavy cream of the days she spent with Rosa.

Alan was skeptical of yoga at first. He was a gym fanatic. Lee knows he would never admit it to anyone, but what really got him hooked on yoga was mula bandha. That much-discussed little "lock" that's supposed to control the flow of energy between the upper and lower halves of the body and, ultimately, the energy between earth and sky. Alan certainly wasn't the first man in history to discover that if you could truly master the mysteries of that subtle inner lifting of the pelvic floor, there were a *whole lot* of energy flows you could control in your body. The benefits sure outweighed those of free weights. Indeed.

She wasn't complaining. She'd never really wanted to go on birth control anyway, and once Alan had his bandhas disciplined, they didn't need to worry about pills or condoms. And back before the twins and before the studio became so demanding, back when they had what seemed like unlimited time . . . well, there are worse ways to spend one, two, sometimes three hours than exploring the limits of Alan's self-control. *Indeed.*

Back then, when everything in their lives seemed to be going so well, the performative aspects of Alan's lovemaking didn't bother Lee so much. "Watch this," he'd say. "Look at me, Lee," he'd say, and she'd happily oblige. *Mula bandha, baby. Go for it.*

Because they felt so connected, because she felt as if he was *hers* and she was *his*, it was all part of their intimate connection. It wasn't about her and him, it was about *them*.

But now, Alan's little stunts and impeccable timing seem different somehow, and on the afternoons he comes by the house, as he's started to do again, she feels less as if it's about *them* than about him having an audience. Any innocent bystander would do.

Lee is actually mulling all this over as they're having sex, and if that's what's on her mind, it can't be a particularly good sign.

"Watch this," he says as he pulls out. "On the count of ten. Watch me."

But really, when you come down to it, it's all self-appreciation more than anything else, at least this part of it.

A few minutes later, she comes back to bed, and he's checking messages on his iPhone. She hates this contraption. Alan seems completely oblivious to the fact that half the time he's talking with her, he's playing with *it*—texting or looking at e-mails or whatever it is he does. It's created holes in their conversations that he fills with meaningless interjections of "ummms" and "yeah yeah yeahs" that tell her, even when they're not face-to-face, that he's peering into it.

"Have you noticed a difference in the boys?" she asks.

"Yeah, ummm . . . I don't know. How?"

"Can you put that down for a minute, Alan? At least while we discuss this?"

"You know it's really insulting to me when you say that. Like you think I can't do both things at once?"

"I'm just asking you if you wouldn't, that's all."

He sighs in an operatic way, but puts the phone on the bedside table. "Happy?"

It chirps. Text message, probably.

"Well, have you?" she asks again.

"Have I *what?*"

"The boys. Noticed a change."

"They're getting older; I mean, I don't know. They're taller. Kids hit puberty sooner these days, but they're only eight. I doubt it's that."

"I mean their personalities. There's less fighting. At first I thought it was because Michael was getting less aggressive, but now I think Marcus is different, too. It's like they're balancing out finally, hitting some peaceful mean. And it began when they started practicing."

Alan puts his hands behind his neck and leans against the headboard. "They're bound to change as they get older. I don't go in for the whole yoga-equals-magic-fix thing. If it's doing something for them, great, but no point in pretending it's going to completely change their personalities. I keep trying to teach Marcus that song I wrote on the ukulele and . . . nothing. Not interested."

"I think we underestimated Barrett. If she can do this with the twins, I think she has real potential." She puts her head on Alan's stomach, that solid plank of muscles. "I've started talking to someone at their school again to see if they're interested in having us start a yoga program there. For the kids, but also for the teachers. With Barrett as my assistant."

"Barrett? I wouldn't get too entangled with her. On top of that, you're signing an exclusive contract. You don't want to start violating that before you've even closed the deal. Zhannette and Frank seem to find out about everything."

Lee senses that she has to deal with this somewhat gently. The last thing she wants is to set Alan off. "I know," she says.

"But what if we tried to negotiate the deal a little differently? We pretty much just agreed to whatever they proposed."

"Are you kidding me, Lee? You know what they're offering for a salary."

"Yeah, but they loved my class, it's what they need. That should give us some room to bargain."

Alan rolls out of bed and storms across the room. "Jesus, Lee. Don't tell me you're going to pull this on me. You hold all the cards here, and I'm just the little nobody in background with the squeeze box. If you decide to bargain, go right ahead. And if it ends up screwing up the whole deal, don't come whining to me about tuitions and health insurance . . ."

"I'm just putting it out there, Alan. Nothing's been decided."

"And I'll tell you something else. If you *do* fuck it up, don't expect me to come around here and do this for you."

"Do what?"

"You treat me like some pathetic pool boy you hired to get you off."

"*What?*"

"You heard me, Lee. You think men aren't capable of feeling they've been objectified? You think I don't feel hurt being treated like your paid companion?"

On the one hand, Lee is so insulted by this, she doesn't know how to respond. And on the other, she sees a hurt look on Alan's face that makes her doubt herself—her perceptions, her motives. It's all so confusing, it's almost a relief when Alan storms out of the house.

Sybille Brent has moved out of the Mondrian Hotel and into a "cottage" she's rented in Los Feliz. She tells Stephanie that the Mondrian was just too ridiculously expensive. Stephanie finds this reassuring. You never know who has money in this business and who's bluffing, and only someone who is so loaded she can afford *anything* would dare complain about a hotel being too pricey. If she'd actually been appalled by the prices, she would have complained of inadequate service or some other pretense or stayed until she was forced into bankruptcy.

And then there's the "cottage." Tucked discreetly off of Mountain Oak Drive, the white Greek Revival house has stunning views of the city, and gardens out back that have been maintained, since the 1930s, to their original design.

"I'm finding this a little more cozy," Sybille says.

They're sitting under the pergola and gazing down the tiered garden where three people are clipping and raking. The pool is somewhere below, perched on a precarious-looking outcropping.

"It's gorgeous," Stephanie says.

"It's adequate. It only has two bedrooms, believe it or not, but they're immense and in completely different parts of the house. Anderson can carry on in any way he likes. I suppose it makes him appear like more of a servant, but that doesn't seem to bother him."

Stephanie doesn't know if this means he is a servant or not, but then decides it doesn't make much difference to her one way or the other. After all, since she's on the payroll, she's technically a servant of sorts herself.

"The house was built for a woman director and her female 'companion.' I suppose it's been renovated a dozen times since, but it still has the feel of a little hideaway constructed for a successful, mannish woman without an excess of delicacy or taste."

There's no mistaking the fact that Sybille is *not* talking about herself. She's dressed this morning in a light dove gray dress that offsets her white hair perfectly and is moving in a striking way in the light breeze. The fabric is rippling like water. She's sipping from a large white cup of cappuccino. Stephanie wonders if Sybille requested a meeting at this time of day so the awkward question of alcohol would not be an issue. Hard to tell and there's no point in going there anyway.

Stephanie's screenplay is sitting on the table in front of Sybille, and sooner or later they're going to have to get to it. The longer Sybille waits to bring it up, the more dread Stephanie is feeling. There are little pink tags sticking out of the script, dozens of them. Hard to know if that's good or bad, but it's impressive that Sybille read the script that closely either way.

Stephanie notices Sybille noticing her noticing the script.

"We had quite a row with the author of this novel, you know."

"I didn't know. You've been generous about keeping me in the dark."

"He's quite the self-possessed young man. I think the reviews and attention went to his head. He was holding out for a ridiculous sum of money. The terms you gave him smacked of desperation on your part, my dear. I'm quoting my lawyer. I hope you don't mind hearing that."

"It's accurate."

"Were we trying to prove something by outbidding someone? A rival?" Sybille cagily picks up her coffee cup and gazes off at the pool, as if only marginally interested in the answer.

"Much more embarrassing than that. An ex-boyfriend."

"Ah." She sets the cup back down delicately and rearranges a croissant on the plate in front of them. Judging from her appearance, this little gesture probably constitutes breakfast. "Boyfriend. How unexpected."

It's not clear from her tone if she's being ironic or not.

"So it was partly an act of vengeance?" Sybille says.

"I'm afraid so. Or trying to prove myself, in a very expensive way."

"You sound so apologetic. I hope you don't think you need to be with me. I assumed it was obvious that a good portion of my motivation in being here was revenge and trying to prove myself. I don't find the fact of it embarrassing in the least. Pretending it was otherwise might be humiliating, but I'm obviously not headed in that direction. A productive life requires motivation of some kind. I don't see why revenge is necessarily a bad motivation. As long as guns aren't involved."

"That's a liberating attitude," Stephanie says. She's been putting off tasting her coffee for fear that her hand is shaking, but now it seems she doesn't have anything to worry about. As she lifts her cup, she notes with some pride that her hand is perfectly steady. "Jesus," she says. "This is amazing coffee."

"You knew it would be, didn't you? The bottom line is, I flew your little author out here to meet with me. Anderson was there, of course, and two of my lawyers. The whole idea was to intimidate him."

"You're putting a lot of money into this."

"I don't believe in doing anything halfway, and besides, it's a huge amount of fun for me. I always thought my ex-husband was a tyrant with his money, wielding power; now I appreciate how exhilarating it is flashing dollar bills."

"Sooner or later," Stephanie says, "you're going to have to tell me what you think of the screenplay."

"Yes, I am, aren't I?" She pushes the cup and croissants aside, draws the script toward her, and puts on a pair of round purple eyeglasses, which, like everything else about Sybille, scream style and money. "As you can see, I've made some notes. I think all the characters need a little more development and precision in their motivations. The mother needs to be more glamorous."

"In the book, she's a waitress with a prescription drug addiction."

"We've taken care of the book," Sybille says. "I see the mother as more the Catherine Deneuve type. I've met her at charity functions in Paris, you know, and I can send her the script. We can explain the accent in a line. Structurally, it's brilliant. I don't think that needs a thing. We've sent the script to Kathryn Bigelow."

"You have?"

"I don't believe in wasting time, and money opens doors, as you know."

Since Sybille seemed motivated primarily by the potential of humiliating her ex-husband through the character of the father, Stephanie is a little hesitant to bring him up. But she must. "What did you think of the father?"

"You did a magnificent job with him. The only change there is we'll have the yoga classes be those überheated things, so we can have him with sweat pouring down. We can cast someone like Danny DeVito and surround him with actors who look like Adonis. The contrast will be mesmerizing. The first act should end with him passing out in a class, drenched in sweat, flushed, completely ignored by the beauties, who don't even see him."

Stephanie is making notes on a pad of paper she brought with her. In some peculiar way, all of Sybille's suggestions make perfect sense. Now that the question of revenge has been elevated to a higher plane, she feels free to toss in some of her own suggestions.

"Instead of passing out, we can make it a minor heart attack."

"I like that. Unless you think it will elicit sympathy."

"Not if it's shot correctly. And the ridiculous boyfriend. I think we should change his name to Preston."

Sybille thinks this over. "I was going to suggest Kenneth. Little Kenneth. But I can live with Preston. In fact, I like. I think we're a very good team."

"I do, too," Stephanie says. And she means it. She wasn't expecting the project would ever be this much fun.

For the past week or so Katherine has been trying to convince herself that, ultimately, Lee will not leave Edendale, no matter how much financial sense it makes for her to sign a contract with YogaHappens. Once you hack your way through the saunas and the towels and the frills, the corporate feeling of the place is downright creepy. And in her own quiet way, Lee has always had a rebellious streak. When she comes into work first thing on Monday morning and tells Katherine she wants to talk with her in her office, Katherine is fully expecting her to say that she's changed her mind and has sent the men from YogaHappens back where they belong.

"I wanted to tell you first," Lee says.

"Okay."

"I've signed the contract with YogaHappens."

Surprisingly, Katherine feels numb. Probably, underneath her hopes, this is exactly what Katherine knew was coming. She looks at Lee and doesn't say anything.

"I know you don't approve. . . ."

"It's not up to me to approve or not, Lee. You've made that clear."

"Don't make it sound so cut-and-dried."

"Well, isn't it?"

"If it were up to me, I would have thrown them out the minute they approached me. You know that."

"To be honest with you, I'm not sure I do. And I suppose it isn't really any of my business, but if it isn't 'up to you,' who is it up to? It's your business. It's your life."

"I can't make unilateral decisions, Kat. I've got the kids. I've got Alan."

Alan. There's a joke. The idea that Alan might make a decision that in any way took Lee into consideration, or anyone other than himself, is completely far-fetched.

"And please don't look at me like that. Alan's going to be moving back in."

The only good thing that Katherine can see in this little announcement is that Lee doesn't make it with any particular joy in her voice. She just reports it as if it's a simple business plan, which may be exactly what it is.

"When was that decided?"

"We went over everything, we went out to dinner, I signed the contract, and then . . . we decided."

Katherine can tell from the look on Lee's face and the oddly apologetic tone in her voice how this went down. *Oh, Lee,* she wants to say, *please don't do this.* Alan basically blackmailed her into signing with the promise of returning home. Katherine hears music and looks out of the office door and into the yoga room, where Barrett is practicing with one of the interns. Hearing Lee's news makes Katherine happier than ever that, whatever mistakes she's made and continues to make, at least she isn't basing all of her choices on a man.

"If it's what you want, Lee, then it's probably for the best."

"We need to talk about you, too. Since we won't be using the studio anymore, we're probably going to sell the building. It isn't the best time, but Alan and I don't feel like being landlords."

There's a little voice inside Katherine advising her to tell Lee what she knows. It only seems fair, after all. But the last thing she needs is to complicate her own life. And besides that, the messenger always gets blamed.

"I probably wouldn't want to be one myself," Katherine says. "It's tough enough *having* a landlord."

"I've talked to a real estate agent, and there's a building about two blocks from here with an office that would be ideal for you. They've been trying to lease it for a while, so I'm guessing they'd negotiate on the rent. It's close to the fire station. I don't know if that would be awkward or not."

"There's no reason it would. Conor's stint in Silver Lake is up. He's in a different part of the city altogether."

"Where?"

"I didn't ask." She can't blame Conor for turning off like he did when he saw Phil at her house. But it would have been nice if he'd waited a couple of days and then called her and asked her to explain herself. Not that that would have been perfect, either. Katherine hates people who fuck up and then ladle out bowl after bowl of excuses, and she's never been able to dish out explanations in that way, even when she knows she's in the right. Conor had his heart broken once. He's protecting himself. She knows about trying to spare yourself more pain—even if doing so hurts like hell.

Katherine gets up to leave, but she doesn't want to walk out of Lee's office with this bad feeling hanging in the air. She turns to Lee and says, "I won't stay upset about this for long. I promise. I owe you everything, Lee. My life, when you come down to it. So if this is what you've decided, I hope it works out the way you want."

She can see into the yoga room, where Barrett and the intern are taking turns spotting each other as they do flips. Barrett is wearing a girly little T-shirt and her hair in pigtails. Katherine wonders if she's heard the news that Alan is moving back in with Lee, and if so, how she feels about *that*.

Imani is sitting beside her pool watching Glenn swim laps in his green Speedo, a bathing suit that manages to be both sexy and nerdy at once. She's bought him different kinds of swimsuits—and suggested he just go in without one—but he picked up the habit of wearing Speedos on the swim team at Dartmouth and he's not about to give it up. It obviously recalls his athletic glory days and makes him swim a little more aggressively. Dartmouth College. It couldn't be more perfect.

If Imani had been able to go into a laboratory and assemble the pieces of her Ideal Man, she would have ended up with a guy who was, in every possible way, shape, and form, absolutely *nothing* like her husband. Where to begin? It might be easiest to start with "A."

Age: Glenn is forty-three, which makes him sixteen years older than her. She'd never really paid attention to the age of her boyfriends, mostly because all the men she went out with had always been within sight of her own age at the time. When she had thought about such things, she'd thought there was something marginally creepy about women who went out with men a good deal older than them. Like, why not just wear a sandwich board advertising your unresolved father issues?

Height: At six foot three, Glenn is officially in the too-tall category in her book, almost a full foot taller than her and looming above her whenever they appear in photos together. She knows this is supposed to be sexy and signify masculinity and power and—let's be honest—a big dick, but she was always drawn to guys under six feet, the ones with the compact little soccer-player bodies, the perfect round little butts. It's more convenient that way—you can kiss them without having to ask to have the drawbridge lowered. And the proportions of their bodies work better aesthetically, are almost always more the Greek ideal.

Weight: Glenn is, by almost any standard, skinny. She's not into chubby, but guys who can wolf down anything they want as often as they want without ever gaining a pound are annoying and inconsiderate and make *you* look fatter. There's a reason von Sternberg surrounded Dietrich with plump actresses in *The Blue Angel*.

Profession: God knows Imani never wanted to marry an actor. She's dated her share of that breed. If they're less successful than you, it's an impossible and doomed situation, and if they're more successful than you, you can't trust them, and it's equally impossible and doomed, just in a different way. But a pediatric surgeon? She usually preferred to date men she thought weren't *quite* as smart as she is. Always best to have the upper hand there.

Race: Let's just say that even though black men are, on the whole, a *pain in the ass*, usually carrying around a chip on their shoulders and pathologically commitmentphobic, she has to admit she's always melted under the gaze of a brother's big brown eyes. All that warm, open, steamy sensuality. And, mostly, just an immediate feeling of a connection and shared larger experience, no matter how different their backgrounds. Not exactly what she feels with a WASP from Columbus, Ohio.

More? Oh, how about the fact that the guy doesn't watch TV, not counting a few playoff sporting events? Or that he likes (she can barely bring herself to say the name) Jimmy Buffett?

But why go on? The truth is, nothing about their relationship makes sense in eHarmony terms, and yet everything works. She just plain old *adores* the guy, and being married to him has made her feel as if her life is right on every level. Maybe for the first time ever.

He swims over to the side of the pool and starts bobbing up and down, then emerges, bit by bit, until his whole too-tall, too-skinny, too-wonderful body is standing behind her chair, dripping onto the ceramic tiles surrounding the pool.

"Don't get too close," she says.

He responds to this by reaching down, cupping her breasts in his hands, and kissing the top of her head. "Too close?" he asks.

"Nah," she says. "Just right."

"You are indeed." He runs his hands up her arms. "Look at this muscle tone."

"Chataranga, baby," she says.

"Maybe I should join you."

"That would work out well," she says. "With your schedule. Anyway, you'd probably be a natural and be able to do everything I've stumbled my way through, and I'd end up resenting you for it. Plus you'd need an extra-long mat."

"I couldn't share yours?" He leans down and whispers into her ear, something about last night.

She sighs and says, "I agree, it was."

She's not sure exactly what he said, but the tone was unmistakable, and last night *was* wonderful. So here's yet another thing that amazes her. They've been married for almost four years now, and while that admittedly can't compete with her parents' thirty-five-year marriage, compared with the relationships in her past, this is major long term. And she's still astonished by the way their passion for each other can go through these dips that feel like the boring end of a movie that's gone on too long and then emerge, so hot and urgent, so fresh and surprising, it is as if it's the first time they've made love and are discovering each other's bodies all over again. It almost makes her think that the long break they took after she miscarried served some useful purpose. It's hard to imagine it could get better than it was last night, but even if there's a cooling off, it doesn't matter. There's the love and tenderness she feels for him that will persevere and sustain them until passion returns.

Maybe she *should* take him to yoga. The classes are fun, but the real pleasure is feeling opened up in some internal way that is almost as addictive as the feeling of flexibility. All those "chest opening" poses that sounded like bullshit to her when she started are paying off.

"How's the script?" he asks.

She happens to know he read the script one night last week when it was sitting on the dining room table. He's a voracious reader, and even though he has zero interest in pop culture and very little in movies in general, he is an amazingly good script reader. He has an intuition for problems in structure and the tone of dialogue that never ceases to surprise her. But he won't give an opinion without first asking her hers. He wouldn't agree with her just for the sake of it, but he'd keep quiet rather than contradict her.

"It's much better than I was expecting," she says. "I thought it was going to be some dreary indie kind of script with too many characters and no tension. But the scenes really move. And it's funny. For some reason, I didn't figure the woman who wrote it had such a good sense of humor."

"The one from yoga?"

"The same. So, okay, your turn. I know you read it."

"It held my interest," he says. "It made me laugh. All the characters seemed to be more or less lying all the time, which I would guess would be very fun for an actor."

How does he know that? It would surprise her if he's ever told an outright lie in his life, and she knows for a fact he's never done any acting.

"You should have been a director," Imani says.

"Too much responsibility," he says. "I'd rather do heart surgery on little kids."

"I'm not completely sold on the role—black actress playing nightclub singer with troubled past. A little bit of a stereotype, don't you think?"

Glenn wraps his shoulders in a towel and sits at the bottom of Imani's lounge chair and starts rubbing her insole. "I assumed you'd be playing the girlfriend."

"That's not what she said."

"I'm sure she could be talked into it."

When Becky Antrim shows up for their yoga date, she sits across from Glenn and starts teasing him about his bathing suit. Becky flirts with Glenn outrageously, mostly, Imani can tell, because she doesn't find him remotely attractive. It's completely safe, and she does it to flatter Imani about her choice in men more than to flatter Glenn. Becky goes for the most obvious types—the pretty, bad boys who have "heartbreaker" written all over their faces. One of these days, Imani is going to sit her down and have a long talk with her. After a class, when Becky is loose and maybe a little bit vulnerable. Glenn has a former college roommate whose wife left him a year ago, and Imani thinks he'd be perfect for Becky. He's thirty-two, short, black, good-looking but not too; plays sax amazingly well; and is trying to make a go of it with a jazz quartet. A yoga fanatic on top of it all. Basically, he's the guy Imani would have made in the lab for herself back when she didn't know a thing.

"Where are you girls headed today?" Glenn asks.

"Your wife is taking me up to Silver Lake," Becky says. "She's bringing me to some yoga class she's been keeping to herself for a while now. After all I've done for her. You should come, Glenn. Lots of pretty girls in tight outfits sticking their butts in the air."

"I'd only have my eyes on one," he says.

"I'm flattered," Becky says, "but not in front of your wife, please."

L ee knows that sooner or later she's going to have to call her mother and tell her the news that Alan is moving back in and that things seem to have settled down. For some reason she's been resisting doing it, but because the house is quiet— the kids are at a friend's and Alan is at the studio getting ready to play harmonium in her class this afternoon—she decides to place the call.

Bob answers the phone. Her stepfather is one of those blustery guys who's always clearing his throat. Maybe he has chronic sinus problems or something along those lines—to complement the chronic "social" drinking—but Lee always feels as if he just likes to punctuate his speech with annoying interruptions, so you have to wait to hear what he really wants to say.

"Mm-hmm, Lee. It's good to hear your voice. Your . . . mm-hmm . . . mother tells me you're getting a divorce."

Ellen married Bob after Lee went off to college, so it's not as if they've ever had a close relationship, but he has a way of being only interested enough in her life to be judgmental. He never gets the facts right, and she's not sure he'd retain them if he did.

"No, Bob. Alan just needed some time alone to get work done."

"Well, I suppose we all need that, as long as that's what . . . mm-hmm . . . he was *really* doing."

"Yes, Bob. That's what he was really doing."

"I am glad to hear it, honey." He says this in a truly sweet voice, the one he uses to make toasts at holidays, the one she hears when (infrequently) he gets sentimental and teary. Then he clears his throat and adds, "You keep telling yourself that."

"Is Ellen around?"

"I'll get her for you. Come . . . mm-hmm . . . visit us, Lee. We need some help with this B and B bullshit of your . . . mm-hmm . . . mother's."

Bob calls out to Lee's mother in a loud and gruff voice. Although Ellen always tries to portray him as a gentle man, he usually seems openly hostile to Ellen. "It's your daughter. I said it's *Lee*! It's *Lee*, for Christ's sake. How do I know? Something about her husband."

"Lee, honey? Are you all right?"

"Yes, Mom. Everything's fine. I just called to say hello. How's it going there?"

"Oh, honey. I know you probably won't believe me, but it's going very, very well. We've started work on the house and it's full speed ahead. I did a little cleaning, and I bought some extra sheets and everything. We're going to turn the old rec room down in the basement into a dorm accommodation. Doesn't that sound like fun? I hadn't been down there in years, what with that odor and everything, but it's cozy. We've got a ton of mattresses on the floor we bought from a motel that went out of business."

"Okay."

"Well, don't make it sound like that, Lee. We had a mold remediator in last week for a couple of hours to deal with the walls and the seepage. And I had Bob spray all the mattresses with Lysol. The more people we can pack in down there, the more money we'll be able to raise to renovate the guest suites upstairs.

"And Laurence and his 'friend' have sanded and polyure-thaned the floor of the barn. It looks so beautiful and professional, honey. You'd be so proud of me. It's turning into a real spiritual haven here."

"I'm glad you're moving ahead with it, Mom." Lee is getting a bad feeling about the whole conversation. Her mother's voice has that tone of hurt and anger that always signals problems.

"I know you're not, but it's a nice little hobby for me. Try not to feel threatened by it, honey. I'm only doing it so I can put aside money to leave to the twins. It's all for you."

"I know, Mom."

"Laurence and Corey—or whatever his name is—have already held a couple of workshops out in the barn."

The last she heard, the barn wasn't insulated or heated. "That's great, Mom. What kind of workshops?"

"I didn't interrogate him, honey. He gets very upset if I press too hard. I'm sure they were wonderful. He got a *huge* crowd both times."

"You didn't go?"

"No, it was only for men. Anyway, Bob and I go to bed around eleven, so it was too late for us. But that's enough about my little triumph. Tell me about you. Are you all right? You know how much I worry about you."

"I'm fine, Mom. Things are much better now than they were."

"I knew they would be, honey. I love you so much, you have no idea. And I have *faith* in you. I really do."

"I know, Mom."

"I know you don't, but it's all right. I told Bob I knew you'd be better off in the end without Alan. He's not good enough for you. He never has been, and no one ever knew what you saw in him, besides his looks."

"Mom, I think you should know that—"

"Now don't get *defensive*. I just mean we all knew you'd been through a rough time back then—I worried so much—so you got married. Your sister cried for hours when she heard you were going to marry him. 'He's a big loser!' she kept screaming. But she got over it. No one ever thought less of you. You couldn't expect your sister to come to the wedding with that fever she had."

"Mom! I called to tell you that Alan is moving back in."

There's a long silence on the other end of the phone, and Lee hears her mother reporting to Bob. "He's *what?*" Bob shouts. "Well, what do *I* care?"

Finally her mother seems to recover her voice. "You know I'll support you, no matter what, honey. And if you tell people you did it for the kids, they'll admire you for it. That's how I explained Bob to people."

Katherine unlocks her bike from the railing along the walk-way in front of her house and pushes it out to the street. It's a lazy, quiet Sunday afternoon, and while she kept planning to go out and get some exercise, buy some bagels, go for coffee, pretty much anything to get her out of the house, she spent most of the day in the little extra bedroom where she keeps her sewing machine and fabrics, working on a dress she's making for Lee. It's one of the most complicated pieces of clothing she's ever tried to design, never mind sew, and the more she does on it, the more excited she gets. It's all black, white, and silver, based loosely on a geometric William Tempest evening dress she coveted the min-ute she saw it in *Vogue*. It's pretty much using every technical skill she has in her bag of tricks and a few others she's never tried, and unless she messes the whole thing up at the last minute, it could be amazing. A boned bodice. Who knew she was capable of sewing that?

She's developed a sort of love for the dress that's bordering on weird, almost as if it's a pet, and it's going to be tough to actually give it away.

On the other hand, her love for it is connected to her feelings for Lee. She sees Lee in it as she's sewing it, and she knows she would *never* have the patience to attempt any of the tricks she's trying if she thought she was making it for herself. She's thinking of the dress as a peace offering to Lee or maybe a going-away, good-luck present.

It's a warm afternoon, and the streets have the quiet, deserted feel of a holiday. She loves biking at this time of day on a Sunday, when it's still and balmy and she feels as if she has the whole neighborhood to herself. With the way the air feels against her skin and the way the breeze feels in her hair, she can trick herself into believing that she has no regrets.

It's so lovely out, she's tempted for a minute to skip yoga class and bike and bike, maybe even head to Griffith Park. But Lee said she was going to make an announcement in class today, and although she didn't specify about what, it's pretty obvious it's about the studio closing. Katherine has been at the studio for most of their big changes and improvements and triumphs, and so she figures she might as well be present for this. It's all a cycle.

She's been trying very hard to tell herself that, *no matter what*, this is a good move for Lee. More money, more prestige, more opportunity to teach without worrying about the business. But she can't get past the feeling that despite all that, Lee wouldn't have done it if it hadn't been to please Alan, to get him back. And that's okay, she supposes—not Katherine's business—but would Lee have wanted Alan back if she knew the whole story?

For weeks now, Katherine has been struggling with this—as a good friend, shouldn't she tell Lee what she knows? But she keeps coming back to the resolution to simply focus on herself, and let Lee and Alan's marriage follow its own course.

She pedals up to the back of the studio and lashes her bike to the fence near the office window. Alan appears in the doorway, wearing a pair of expensive little gray yoga pants and a tank top. How is it, she wonders, that someone with such a great body, beautiful hair, and those strong, chiseled features can be so physically *unappealing* to her? For all the trouble she's made for herself and other people through her life, Katherine has never been even remotely attracted to married or otherwise-engaged men. Well, not counting the infamous guy she was in love with for six months. But she didn't *know* he was married, and she dumped him as soon as she found out.

"Beautiful day," he says. "Coming to class?"

"That's the plan," Katherine says.

"Lee will appreciate that," he says. "She's kind of emotional about the announcement and all. And I'm doing the live music."

Katherine doesn't say anything to this. There's a little edge in Alan's voice that makes her feel as if he's goading her, trying to get her to say something so he can make a comment. Not buying into it, thanks.

"She told me you're not thrilled about our decision."

Katherine shrugs. "It's not my business, Alan."

"Well, it seems to me you've gotten into our business before. I haven't ruled out the idea of having my lawyer do a closer audit of the books, you know."

"I wish you would," Katherine says. "Ease your mind once and for all."

"I would have done it sooner, but it's not cheap."

"From what I hear, Lee is going to be making enough to cover lots of extra expenses."

"*Lee* isn't the only one making money in this family, Katherine." He leans in toward her and his long hair swings out from behind his ears. The hair and the expensive tank top and all the other vain little touches really don't go well with anger and pettiness. "So get it right. And I'm sorry you're going to lose your massage space, but I'm sure you can find another. Especially if they don't find out what you *really* get paid to do in there."

When Katherine first opened her practice at Edendale, she used to pay her rent by giving massages to Lee and Alan. It had been Lee's suggestion, and even though Alan was against it, he made use of her services more than Lee did. Although it's something she's tried her best to forget, she had to fend off Alan's naked advances more than once. She finally took out a loan so she could pay rent and refused to book him. The whole request for "release" from male clients is so common—like, *Oh, poor me. Look at this* problem *I've got. Help me out!*—she's bored with it by now and knows how to handle it by making a joke and defusing the situation with humor. But especially galling was Alan acting as if she owed it to him as part of their deal.

"I don't get paid to do that," she says. "You didn't know? I do it for free. Unless the idea of touching the guy makes me feel like throwing up."

"You know what your problem is?" he says. "I don't think you like men at all. You should just come out and get it over with. You're in love with Lee."

"Well," she says, and slings her pack to her shoulder, "that makes one of us."

Alan stomps back into the studio and then storms back out like the petulant child he is. "And don't leave your bike back here. It clutters up the patio and the YogaHappens guys might be around this afternoon, and I don't want it looking like shit back here."

She could just leave the bike where it is and he'd keep his mouth shut, probably for fear she'd go to Lee. But the thing is, once you get in the habit of owing people nothing, you get addicted to it. She unlocks the bike and sits sidesaddle on the seat and coasts out to the sidewalk. She locks it to one of the street signs—*out of view of the studio, Alan, okay?*—looping the chain through both wheels. She pats the bicycle seat and says, "Now you be a good girl and don't *go* anywhere. I'll be right back."

Lee is so rattled and agitated by the phone call with her mother that she arrives at Edendale ten minutes later than she planned. She can see that there's a crowd assembled in the yoga room, and she can hear Alan playing, warming them up, in a sense. He claims not to like the harmonium—it's perfect for classes, but not terribly versatile—but he took to it quickly, and when he starts playing, he seems to lose himself and go into a trance. Listening to the haunting, repetitive sound of the instrument, students in classes seem to go inward as well.

Hearing the beauty of his music is reassuring to her. She doesn't pretend to think Alan is perfect—any more than she is herself—but her mother really ought to give him credit where it's been earned, and in terms of musical talent he clearly has earned credit.

"Lee," Tina says from behind the product counter, "I know you're going into class, but could you come here for a minute?"

Brian/Boner is standing off to the side of the counter, and if Lee didn't know better (by which she means she hopes she's wrong) she could swear he's flirting with Tina. *Oh, please, Tina,* she feels like saying, *don't fall for this guy.* He's got that exhibitionist streak, and he must be close to twenty years older than Tina.

"Hi, Lee," he says. "You've got a good crowd today. I think you're going to be happy with it."

"Sundays are unpredictable," she says, "but it looks that way. I'm happy to see you're here."

"I'm trying to come three times a week," he says. "It gets me in touch with my spiritual side. Especially with the music. It really opens me up."

Hopefully not too much, she wants to say. "That's great. What did you want to discuss, Tina?"

"Brian has an issue with the merchandise, and . . . maybe you should explain it yourself."

It would be a lot simpler to count up the people who *don't* have an issue with the merchandise. If Tina had stocked bubble gum and chocolate it might have been simpler.

"It's not a big deal," he says. "But the thing is, Lee, you're not selling any products for men here. The outfits, the Kegel exercisers, the toe rings, the bags. All for women."

Lee hates this kind of argument. Does he really feel left out, or is he just trying to make trouble? The funny thing is, though, thinking about the fact that this annoying business with the merchandise is about to end when she closes the studio, Lee is suddenly filled with melancholy.

"Was there something in particular you wanted?"

"Well, if you're going to stock women's underwear and bras, I think you really need to stock jockstraps as well."

"I see."

"Otherwise it just looks sexist, and it's tough enough for us men being so outnumbered by women in classes."

Oh, boy. Where does she even begin with this one? It seems like a given that one of the reasons he comes to classes is to be surrounded by women. Could it be that he feels he's not getting enough attention? *I know of some workshops in Connecticut that might interest you,* she's tempted to say. *I have a feeling you'd get a lot of attention there. And probably wouldn't need to wear* anything.

"There's still a stigma in a lot of places about men taking yoga classes," he goes on. "It takes a lot of guts, Lee, for men to come to classes. You have to be secure in your masculinity."

"Oh, God," Tina says. "I really didn't mean to offend anyone, I swear. But honestly, Brian, no one here questions your masculinity."

Tough to do when constantly presented with the evidence of same. Lee is tempted to tell Brian that if he'd actually wear underwear of any kind, she'd be happy to buy it for him herself.

"The thing is," Lee says, "I'm going to make an announcement in class today, so you'll be finding out anyway. I'm afraid there are going to be some big changes here in the next month. I don't think you should do any advance orders . . . well, on anything, Tina."

Tina's pinched, pretty face crumples. "You're closing the studio?"

"I'm afraid so, Tina. I'm sorry. I was planning to tell you before I made the announcement in class, but I got here a little late. . . ."

But Tina is already starting to cry, so there's no point in going on. Brian seizes the opportunity and has her in a bear hug, petting her hair, telling her it's all right, and glaring at Lee.

It's definitely time to start class.

Midway through class, Katherine begins to feel hypnotized by the sounds of Alan's portable harmonium and the improvisational chanting he does to go along with it. Given the way she feels about Alan, it's a real testament to his talent that she's able to get lost in his music. The vibrations of the notes as his fingers play over the keyboard have a way of getting under your skin, and the little bellows at the back of the instrument that he pumps with his left hand make it even easier to sink into the breathing instructions that Lee is giving. In fact, there's a way in which the two of them seem to be more in sync than she's used to seeing. It's doubtful they worked out the routine ahead of time; they've just fallen into it naturally. Maybe this bodes well for the marriage. You never know what goes on in people's lives behind closed doors, and if this synchronicity of theirs in class is an indication of their private chemistry, she can only be happy for Lee.

Men cheat. (And it's not as if she has a perfect fidelity record.) Someone as narcissistic as Alan is probably capable of doing so without feeling anything for the person he's cheating with. He'll move back in, and poor Barrett will have to nurse her own wounds. Some things are better left unknown, unspoken. If husbands and wives confessed every indiscretion to each other, the divorce rate would be even higher than it is already.

And when she looks at the class, it's as if everyone is flowing and dancing, hearing Lee's words and Alan's music and letting their bodies respond. The deep lunges, the long stretches, the beautiful silent floating, the arching back bends, and the magic of thirty people breathing in unison creates a feeling of connection and community that goes far beyond anything that can be deconstructed.

It will be sad to lose this. There are plenty of other places to practice, but this feeling of community is going to be a lot harder to find. Graciela and Stephanie are in class, and Imani finally made a return visit, this time with Becky Antrim in tow. There was the initial murmur and gasp of recognition, but eventually everyone settled down.

At the end of class, Lee slowly brings them out of a deep

meditative savasana and has them sit up with their hands on their knees. Katherine knows what's coming and feels a little anxiety deep inside. This will make it all too real. No turning back.

"As you know," Lee says, "we spend a lot of time in class talking about letting go. Letting go of tension, letting go of expectations, letting go of fear. Because the truth is, you can't advance in your practice unless you let go of your fear of falling over or turning upside down, your fear of looking foolish or failing. Or farting, for that matter! If you think about the first time you did a headstand, you can maybe remember the leap of faith it took to finally feel your feet lifting off the floor and realize that you're still standing. Just not the way you usually do.

"But as you know, the physical postures are just the vehicle to achieve the deeper changes elsewhere in your life. So I've come to a moment in my life when in order to move on, I find I have to let go of something I love. Specifically, this studio.

"Alan and I have an opportunity to do our teaching and music in a different setting, and in order to do that, we will be closing the studio in two weeks."

Katherine had no idea what to expect, but she wasn't prepared for silence. She makes eye contact with Lee and shrugs.

"Does anyone have any questions?" Lee asks. One hand goes up. "Carol?"

"I lost a pair of sunglasses here last week, and I'm wondering if anyone found them."

"What did they look like?" a dark-haired woman who frequently naps during savasana asks.

"Cheap red plastic. I got them at the drugstore, but I like them."

"We'll look in lost and found," Lee says. "Any other questions?"

"I might have a class or two left on my ten-pass," Roger says. "What am I supposed to do with it?"

"We'll deal with those individually as they come up," Lee says. Alan, Katherine's been told, has devised a plan for this. "Anything else? Sharon?"

"I'm assuming you're going to have a clearance sale on mats and some of the other stuff up front. Any idea what the markdown will be?"

"You should talk with Tina next week. She and I will try to figure something out."

People have already started to roll up their mats, and Katherine can tell from the look on Lee's face that she's feeling a little foolish for having made such a big deal about the announcement. She sees a few sad faces, and then Andrea, a woman who has been a regular for years now, raises her hand. "Andrea?"

She looks at Lee for a moment, and the activity in the room comes to a stop. All the students turn toward her. She looks a little lost and dumbfounded.

"Did you want to ask something, Andrea?"

"What—what are we supposed to do?"

"How do you mean?"

"What are we supposed to do without you?" she asks.

That's when Tina starts crying loudly and runs to Brian for comfort.

After class, Stephanie, Graciela, Imani, and Becky decide to go to Café Crème across the street, and they ask Katherine to join them. Katherine can tell that Lee wants her to stay and talk with her, to help her process what happened at the end of class, but for the moment, Katherine feels a stronger allegiance to her other friends. It's as if they've all been abandoned by Lee and need to band together. Besides which, Katherine's been a big fan of Becky Antrim for years. She's not going to pass up the opportunity to sit across from her with a latte.

The weather is still beautiful, and as they walk, she notices the way people stop and turn around, point, and pull out their phones to snap pictures of Becky. What would it be like to be so visible and under a microscope? More to the point, why would anyone want to be? Becky seems to have made peace with it. She walks with a combination of disregard and haughty imperviousness that only draws more attention to her.

At the Crème, they get their drinks and sit at a table on the sidewalk.

"Somehow," Stephanie says, "I didn't think Lee would go through with this. How long have you known, Kat?"

"She told me a few days ago. She's already signed the contract."

"I'm still floored by how good she is," Becky says. "I'm the most promiscuous yoga *slut* in this town, so when I say she's good, you can believe she's *good*."

"I still don't see why she can't teach here, too," Graciela says.

"YogaHappens only wants her to do an exclusive contract," Katherine says. "She's worth more to them that way. And they're giving Alan a contract to play live music at classes."

"He's cute," Imani says.

Katherine decides to hold her tongue.

"You know," Stephanie says, "I used to think you were screwed once you'd signed a contract. But all you need is a good lawyer. The woman who's producing our movie has lawyers who seem to be able to do anything. Break any contract."

Becky is sipping an enormous cup of coffee to which, Katherine noticed, she had a double shot of espresso added. High-octane movie stars. She spills some coffee on her T-shirt and blots it with a napkin. It's funny how someone can be so glamorous and famous and completely casual and unaffected at the same time.

"A friend of mine," Becky says, "had a little studio in Santa Monica. Big following, packed classes. Alan Cumming took me to her years ago. Anyway, YogaHappens gave her a fat contract, forced her to close her studio, and then a few months later they claimed she broke the terms she'd agreed to over some ridiculously minor thing she said in class, probably about the fucking water bottles. She had to renegotiate the contract and ended up making half the original offer. They started up in Denver, and they did it all over the place there. I guess word hasn't really gotten out here yet."

"Sleazy!" Stephanie says. "It figures."

"Has she met the owners? Zhannette—with a 'Zh'—and Frank—with an 'a,' one assumes. I've heard they're weirdos."

Although Lee never quoted an exact figure to Katherine, she knows that it's something outrageously high. And on top of that, the contract with Alan. So it makes sense that something that sounds too good to be true actually is a setup, a trap, and one that Alan led her into. Blackmailed her into, in fact.

She feels a new rush of anger, this time not at Alan or YogaHappens or anyone other than herself. She should have told Lee what she knew a long time ago. She finishes off her drink and gets up from the table. She isn't going to make that mistake again. She can at least pass along what she has just heard.

"I have to head back to the studio," she says and rushes out. She tries not to run to the studio, but she can't stop herself from doing some crazy speed-walking that's close to a jog.

Lee is still there, in the yoga room, straightening up and talking with Alan. She'd rather tell Lee alone. She pushes open the glass doors.

"You rushed out," Lee says. "I wanted to ask you how you thought that went."

"It went all right. I mean, a lot of people were shocked, but what can you . . . Listen, Lee, I just had a conversation with Graciela and Stephanie and . . . Anyway, Becky Antrim said something about YogaHappens. . . . Can I talk with you for a minute?"

"Of course."

Alan turns around from the wall where he's stacking blocks. "You can talk to both of us," he says. "We're in this together, something you keep forgetting."

Later, when Katherine goes back to revisit this moment, she realizes that she probably did sound a little crazy. Her delivery was too rushed, and maybe hysterical. The wacko owners, the sleazy business practices. The fact that Stephanie has been working with someone who has lawyers who can get you out of a contract with Satan if need be. She didn't make a strong case for the information she had. So, in retrospect, it wasn't really a surprise that Alan accused her of making this up, of coming up with a desperate attempt to get them to keep the studio open for her own selfish reasons.

He goes to Lee and puts his arm around her shoulder. "Did you really think we'd believe you?" he says.

Lee doesn't say anything. She doesn't have to. The look she gives Katherine says it all. She feels bad for Katherine. Bad for her that she has to go to this extreme to try to change their plans. Even in the moment, Katherine understands. Lee and Alan are a team again, and if Alan is playing captain, Lee has to go along with him. Couples. It happens all the time, and if she were ever in a position to actually be in a solid, lasting couple, she'd probably behave the same way.

She leaves the yoga room and walks outside. You just learn to accept the things you can't change, even if you never learn to love them. She'll go for a long ride and work it out of her system. Then she'll go home contented and finish the dress for Lee.

She walks up the street and when she's halfway to the sign where she locked her bike, she notices that it's gone.

Sitting in Café Crème nursing an iced tea, Graciela starts to feel overwhelmed by the company. She's disappointed in herself for feeling this way. After all, she is now officially a person who has credentials and standing in her field, a person whose talent has been recognized. She beat out hundreds of dancers and made it into a major video shoot. She was selected by Beyoncé herself. When the great lady (exactly the way Graciela thinks of her) met her for the first rehearsal, she looked at Graciela closely, shook her head, and said, "I might have made a mistake." Graciela's stomach dropped, but Beyoncé laughed and said, "Relax. You're just so *gorgeous* it's going to be tough dancing next to you."

Graciela doesn't know if that comment was calculated, but it made her feel more confident, more of an equal somehow. It made her dance better, all in an attempt to live up to the confidence everyone had in her.

Since then Graciela has heard rumors—little whispers from the choreographer—that she's being considered for one of the backup dancers on the upcoming tour. That would take her to a whole new level. She can't even let herself dwell on it.

Still, you would think she wouldn't feel *so* intimidated by these women, still hear echoes of her mother's insulting criticisms telling her she's stupid and unworthy every time she's about to open her mouth and add to the conversation. Too bad that voice is still so loud.

"I just hate pigeon pose," Becky says. "You know what it reminds me of? It reminds me of lying down on a really cheap pullout bed—you know, where you feel the metal bar across the middle of your stomach?"

Imani bursts out laughing. "When was the last time you were on a cheap pullout bed, honey?"

"For your information, I had a boyfriend in college who lived in a group house and slept on a convertible sofa in the living room. I should have married him."

"Sounds kind of romantic," Stephanie says.

"Uh-huh," Imani says. "Now, let's talk about what you were doing lying facedown."

Graciela wants to say, *Maybe she just had her hair blow-dried.* Not a brilliant comeback, but at least it's *something.* But what if it comes out sounding as lame to them as it does to her? What if no one laughs? If Daryl were here, she'd at least have company in her silence; he rarely speaks up during these kinds of conversations, either. Their shared insecurity is a bond.

"I used to feel that way about pigeon, too," Stephanie says, and the moment for Graciela's comment has passed. "Then I started pretending I was lying down with a cozy pillow under my chest."

"Oh, God," Becky says. "If I started thinking about my thigh as a 'cozy pillow' I'd probably have a panic attack."

Graciela's waiting for the day when her success in the past month will sink in and make her believe she deserves to be real friends with these women, not a mascot. (*Como una animala.*) Obviously she's going to have to wait a little longer.

Not long ago, Graciela could have counted on Stephanie to be her supporter in a situation like this, but since Imani is so excited about Stephanie's screenplay, Graciela feels on the outside there, too.

"Since Lee brought it up," Imani says, "what pose makes you afraid you're going to fart?"

"Halasana," Stephanie says. "Every time."

"Burrito-asana," Becky says. "Especially with sour cream."

"Right," Imani says. "You skinny thing, what do you know about *sour cream?*"

"You *gringas*," Graciela says. "What do you know about burritos, period?"

To her huge relief, they all laugh. Her phone starts to ring, and she gets up from the table to answer it. It's Katherine, her voice low and hesitant, as if she's upset.

"Are you still in Silver Lake?" she asks.

"Still here at the Crème," Graciela says. "What's up?"

There's a long silence on the other end of the phone, and then Katherine says, "I hate to pull you away, but when you're done there, would you mind driving me back up to my house?"

It's a relief to have an excuse to leave the café and her impressive friends, especially since she managed to say *something* before she left. "I'll be right there," she tells Katherine. She goes back to the table, picks up her pack and her yoga mat, and apologizes for leaving.

"Katherine needs a ride home," she says. She bolts down the last of her iced tea. "It was really great meeting you," she says to Becky. "I know it's nerdy to say so, but I'm a huge fan."

Becky gives one of her trademark pouts, an expression Graciela has seen dozens of times on TV and in movies. "We didn't get a chance to talk," she says, and she really seems to mean it.

Graciela can feel herself blushing, as if she's a kid being lavishly praised for a small, insignificant accomplishment.

"Imani told me you're in the new Beyoncé video," Becky goes on. "I was dying to hear what she's really like."

"Let her go," Imani says. "She can tell you next time. Or you could just ask me."

As Graciela is going to get her car, she realizes that while she was feeling intimidated by Becky, Becky was dying to ask *her* about *her* experiences. Who would have guessed it? Maybe Becky was feeling a little intimidated by her.

Katherine is sitting on a bench a few doors down from the studio. She has on her cheerful little yellow print sundress and she waves and smiles at Graciela, but when she gets in the car, Graciela can see right away that something's wrong.

"Everything okay?" Graciela asks.

"Someone was supposed to give me a ride home and she bailed. I could walk, but I'm a little tired after class, and it would take almost an hour."

Graciela can tell this isn't it at all, but she figures it's best not to push. As upset as everyone is about the studio closing, Katherine has reason to be most worried. Her business is there, and she's known Lee the longest by far.

She drives up the hill slowly, silently watching as the neighborhood gets quieter and prettier as they go. Katherine once mentioned that she lived in a nice place, but Graciela didn't imagine it as being this lush and exclusive. How much do massage therapists make, anyway?

"It's this one," Katherine says, pointing to a beautiful little bungalow half hidden by purple bougainvillea.

"Wow" is all Graciela can manage. There's something unbelievably romantic about the house, and even more so knowing that Katherine lives here alone. Why is it, Graciela wonders, that being single looks so appealing to her these days? She knows very well that if she were solo she'd be miserably lonely and spend half her time looking for a boyfriend anyway.

"No one can believe I live here. It makes more sense when you consider that I could be asked to leave any minute. The terms of my lease, so to speak. And with the way things are going, I probably will be."

"Bad day?" Graciela asks.

"You could put it that way."

"It must be tough for you with the studio closing. Do you think Lee's really making a wrong decision?"

Katherine seems to be thinking this over, not as if she's unsure of her opinion, but as if she's not sure she wants to share it. "I think she's making a decision for the wrong reasons."

"Alan?" Graciela asks. She's a little surprised she said this. The topic of Alan is one she hasn't wanted to go near. But it just popped out.

Katherine shakes her head and laughs in a sad way. "It's always the quiet, shy folks who know everything. What do you think of Alan?"

Graciela realizes, as soon as she hears Katherine's question, that she's been waiting to be asked this by someone for a while. She hasn't spent much time around Alan, but when she has, she's noticed something familiar in his attitude, a strutting kind of confidence that isn't remotely convincing. She's heard him throw in his own credentials when someone praises Lee's teaching, even when they have nothing to do with the conversation. She's seen this in Daryl and has always tried to make excuses for it. Watching Alan has made her realize just how desperate it seems and how hurtful to Lee. Still, she's not yet ready to say everything she believes. "I guess it's good they're getting back together if it's what Lee wants. If it were me, I wouldn't trust him, that's all."

Katherine looks at her and then says softly, "Don't tell me he made a pass at you."

"It isn't that. I mean, he makes little comments when I see him, but I just ignore them."

"Excuse me for saying so, but with that face and body, you must hear 'little comments' a lot," Katherine says.

"I never heard them from Conor," Graciela says. Another remark that just popped out without her meaning to say it.

Katherine glances through the windshield and then opens the passenger door.

"Wait," Graciela says. "What happened with Conor? He's crazy about you. You know that."

Katherine leaves her door open, but falls back against the car seat. "Conor's not 'crazy' about anything. He's the most sane person I've ever met. He's afraid of being hurt; I'm afraid of hurting him."

"Really? And it has nothing to do with you being afraid of *getting* hurt?"

Katherine gives her a weary gaze. "I'd invite you in, but the place is a mess and I'm all out of Diet Coke."

I'm not the most together person in the world, Graciela thinks, *and I'm not the brightest, and I'm not the most accomplished. But I'm not* una animala *and if I can tell Becky Antrim something she doesn't know about the biggest celebrity in the world, I can tell Katherine that she's acting like a fool.* She starts to close up all the windows of her car. "I don't care about the mess," Graciela says. She unbuckles her seat belt. "And I don't drink Diet Coke anyway. You and I need to talk. You're inviting me in and you're going to tell me the whole story."

That said, Graciela gets out of the car and strides down the walkway toward Katherine's house. When she doesn't hear footsteps behind her, she turns around and says, "Katherine, I said come on. I'm not taking no for an answer, and I don't give up easily. How do you think I got in that video?"

You don't think Katherine has a point about YogaHappens, do you?"

"What? That they're the evil empire? Jesus, Lee. Look at the money they're offering us."

"But maybe it's a trap," Lee says. "We close the studio and . . ."

"Honey," he says. "That's paranoia. It's hippie, druggie fantasy. Katherine would say anything to keep you here. You can't believe her."

The phone in the studio rings, and he goes out to the reception desk to answer it. When he comes back into the yoga room, his face is flushed.

"Something wrong?"

"That was Zhannette and Frank's private secretary. You're not going to believe this."

They're canceling our contract, Lee thinks, with more relief than regret.

"We're invited up to their house in Laurel Canyon next week. For cocktails."

Lee knows better than to show her disappointment. "Oh. Well, that's nice. It should be interesting."

"Nice? Interesting? Are you kidding me? These people are so reclusive and private, even Dave and Chuck haven't met them. This is amazing. It's huge."

"I guess I shouldn't wear a T-shirt, huh?"

Stephanie's neighbor Billie has three daughters—Danni, Frankie, and Bobbie. The two oldest moved out of state, but Bobbie lives closest, up in San Francisco. Even so, she, like the others, never seems to visit. Earlier in the week, someone from the yoga studio where Billie practices called Stephanie (Billie had listed her as the emergency contact) to say that Billie has been passing out routinely in their superheated classes. There's concern that she's dehydrating in a severe way and is possibly at risk for a heart attack. Before they try legal intervention of some kind, the studio is hoping a family member can stop her from taking classes.

Stephanie went to talk with Billie, but when that proved fruitless, she finagled Bobbie's number and gave her a call. Bobbie was surprisingly nice on the phone (Stephanie had been imagining that the daughters all had a grudge against their mother; how else to explain the fact that they never visit?) and, more surprising still, she showed up in L.A. a couple of days later.

When she knocked on Stephanie's door to thank her for calling, for helping out, for being around to do chores for her mother, she was dressed in a pair of jeans and a man's sleeveless T-shirt—a "wife-beater," to use a term Stephanie has always found disturbing on about six different levels. Given the androgynous outfit, the lean, strong build, the flattop haircut, and the fact that Billie has told her her youngest daughter is a plumber, Stephanie was expecting someone fairly . . . aggressive? Instead,

Bobbie—"If you don't mind, I prefer Roberta"—is a soft-spoken woman in her late thirties with gorgeous blue eyes and a completely appealing manner. When Stephanie invited her in, she saw that she has about her some of the unexpected vulnerability that Stephanie has noticed in a lot of the more (why not say it?) butch women she's known. Maybe everyone is always playing against type. Roberta (even though "Bobbie" suits her better) sat opposite Stephanie, her legs spread and her hands hanging between her knees, and poured out her concern for her mother, especially given her stubbornness. In case Stephanie was wondering why neither she nor her sisters ever shows up, it's because Billie banned them from coming—she doesn't want people to know she has such old daughters.

"Let's face it," Roberta said, on the verge of tears, "she's headed into some kind of dementia here. I've been trying to get her to move up to San Francisco with me. My girlfriend, the bitch, just moved out, so I've got the room. But you can imagine how that went over with Billie."

When Stephanie asked her if she wanted to grab a sandwich, Roberta said okay, but only if she let her pay. It's the least she can do.

They go to the self-consciously homey place on Melrose, walking distance from Stephanie's apartment, where she wrote a lot of the screenplay for *Above the Las Vegas Sands*. The snippy little waiter who usually treats her like a tourist is civil to her. Maybe he's intimidated by Roberta's biceps, more nicely shaped than his own.

"How are the burgers here?" Roberta asks Stephanie, studying the menu.

"Well, to be honest," Stephanie says, "I became a vegetarian about a year ago, and this place only opened eight months ago."

"Again: how are the burgers?"

Oh, well. "Amazing," Stephanie says. "Especially the one stuffed with onions."

It isn't until Roberta orders the cheeseburger that Stephanie realizes she hasn't used her anti-Preston mantra in weeks now. Hasn't needed to. Not that she hasn't thought of her ex, it's just that since she stopped drinking, since she started writing the screenplay for Sybille, she hasn't felt that same urgent desperation about him, the desire for revenge, all of it. Being happy in herself really is the best revenge, except she doesn't even think of it as revenge. It's just nice to be in control of her life again. None of it has anything to do with Preston.

"It's funny," Stephanie says. "I used to chant the word 'cheeseburger,' like a mantra, whenever I thought of my ex-boyfriend. It helped me get over him, in a way."

"Every time I think of my ex, I chant something, too, but it isn't working. Maybe I need a new mantra."

"What is it now?"

" 'Cunt.' " Roberta shrugs. "She left me for a twenty-year-old figure skater."

"I didn't know there were any lesbian figure skaters," Stephanie says and then worries that maybe that's offensive somehow.

"Eh, she's not much of a lesbian, if you ask me. She'll be with a man in six months. She's not much of a skater, either, now that I think about it. What happened with Mr. Cheeseburger?"

"I never really knew, which was a big part of what was so painful. We were together for three years. He said I was cold, I was distracted."

"I hate when they think they have to blame *you* for their leaving instead of owning up to the fact that they're unreliable, promiscuous sluts."

When Stephanie's garden salad is set down in front of her,

it looks bland and unappetizing somehow. Not what she really wants to be eating. Roberta bites into her cheeseburger and gives a thumbs-up. When the waiter says, "Anything else I can get for you ladies right now?"

Roberta mops at her mouth and says, "Bring her a side of the onion burger. With Swiss."

Stephanie is about to protest but has a sudden insight that she likes the idea of being a vegetarian more than the fact of it. (Why else did she sneak in here in her more looped moments and wolf down the burgers?) But it's so clear that it doesn't matter to Roberta one way or the other, she lets it go.

"I had a thought about your mother," she says. "Maybe if, instead of getting her to stop going to yoga altogether, I could try to take her to a different kind of class. I go to one up in Silver Lake that's great, but not heated. And the teacher is incredibly sensitive to everyone's particular body. She has some background in medicine. Billie met her."

Roberta puts down her food. "Something wrong?"

"Not really. Why?"

"My mother would say it looks like someone just stepped on your grave."

"I realized the place I've been going to is about to close, that's all. I'll miss it. A lot." There are also the circumstances under which Billie met Lee, but best not to revisit that unfortunate moment. She can't know if Billie told her daughter about all that (probably not), though Stephanie is pretty sure Roberta wouldn't condemn her for it. "But it should be open for another couple of weeks. Maybe you'd like to join us?"

"I'm heading back to San Francisco in a day or so. On top of that, the idea of watching my mother put her foot behind her head is something I'd rather not discuss over lunch. Maybe next time I'm in town."

"You're coming back?"

"There's no point in keeping up the charade about her age, and she's getting too unreliable to come up and visit me. I'll be around more often."

The snippy waiter delivers Stephanie's burger. Stephanie holds it up. "Here's a toast," she says. "To cheeseburgers."

Roberta taps hers against Stephanie's. "To cheeseburgers everywhere."

For days, Katherine has been mulling over her conversation with Graciela. As soon as they got into the house, Graciela started asking her questions about what had really happened with Conor, and why, and what she planned to do about it. It was funny, really, seeing her be so assertive and insistent about getting answers. It was almost as if she was playing a role, like a kid suddenly interrogating her parent. It wasn't a role that suited her perfectly, but maybe that's why Katherine found herself opening up completely, telling her all her fears about her past and what Conor would make of that, and then forcing herself—though it was torture to do so—to describe what had happened with Phil, the whole stupid, awful, humiliating series of events.

Graciela looked at her for a few silent, unnerving moments and then said, "I hate to tell you this, Kat, but you're not nearly as bad and unreliable and nasty as you seem to want to believe. You're one of the most solid, together people I know. Look around. Whoever is living in this house is *not* out of control, crazy, or currently self-destructive. Write him an e-mail. Tell him what happened. You don't even need to apologize. And let me know as soon as you've got it done."

Katherine had tried to do just that a number of times but had always stumbled over apologies, lame excuses, the crazy details.

She's lying in bed, and it's almost dawn, and she can see the strange, magical blossoming of light in the sky outside her windows. The blue seems to deepen and then start to bleach out into paler shades. She'd love to stop the day right here, when it's silent and still, cool and full of possibilities. Graciela was right. Of course. She isn't afraid of hurting Conor. Not entirely, anyway. She's been terrified that he's going to hurt her, reject her, leave her stranded. It's not like it hasn't happened before. But it's not so bad when you're dating a creep and it's a *given* from the outset that he's going to wound you somehow or other.

But how many possibilities can the day hold if you don't stick your neck out? If you're not willing to take a few risks, you have to settle for things as they are.

She gets out of bed and goes into the dining room. She sits in front of her computer, an ancient Mac desktop thing that is so chunky and heavy, the screen so weirdly small, that it has the look of another era altogether and fits right in with all her vintage clothes and décor. She folds herself into a lotus position on the chair and starts to type.

Dear Mr. Ross

1. Nice weather we've been having, eh? 2. My bike got stolen from in front of the yoga studio. Boo hoo. 3. I watched Casablanca on TV the other night and had a good long cry. 4. There are a lot of things in my past I wish I could change but I can't. I'm just trying to make

sure I don't make the same mistakes again. 5. The sun is coming up and there's a little orange glow on the horizon, and to tell you the truth, Mr. Ross, I would do almost anything you could name to have you here with me right now.

　　　　　　　　　　　　　　　　　　　Brodski

Now, now, now, before the sun comes up and all that light starts flooding in. She hits the "send" button and goes to make coffee.

S inew and Fireplug made it clear, to the point of being insulting, that it's an honor to be invited to Zhannette and Frank's house in Laurel Canyon. After a while, Lee began to feel that the two men were crazily jealous that Lee and Alan— unworthy newcomers—had received an invitation. *They usually don't invite teachers out to their place. None of the employees gets a personal invite.*

"You're just picking on nothing," Alan says. "Probably because you're a nervous wreck about meeting them."

There's something about the term "nervous wreck" that Lee finds insulting, especially since it's clear that Alan is the one who's anxious about this meeting. He spent half an hour trying to figure out what to wear, he has been scratching his neck a lot, and he's even been ignoring the chirping sound his phone makes when he gets a text message, something that's been happening about every ten minutes since he came by the house to pick up Lee and the kids. Apparently his friend Benjamin wasn't happy when Alan told him he was moving back home in two weeks, especially since Benjamin kicked out one of his roommates to make space for Alan. They're driving the kids to the studio, dropping them off with Barrett, and then continuing on to Laurel Canyon. The kids are strapped into the backseat, and they have the windows down and the air conditioner on. Wasteful and not very green, but one of those indulgences Lee allows herself from time to time, especially when Alan is so stressed.

"Just remember, no matter how rich and successful they are, they're just people."

"I didn't think they were deities," Lee says.

"Jesus Christ, Lee. Can you try to curb the irony for maybe one hour? I know you're a bundle of nerves, but come on. Don't try and get me upset, too."

Lee wants to correct him and point out that she's not a "bundle of nerves," she's a "nervous wreck," but better just to change the subject. Chirp. Another text message.

"How many messages is he sending?" Lee asks.

"He's nuts. I told him it was temporary lodging. I never even *implied* to him, or *anyone*, that we were getting a divorce. People are so fucking conventional, as if taking a little breather means some big thing."

There's something disturbing about this comment, but Lee lets it go. *Let it go, let it go, let it go. Just move forward.*

"You kids looking forward to the class?" she asks.

This starts Michael and Marcus on their new favorite pastime, which is competitive chanting of "om" to see who can be the loudest. It can be irritating, but it's cute, too, and it's certainly a lot better than the pushing and shoving and swatting each other they were into before they started practicing. When they get close to an intolerable volume, Lee joins in, as if they're all singing together, and then Alan adds his best rolling bass. *Okay,* she thinks, *nothing's perfect. But at moments like this, we're at least a happy little family.* If she has to close the studio for this, so be it. In the end, this is more important.

As they're about to walk into the studio, Lee takes Alan's hand and kisses him. "I'm not a nervous wreck when you're around," she says.

He leans his shoulder against hers and says, "Lend me a little of that calm, then. I'm tense."

Barrett is sitting behind the registration desk scribbling on a piece of paper with one hand and, with the other, doing something with her BlackBerry. Like everyone else, she's been a little grumpy and uncommunicative, and in truth, Lee can't say she blames her. She expected there would be a lot of this once word got out. Lee's been doing her best to find places for everyone, and last night she sent an e-mail to Barrett telling her it looked about ninety percent sure that the school system was going to hire her to teach yoga to the kids, three times a week, as part of the physical ed classes. It's a little bit of a shock that she didn't respond. She doesn't even look up when they walk into the studio.

The kids rush behind the desk, and Alan, iPhone in hand, walks through the glass doors into the yoga room.

"Ready for chaos?" Lee asks, nodding toward the kids.

Barrett shrugs. "Whatever."

"Did you get the e-mail I sent you last night?"

"Yeah, I got it. Thanks."

"You know, I really worked hard to make that happen, Barrett. It wasn't easy. It's going to be great for the whole school, but it's going to be a good thing for you, too."

"I just *said* thank you."

"I know you did, but it might sound a little more sincere if you'd look at me when you say it."

Now Barrett's phone is chirping, too. Someone ought to do a

psychological analysis of the world's most annoying ring tones and cell phone signals and how people choose the ones they choose. Barrett checks her message and then does look at Lee, right in the eyes. "Thank you," she says. She grabs the pad of paper she's been scribbling on and stomps out to the sidewalk.

"Mood alert! Mood alert!" Michael and Marcus chant, echoing the phrase Lee and Alan having been using around the house for years.

Lee goes behind the desk to check the computer. There's that chirp again! Is she hearing things? No, Barrett walked out without her phone and it's sitting on the desk chirping and blinking. Lee moves it to the far end of the desk, and in doing so she notices that it has an alert for an incoming text message.

From Alan.

Interesting.

Zhannette and Frank's house is one of those miracles of modern architecture clinging to the side of a hill in Laurel Canyon. From the street, it looks almost like a little glass box that would be too thin to stand up in. Obviously an optical illusion. But even from below and even though there are other houses around it, it exudes some feeling of peace and balance, both things Lee is feeling the need for right now.

Alan chatted pretty much the whole drive out here about some changes he wants to make on *their* house—basically: install a home gym in the basement, a career investment since he's planning to start auditioning for performing gigs in a more active and aggressive way once they get the monkey of Edendale off their backs and a little more money in their joint account. He didn't seem to notice that she was saying pretty much nothing the whole way. In fact, Lee felt a strange and welcome kind of peace come over her as soon as she got into the car with Alan and started to mull over what she'd seen. And what she'd seen—and *all* that she'd seen—was Barrett's BlackBerry indicating that she'd received a text message from Alan. Lee has received text messages from Barrett on many occasions, hasn't she? Wouldn't it be dangerous to leap to assumptions and make accusations? Yes, it would be.

"Is this amazing or what?" Alan says, looking up at the house reverently.

"I'd have to have curtains," Lee says.

"They probably don't have anything to hide."

"Everyone's got something to hide, Alan."

They climb up the steep steps and are met at the top by a slim man with a blond crew cut. Definitely a yoga fanatic, Lee can tell by the build, and definitely a fanatic in some other ways, she can tell by the too bright, unblinking gaze. "You must be Lee and Alan," he says, hand out. "I'm James. Zhannette and Frank are very eager to meet you. They've been waiting."

"Are we late?" Alan asks.

James makes an amused frown. "You're seven minutes late, Alan. Hardly worth mentioning. Don't even think about it. They know you wouldn't be even a minute late for classes."

"Traffic," Alan says.

James lays a hand on Alan's arm and his gaze grows even more intense. "Don't even think about it, all right?"

Lee takes a small measure of comfort in knowing that she is not responsible for this horrible seven-minute faux pas. There's also something about the treatment they're receiving that makes it clear, in case there was any doubt, that this is a business meeting more than a social call. When was the last time Lee called out any guest for being a few minutes late? For being late, period?

The first thing Lee notices about the inside of the house is that it's the most perfect temperature she's ever felt. There must be a sophisticated climate control in here that regulates the temperature and the humidity and the ions. Maybe the scent as well; there's a fragrance in the air, like roses, but lighter. And there are soft sounds, too, something between wind chimes and the chirping of distant birds. Even in her less-than-spectacular frame of mind, Lee feels calmed and reassured by the atmosphere.

The house is so clean, all the marble and polished wood floors gleaming, and so minimally furnished, that it's a little hard to believe anyone lives here. From inside, it's clear that the gardens have been so lushly and amply planted, there's no need for curtains. It feels a little like a terrarium, but there's such a flow from inside to out, it's hard to tell if you're inside the terrarium or outside looking into it.

The living room juts out at the back of the house like the prow of a ship, and, sitting at the far end of it, with the milky white sky behind them, are Zhannette and Frank. They're sitting on invisible chairs that must be made of Lucite, so they appear to be floating in this room, which is itself floating.

They stand in unison and come forward to greet Lee and Alan. Given the buildup, the reputation, the house, the names, and the smell of roses in the air, Lee was expecting two lithe gurus in white robes. What a surprise then that Frank is a perfectly ordinary-looking man, probably in his late fifties, wearing a pair of jeans and a V-necked sweater with nothing underneath. There's some graying chest hair sticking out the neckline, and the suggestion of a gut above his cinched belt.

Zhannette is one of those extremely well-put-together women

who looks as if every inch of her body is pampered and preserved by expensive treatments—soft hair, a lovely complexion, perfect nails. But there's something about her features and the shape of her face and body—a little chunky and fleshy—that suggest she wasn't born into this wealth. She could be fifty, but who knows? She has on a pair of jeans and a white shirt that appears to be one of those six-hundred-dollar knockoffs of a man's business shirt. Everything about her looks clean, and you can tell she's covered in a thin layer of an expensive and lightly scented moisturizer.

She puts her hands in prayer and bows a little to Alan and Lee, as if this is what they expect as a greeting. Really, a handshake would have been fine.

"You have such a beautiful aura," she says to Lee. "It's radiating all around you, like a brilliant evening star in the clear northern sky."

Lee supposes she ought to say thank you, but the whole point of the comment seems to be to show Zhannette's own abilities, not to compliment Lee. "It was warm in the car," Lee says. "That's probably what it is."

"Isn't she lovely, Frank? We're so lucky to have you on board. Both of you. James will bring out some drinks in a minute. Sit."

There are four identical S-shaped Lucite chairs, and as Alan begins to sit in one, Frank says, "That's mine."

"Oh. Sorry about that."

Frank is one of those preoccupied businessmen who seems to have at least a dozen things he'd rather be doing than this and who views this meeting as an obligation, either to the business or to keep his wife happy. Although something in Zhannette's appearance suggests to Lee that the antidepressants do the happiness trick on their own pretty effectively.

"We have been wanting to meet you for so long now," Zhannette says. "As soon as we heard about your studio, I said to

Frank, 'We have to get these wonderful people.' I wanted you to know that while you probably felt like you were working in a mine somewhere, you were noticed and that people like us were aware of your existence! I want to know everything about you, Lee. Everything.

"But first—you're probably wondering how we got into the spirituality industry. Do you want to tell them, Frank?"

He folds his arms across his chest, resting them on his little belly. This is apparently sign language for *You tell them*, so Zhannette continues:

"About ten years ago, everything came together for us, Lee. I won't bore you with the details, but let's just say that we were suddenly among the most admired people in this town. Do you have any idea how difficult that is when it first happens? When money and success thrust one into the stratosphere? I'm just guessing you don't know what it's like to be wealthy, Alan, and invited to every A-list party and jetting off to Morocco for 'someone's' birthday party. I know it sounds marvelous to someone like you, Lee, and okay, I'm not going to deny—partly it *is* marvelous. But the whole truth is always different from what we see on the glittering surface."

She clasps her hands and gives another little bow, although it's not clear who she's bowing to. Truth? The glittering surface?

"Back when we were just rich, it was relatively carefree. But when you get into the category we're in now, Lee, the obligations and the pressures mount exponentially. Just stop and think about it for a minute, Alan: if you had the ability to do whatever you wanted, *whatever* you wanted to do, how many decisions would you have to make on a minute-to-minute basis? Dozens? Try hundreds, Alan. Think about that.

"But you know what, Lee? I have always faced adversity head-on. I have *never* been one to let a crisis like this roll over me and pull me under. So many of the megarich are swept away by the difficulty of their positions, just like those unfortunate little people who were pulled out to sea by the tsunami."

James arrives with a glass tray of juice and clear bowls with colorful fruits heaped up in them. He sets it on a glass table beside Zhannette, but she doesn't acknowledge it or James, a shame really, since Lee is dying of thirst and didn't have much for lunch.

"So I began meditating. And from the minute I first went into a deep meditative state—and I had a real talent for it—I saw the path in front of me. Can I tell you how I view you, Lee? I don't want to embarrass you—I know how modest you are, I can read it in your beautiful aura—but I know I can be honest with you.

"You are a work of art. No, really, you *are*. And you are, too, Alan." She reaches out and takes both their hands. "And when you think about it, it's always been up to the wealthy and privileged people of the world to buy art so that it can be protected and made available to everyone. So that's what I began doing, Lee. I began buying the most wonderful, masterful works of art in the world. The truly *precious* things in the world. Things like *you*."

She drops their hands and signals to James, who, apparently, has been somewhere on the periphery, watching. He appears, and Zhannette says, "If you wouldn't mind taking this away, dear. I'm not thirsty now. *Namaste*." That said, the food and drink disappear.

"But what do you *do* with art, Alan? Oh, don't look worried, I don't mean you, I mean *one*. What does *one* who can afford to acquire art do with it? Well, you either keep it hidden away or you put it in a museum. So that's where YogaHappens comes in. You see, the Experience Centers are museums. That's why they're so gorgeous, Lee. They're museums, Alan. And I know people like you probably think we have a lot of rules and regulations and such, but when you think about it, doesn't the Getty? Doesn't the Prado? Doesn't the Louvre? How else can all the lovely things they hold, all the wonderful objects on exhibit, be protected from the people they are there for?

"So now I've babbled on here, I know, but I really want you to know where I'm coming from. Some people say—and we hear the rumors, Lee, all the way up here in our cottage and even down in Malibu, where we have our real house—people say: 'Oh, Zhannette and Frank are taking the best teachers from the little yoga studios.' Well, number one, we're not *taking* anyone, we're *buying* them, and number two, if a beautiful, priceless Picasso like you, Lee, or a charming little sketch like you, Alan, were sitting around some moldy old junk shop in the middle of nowhere, wouldn't you want to rescue them if it was in your power? Wouldn't it be almost a moral obligation?

"Aren't I right, Frank?"

Frank unclasps his arms. "We're raising the class fee to thirty-eight dollars next month," he says.

"He's the businessman, Lee. I don't get involved in that, and you don't need to, either. That's the beauty of it. Do you see what I mean, Alan? I *envy* you being in the position you're in. No, really, I do. It's like my dogs. Sometimes I look at them and I think: Aren't they lucky? The food just appears in their bowls!

"By the way, my name. Let's just get that one out of the way, okay? Once I became a Buddhist, Lee, the name Janet just didn't sound right to me. It was fine for Milwaukee, where I grew up, but I felt like a new person and I wanted a name to suit me. So I was in Paris and all the little women at the couture houses were saying *Miss Janet* this and *Miss Janet* that, but, naturally, they pronounce it 'Zhannette.' Have you ever been out of the country, Lee? The French speak English so beautifully, even the peasants. So I embraced it and changed the spelling.

"I really *have* gone on too long. Please. Do you have any questions, Alan? What about you, Lee? Is there anything you'd like to ask?"

"Well, in fact, I do have one question," Lee says. She turns to Alan and says, "You've been fucking Barrett, haven't you?"

H ow could you do that to me?" Alan asks.

"What are you *talking* about?"

"In front of Zhannette and Frank! Did you see the looks on their faces? They were so embarrassed they didn't know what to do."

"Do you really think I give a *shit* about Frank and *Janet*? Just start the car, Alan. Start the car and drive me home."

"Fortunately, she has enough social skills to pretend you hadn't said anything."

"Fortunately, she's so pathologically self-absorbed, she wouldn't have noticed if I'd pushed you through one of those windows, which is what I felt like doing."

"You're jumping to conclusions."

"Start the car, Alan."

"I'm trying to find my keys."

"Try *harder*."

There are so many zippers and tiny Velcroed pockets on the pair of yoga pants Alan is wearing, he keeps losing track of where he's already looked and where he hasn't. What, Lee wonders, did the designer have in mind: a different pocket for each coin?

"And you haven't answered my original question," she says.

"I'm not going to honor that with a response, Lee."

"Oh, yes, you are. And you're going to honor it right now." For so many years, Lee has been practicing equanimity and calm, breathing into anger, releasing, relaxing, letting go. But she feels a completely unfamiliar rage churning inside her, almost as if she's losing control of her thoughts and her actions. It's a physical sensation as much as anything else, a tingling in her arms and legs and across her scalp. "In case you've forgotten, I asked: You've been fucking Barrett, haven't you?"

"I haven't *slept with her*, Lee," he says, pulling the keys out of a pouch below his knee. "And we're not *having an affair*, either."

"Oh, my God," Lee says. "Oh, my God! In other words, you've been having sex." She punches at the button on the glove compartment, and when it doesn't open, she fishes through her bag until she's found her own keys. "She's a *kid*, Alan! She's a senior in college!" Lee opens the glove compartment and roots around until she's located the pack of cigarettes she stashed there that night Alan moved out, months ago. She knew they'd come in handy sometime. "And she's *our* kids' babysitter. That is so . . . fucking . . . tacky and clichéd."

"What the hell are you doing?"

"I'm lighting a cigarette," Lee says. "Isn't it obvious?" The Marlboro is bobbing up and down in her mouth as she nervously tries to strike a match. "And once I have it lit, I'm going to *smoke* it. Right down to the goddamned filter."

"Are you out of your mind? What if Zhannette and Frank saw you?"

"Do you really think I care about them? Do you really think I have *any intention* of working for them? They're horrible. I mean, he's a complete corporate pig, and she's so clueless, I'm tempted to feel bad but am resisting the temptation. She just referred to us as *dogs*, Alan. Which is actually completely true in your case, but not for the reasons she thinks."

Alan puts the car into drive and slowly pulls away from the house, glancing up just to make sure no one spotted them. Lee rolls down her window and sticks her head out and shouts, *"I'm smoking a cigarette down here,* Janet! *Want a puff?"*

"You're out of your mind. You're so full of hostility."

"And what do you call fucking the girl—*girl,* Alan—who works for us? For *me?"*

"It only happened three or four times."

"Oh, well. Is that all? Only three or four times? Gee, I guess in that case it doesn't *count,* does it? In that case, I can just *forget* it. In that case, I can let you move back in so we can be a happy little couple and go work for the animal trainers. Bow wow, baby. You should have told me sooner! If I'd known it was only *three or four* times, it wouldn't have even *bothered* me, darling. I wouldn't have *cared!* And I'm sure Barrett doesn't care, either, does she? She doesn't have any feelings, either, does she? I'm sure you didn't tell her we were *getting a divorce,* did you? Just so you could get in her pants."

"I did not *tell* her that. If she got the idea somehow that—"

"You're despicable. You're horrible. And do you know what's almost the worst of it? Any idea, Alan? My mother knew you were a creep all along, and I didn't. Blinded by love or stupidity or self-righteousness because I'm such a good and goddamned *centered* person. So now I not only have to reevaluate my entire opinion of you, I have to start thinking of *her* as someone with more insight and better judgment than me. And I *hate* that!"

"We have a contract with YogaHappens, Lee. It's signed. It's a done deal. You know what that means, don't you?"

Lee is getting a little out of breath and the smoke is starting to make her dizzy and a little nauseated. "I do, darling," she says more softly. "I do, indeed." Lee tosses the half-smoked cigarette out the window. If you're going to be bad, you might as well litter, too. She shakes all the remaining cigarettes out of the pack. "It means I'm going to have to get a really, really good lawyer. And guess what? Stephanie, one of my most devoted students, just happens to know one. And while he's breaking that little contract, I'm going to have him negotiate me one amazing freaking divorce."

She rubs her hands together until she's got a fistful of tobacco and then she rubs it all over Alan's face. "So put that in your pipe and smoke it."

In most ways, Graciela is relieved that the shoot is over, even if it was, no question about it, the most fun she's ever had in her life. Ever. And not only the most fun, but also the most challenging and the most rewarding. But at the same time, it was exhausting on a day-to-day basis in ways she's never experienced before. It drained her physically, and pushed her emotionally, and there were times she thought she'd crack. She literally did start doing some of the routines in her sleep, thrashing in bed, flailing her arms and legs to a soundtrack that only she could hear. Many times, she woke up Daryl in the middle of the night. It amazed her how sweet and supportive he was about the whole thing, the entire time she was doing it, starting with rehearsals. Sometimes she'd see a little flash of anger or resentment in him, but the important thing is, he held it in check. Many days over the weeks she was doing the shoot, she'd come home and he'd have dinner prepared for her and a bottle of wine open. He'd give her a massage and serve her her meal. There was a moment, all those months ago now, when she thought she might have to leave. But suddenly, everything just fell into place.

For a while.

As she's driving to Edendale for Lee's class, the first one to celebrate the reopening of the studio, she tries to piece it all together. Yesterday she got a call saying that the editor of the video was in love with her work on the shoot and that everyone is talking about how good the video is turning out. Much better than anyone expected. Does she have any idea how amazing she looks in that silver corset? What her hair looks like when the lights and the wind machines hit it? "The next 'Single Ladies'" is what they're all saying about the video.

She isn't going to get her hopes up about that, but if it's even one-tenth as good and one-fifth as popular, it will transform her career. And she knows, given the life expectancy of most dance careers, that she is going to have to drink it all in and enjoy it for what it's worth.

The choreographer who called yesterday went on and on about the video and then casually (*casually!*) told her they were contacting her agent to officially offer her a job as one of the dancers on Beyoncé's upcoming tour. About ten minutes after she put down the phone, her agent called. The money, compared with what she's been making, is incredible, and the exposure is more than she ever thought possible. Naturally all the dancers will be in the background, only there to support Beyoncé, but between this and the video, well, suddenly Graciela's agent, who's always treated her with lukewarm enthusiasm, the way you might treat a promising student, is sounding excited, talking about playing "hardball," and calling her "honey."

"I don't care about hardball," Graciela said. "I just want to make sure I get a contract!"

With a contract and a steady paycheck for the tour, she could take Daryl on a vacation, a real vacation, something they've never done the whole time they've been together. Maybe Hawaii. And she could afford to hire someone to clean her mother's house a couple of times a month. A way of helping her out that doesn't involve putting her own mental health on the line. And then there are the blinds for their windows.

She was the one who prepared a special dinner for Daryl last night—a complicated recipe her mother had taught her. She'd shopped and cooked all afternoon and had the apartment looking beautiful. She had flowers on the table. She told Daryl about the tour over dinner. The first thing he said was, "How long will you be gone?"

"I don't know," she said. "I didn't get all the details. But they said there would be breaks in between some of the dates. It's not like I'd be gone for six months straight. Plus you can come with me some of the time."

"I guess you're really at a different level now, aren't you? Are you still going to love me? You still going to be mine?"

"Always," she said.

Then he took her in his arms and carried her to bed. When he made love to her, it started off so tender and sweet, she thought Daryl had tears in his eyes at one point. "Are you still going to be mine?" he whispered in her ear again.

"Yes," she whispered back.

"Are you?" he said again.

"Yes," she said, a little louder.

But he kept asking, not as if he hadn't heard her answer, but as if he didn't believe it. As if she was lying to him and he'd caught her. There was something so intense and urgent in what he was doing that at first she found it incredibly exciting. He was taking possession of her, and it felt more passionate than they'd been in a long time. But as it went on, it became something else. It was as if desperation had come into their sex, as if he was punishing her for something she'd done, not making love to her. She'd tried to pretend she was enjoying it, pretend that everything was fine, even though she knew it wasn't, even though he was hurting her.

When it was over, he'd rolled onto his side of the bed and curled up in a ball and started to cry. "I'm sorry," he'd said, over and over, until finally she was the one who'd ended up comforting him and apologizing to him, although she wasn't sure she knew what she was apologizing for.

She pulls up in front of Edendale and does her best to park. She'll work through whatever bad feelings and doubts she has in yoga. It always helps her clear her mind. At some point, she's going to have to confront a few facts about her relationship, make a few decisions, but for now, this is what she needs. A few sun salutations, ninety minutes of moving meditation. That will have to be enough for the moment.

Imani is driving to Lee's class when her cell phone rings. She listens calmly, says thank you, and hangs up. Her first instinct is to turn the car around and head back home. Glenn is in surgery most of the day, but sometimes she can get through to him if it's an emergency. When she had the miscarriage, he did his best to make her believe that it was his loss, too, and that she had to let him carry some of the burden of what happened, that if she didn't try to absorb the whole blow and all the blame herself, it would be easier for her to deal with it. She hadn't been able to hear it at the time or even fully understand what he meant. *She* was the one who wasn't able to carry her baby to term.

But something has changed in the past three months, and

now she knows what he means. She was so caught up in her own pain and despair, she forgot that it was his baby, too. She isn't going to make that mistake again.

She tries to find a place to turn, but the traffic is heavy, and she's swept up in the flow of it, and there's no way she can do anything but keep moving in the direction she's headed. *Maybe it's for the best,* she thinks, and settles back in. She'll take the class anyway. Yoga has been her solace, and she can count on it to calm her down now. More than anything, she needs to calm down. And maybe, while she's lying in savasana, she'll think of exactly the best way to tell Glenn. In class, she'll find the right words and she'll practice the way she's going to say them. But as she's driving, she starts going over her lines:

I don't want to jump the gun . . .

I don't want to make us both crazy . . .

I want to be realistic about the chances . . .

She pulls up at Edendale and it really is her lucky day—a parking space directly in front!

I have something to tell you, Glenn, and I don't want you to . . .

She reaches into the backseat and grabs her yoga mat. *Fuck it,* she thinks. She knows exactly what's going to happen. As soon as she sees Glenn she's going to start screaming, "It's what we thought! We're going to have a baby!"

The bad thing about spending so much time with Sybille is that Stephanie has started getting used to the perks. (The good thing is everything else.) The car and driver, for example. What could be more wasteful, unnecessary, decadent, and spoiled? And *what* could be better? Stephanie was shocked when Sybille agreed to attend Lee's class, but Sybille explained that she's in L.A. to have fun and since she's starting to get bored with her private Pilates instructor, she might as well try something new. She didn't even object when Stephanie explained that she was bringing her elderly neighbor to the class. "I owe her a favor," Stephanie explained. "Something she did for me when I was at . . . a low point."

"We all have those," Sybille said. "Even I've had my dark nights of the soul. Bring her along."

"Her daughter is becoming a friend, too," Stephanie says. Not exactly true, but she'd like to think it could be.

So she drives up to the "cottage" in Los Feliz, and then Sybille, Stephanie, and Billie pile into the back of the town car. Sybille has a look of nonchalant horrified fascination as she listens to Billie.

"They made me leave the other yoga place I was going to because I was too good. Did Stephanie tell you? All the teachers were threatened by me."

"I'm sure."

"It happens all over the place. What the hell? I figure since this place is out on the fringes anyway, I wouldn't ruffle anyone's feathers. I'll bet you're good, too. Look at those long, skinny legs."

"Thank you," Sybille says. "They could use a little better tone, I suppose."

"You don't want to get muscle-bound, sister."

"I was referring to my self-tanner."

"People always ask me if I've had work done," Billie says. "A compliment, isn't it? I'm not saying I *wouldn't* have work done, it's just that I wouldn't let them touch me until I turn fifty. And I don't have to face that anytime soon. We nearby? I need to do some meditating."

When Billie starts snoring, Stephanie tells Sybille that Lee is eternally grateful to her for referring the lawyers. She doesn't mention anything directly about the fact that Sybille picked up the tab for breaking the contract with YogaHappens. It's up to Lee to do that, if she wants to, and Sybille has an unexpected streak of modesty Stephanie has noticed from time to time.

"It was incredibly generous of you. I'm still not sure why you agreed to get involved."

"Number one, I'm very fond of *you*. You've completely underestimated your talent and skills and appeal, and that is so much more endearing than overestimating, it made me want to help out your friend, since it obviously meant so much to you. Number two, this Frank person was a real estate developer in Las Vegas. That's where the money comes from. Having lived with a real estate developer for all those years of my horrible marriage, I knew it would be easy to find something on him, wave a threat in his face, and get him to back down. It was about twenty hours of billable time. My lawyers are very familiar with this territory. How do you think I got the divorce settlement I got? Especially since I was the one having the affair.

"And by the way, I was surprised by the final revision of the script."

Stephanie has been expecting this comment and is prepared with a response. "It wasn't exactly what we discussed," she says, "I hope you didn't mind."

"No, it was brilliant. You toned down all my excessive suggestions. And I respect the fact you didn't tell me in advance. I would have objected. As I was reading it, I realized I actually do care about making a good movie—even more than I care about humiliating my ex-husband."

"Are we still talking about starting a shoot in October?" Stephanie asks.

"Definitely. From what I've heard, we should expect several months, possibly years, of setbacks and delays, but I'm extraordinarily tenacious. I hope the tenacity carries me through this yoga class."

"Don't be silly," Stephanie says. "You can do as much or as little as you choose. Lee leads the class, but you're free to do what you want."

Sybille gazes out the window, as if she's taking this in. "In that case," she says, "I might just drop the two of you off and try to book myself a massage."

Katherine stayed up most of last night finishing the dress for Lee. It was supposed to be a going-away gift, but now it's a welcome-back gift. Not that Lee ever went anywhere. It's more that Katherine's been away herself, still hurt by the look Lee gave her that day in the studio when she tried to warn her about the owners of YogaHappens. She's carried that grudge about as long as she wants to. It's time to get rid of one more burden.

She slips the dress on and looks at herself in the mirror. It's gorgeous, but not really her style. It will need some alterations, but it will look amazing on Lee. She's going to need some clothes to start going out, now that she and Alan are officially separated. Maybe she and Lee can go out to some clubs together.

Katherine sent Conor her sunrise e-mail, as she thinks of it, over three weeks ago. Not a peep. She is surprised he didn't answer, but she understands, too. Or at least she's stopped checking her e-mail on an hourly basis to see if there is anything from him. If it wasn't meant to be, it wasn't meant to be.

She takes off the dress and, using tissue paper, folds it carefully and lays it in a box. She loves all these little accoutrements that seem so outdated in a way—tissue paper, the dress box with a handle. She'll present it to Lee after class today.

She slips into a faded blue sundress she did a little reconstructive surgery on a couple of days ago. Not especially chic, but more her style.

It's going to be a warm day, and as she's gathering up her mat and water for class, she looks out the window to the slope of the hills and the sparkling reservoir. Who's kidding who? It would be nice to share this view, this house with someone else. Sometimes she feels an aching for that. But she can cope with aches. She really can manage alone.

As she's locking the deadbolt on her door, she hears a little ringing somewhere down the street, like maybe an ice cream truck, something she's never seen in all the time she's lived here. The bougainvillea has grown up so high, she can't see the street clearly. She really ought to cut it back. She hears the bell again, a little closer this time, and more familiar. Almost like the bell she had on . . .

She walks to the sidewalk and looks down the street, and that's when she sees him—Conor, pedaling up the hill on a big Dutch bicycle, not pink, but green, with a big red bow on the handlebars. He's breathing heavily and grinning, and he waves.

I can't, she thinks. *I'm doing so well now. It isn't going to work out, and in the end, everyone's just going to get hurt.*

"Brodski!" he calls out, puffing. "Do you know how long it took me to get this bike? Sorry about the color, but the pink would have taken another two weeks. And I didn't think you should be without wheels that long."

Don't, don't, don't, she hears in her head. And then she slips out of her sandals and drops what she's carrying and starts running toward him, feeling as if her heart is going to burst.

L ee had been hoping for a big turnout, but only about fif- teen people showed up for the class. Maybe some of her stu- dents are still angry at her for announcing that she was going to close and then doing an about-face and telling them she wasn't. Or maybe they just fell out of the habit of coming during the two weeks she did close so she could go away with the kids and explain everything to them as best she could. How their lives were going to change now, how she and Alan would always be their parents, their real family, even if they would be living in different places permanently, not just for a little while as she'd said before. Forever. That was a tough one to swallow herself, but the sooner she lets go of "maybe there's a chance . . . ," the sooner she'll start to heal.

Fifteen isn't a bad number, really, and the others will drift back. Some of the students she feels closest to came in support. She has them all on their backs in savasana, their eyes closed, and she goes around to each and cups her hands over their eyes and gently touches their temples.

"Thank you for being here," she whispers to each, offering something up, but trying to draw strength from them as well.

Graciela reaches up and grabs her hand as she touches her; a smile trembles on Stephanie's lips; and Imani whispers back, "I have something to tell you after class."

It would be perfect if Katherine were here, but she understands that she needs more time. She'll give her however long it takes.

Lee goes to the front of the room and sits in lotus, her hands on her knees and her fingers touching in a loose bhudi mudra. She closes her eyes and tries to get her breathing in unison with the class, but she feels a little clutch of panic at her chest. There are so many details to work out, so many knots to untie. What will it mean for the kids? And how is she going to move forward and face everything alone? She's always wanted to think of herself as being such a strong, independent person, but the truth is, she's been connected to someone—even the wrong someone— for so long now, she isn't sure if she's going to be able to cope.

She presses her fingers together a little more tightly and breathes as slowly and steadily as she can. She instructs the class to roll onto their sides, to sit up, to give thanks, and then she opens her eyes.

The first thing she sees is Katherine standing at the back of the room, a dress box in one hand and Conor's hand in the other. They're both smiling, their cheeks flushed in an unmistakable way.

There are moments in life when you understand with certainty that no matter how difficult the immediate future is likely to be, you are going to be able to face it. You are going to walk into it with calm and conviction. You might not get through it unscathed, but you will get through it. Your life isn't the way you thought it would be, but you know for sure you're not alone. And looking into her friend's kind eyes, Lee has one of those moments.

All right, she thinks, *let's begin.*